AN UNNAMED PRESS BOOK

www.unnamedpress.com

Unnamed Press, and the colophon, are registered trademarks of Unnamed Media LLC.

ISBN: 9781951213411
eISBN: 9781951213374

Library of Congress Control Number: 2021941547

This book is a work of fiction. Names, characters, places and incidents are wholly fictional or are used fictitiously. Any resemblance to actual events or persons, living or dead, is entirely coincidental.

Designed and Typeset by Jaya Nicely

Manufactured in the United States of America by McNaughton & Gunn
Distributed by Publishers Group West

First Edition

ADMIT

STORIES

THIS TO

LESLIE PIETRZYK

NO ONE

The Unnamed Press
Los Angeles, CA

TABLE OF CONTENTS

Till Death Do Us Part........13
Wealth Management........27
We Always Start with the Seduction........43
Stay There........55
I Believe in Mary Worth........77
People Love a View........99
This Isn't Who We Are........117
Hat Trick........123
Anything You Want........143
Green in Judgment........147
My Father Raised Me........165
Admit This to No One........189
Kill the Fatted Calf........209
Every Man in History........235

Acknowledgments........254

Previously published in slightly different form:

"Till Death Do Us Part," Great Jones Street literary app; "Wealth Management," *Ploughshares*; "We Always Start with the Seduction," Southampton Review online; "Stay There," *Southern Review* and *Pushcart Prize XLIV: Best of the Small Presses 2020 Edition*; "People Love a View," *Arts & Letters*; "This Isn't Who We Are," published as "#How2BSuburbanWhite21 #DMV," *Little Rose Magazine*; "Hat Trick," *Story Magazine*; "Anything You Want," *Phoebe* and *Boog City: The Baseball Issue*; "Green in Judgment," *River Styx*; an excerpt from "Admit This to No One," *This Is What America Looks Like: Fiction and Poetry from DC, Maryland, and Virginia* (anthology).

Author's Note:

Quoted dialogue concerning "Beau" in "We Always Start with the Seduction" is sourced from Ed Rollins, *Bare Knuckles and Back Rooms*, and the *Washington Post*, "GOP Battler Lee Atwater Dies at 40," March 30, 1991.

This book is dedicated to
everyone in DC who scanned the room
during the party while asking me,
"So, what do you do?"

this

ADMIT THIS TO NO ONE

TILL DEATH DO US PART

I'm meeting my stupid father "preperformance" at the Kennedy Center bar on April 15. Which happens to be his wedding anniversary to my stupid mother. I know, who gets married on *tax day*? Who meets their *kid* on his wedding anniversary? They're not married now, but still. I'm supposed to be there at six o'clock sharp. That's how he still talks, like he's a hundred-and-ten years old, like people say "sharp" every two seconds. I don't even know what show we're seeing, ballet or symphony or whatever. He brings the tickets.

I shoot for 6:15. He'll be late. Plus, it's a *bar* and I know I look like I'm *at least* eighteen, but I'm fifteen, and sometimes people act like I'm a child and sometimes I catch grown-up men staring like they want to hike my skirt with one hand and fuck me, like they're imagining no underwear in the way. Anyway, either makes sitting around a bar waiting for his entrance exactly what I'm not in the mood for.

He's always late. He's a very important man in Washington, DC, always "running behind," with some assistant whose whole job is texting bullshit about how late he'll be. Delete.

I'm supposed to take a taxi but obviously that fare's in my pocket and I'm riding Metro and the free shuttle bus from Foggy Bottom. My income's gonna tank the minute someone on his staff explains Uber. Once a month I meet my dad at the Kennedy Center because, he says, culture will be my savior, and because he likes people seeing me with him, people seeing him "culture me up." Honestly, I think he pretends I'm his *date* or something super-uniquely insane like that. I don't say this because of course *I'm* not stupid.

So, at 6:15 I'm on the elevator with a flock of lady tourists wearing what my dad might declare their so-called finery, fake-leather high heels with rolls of foot fat spilling over the sides; shiny, thick-fabric skirts that are too tight but also too baggy; polished, wire-wrapped, purple stone earrings from a spin-rack at a bad mountain-town gift shop—and it practically damages my eyes looking at them. But no floor numbers to watch lighting up above since this elevator only goes one place, to the roof level where both restaurants are, the fancy one, where I'm headed, and the one where you pile crap on a plastic tray, which guess who will be going there? So I close my eyes, trying to imagine my parents in love, imagine my father creaked down on one knee, all, "Will you marry me, my darling?" and my mother's eyes not their usual bloodshot fury, but starry, like a teenage girl watching a movie about herself, which she was, being nineteen. Fifteen years ago this happened, which is a whole lifetime—*my* whole lifetime—and, *yes,* I get the math and get why they got married. So I should stop with picturing flowers in her hand, a veil, an organ pumping out that stupid song. Stop thinking there was any love at all. There's none now, that's for sure. I don't even know what love is or why bother.

The elevator door dings finally, and my eyes snap open. My mom's mascara feels stiff on my lashes, but no touching or it'll smudge. I flounce my way out of that elevator on *very* high heels that make me look *at least* eighteen and I go left as the Oklahomans or Iowans or Ohioans or whatever the fuck they are stare in cow-faced confusion at a sign, as if an ant-stream of people balancing sodas on plastic trays doesn't clue them to *go right,* and definitely far, far away from me.

I like the bar at the Kennedy Center. *Not* because it's almost always where I meet my dad since I informed him mall lunches are an embarrassment but because there are these tiny round tables about as big as cookies dotted around what my dad calls an "alcove." You sit on either white leather cubes or a short, stiff couch with fringy hippie pillows, and the lights are way low and the candles, which are real wax, flicker differently in here, kind of slower and moodier. We always snag a table in the "alcove" where I'm the youngest person *by far* and I love everyone staring at me through the shadowy light pretending they're not. I love how a waiter might smirk something like, "Sure you're in the right place, 'miss'?" and I get to go all snot-bitch about how I'm meeting my *father*, and give his name, and their mouth pops like a blowfish.

I love the Kennedy Center bar, the "alcove," and if not my father, at least his name. I wouldn't tell anyone this, ever, but I keep a secret scrapbook of our meetings, each ticket, each program with every single sheet stuffed in the program ("Tonight the part of Tobias Ragg will be played by . . . "), and the bar receipts, which finally, finally my stupid father figured out to just hand over to me instead of me shooting into a pout to make him agree one missing business receipt won't collapse him down into financial hell. Also, the pout is because why is meeting me *business*?

There's so much money on those receipts—I like adding it all up. Then tossing in the ticket price. And the taxi money getting here, and the taxi home which I can't ditch with him hovering around the line outside the Kennedy Center, working it, then doing the "last wave" when I get driven off, like a salute, like I'm off to war. What that money adds up to is a satisfying figure, almost a super-tremendously huge figure. That's me knowing how much he loves me, which might be pathetic if the figure weren't so satisfyingly huge.

He's not there yet, and the best table in the alcove is waiting for us, the one up front with perfect-frame view of anyone strolling up to the host stand or leaving the restaurant, anyone in the bar, and my father also in a perfect-frame, with me at his side. I snag that table, wedging in front of a wavering couple deciding drinks versus a real dinner in the restaurant, so I show them a thing or two, flinging myself onto the couch, then rearranging into a decorative pose with my arm draping along the back edge. I like how my tinkly bracelets puddle down my wrist, and I give a little shake to rev them. I've practically memorized the menu so I decided on the Metro I'm ordering tuna tartare, a dish not in my mother's repertoire, and french fries, which he's too chickenshit to order after his doctor said staying clear of fried foods would add years to his life. So he wolfs half mine and talks tough, going something like, "I think the man means it will feel like years." Haha, ha-de-haha. He's a little too used to people jumping to laugh their asses off at his dumb jokes.

The waiter is new, tall, thin, kinda toothpicky, but he doesn't get on me, just hands over a menu—and wine list—and when I use my haughtiest voice, "We will be two," hands me another. He doesn't care. Good for him. I like people who don't give a fuck. He looks barely older than me, like he's supposed to be working a hipster cidery on H Street, wearing a vintage '94 World Cup T-shirt instead of this tidy little ensemble of black poly pants, shirt, and skinny tie. He goes away. He's in charge of the alcove tables.

I read over the wines. My father drinks red if we're ever somewhere private, which we aren't anymore, and white if we're out because he's all, "Red wine stains the teeth." It's only repeating what some top-dollar K Street consultant said, but in his voice like the deep-deep-blue sea, it sounds very true. He's like a hundred and ten but that voice of his won't quit. My mother drinks whatever. She couldn't give the littlest fuck about stained teeth. She'd be on like her fifth glass already. She's drinking herself to death. Last month, at this exact table, I told my father that, those words. He said, "I am not your mother's keeper."

"Me neither," I said.

One of those lonely, late-nightish-feeling silences. Then I said, "It's like stepping right over a homeless man in the doorway of the Starbucks where you're going for a vanilla latte," which he totally would do, totally, which I also told him.

"I would not step over a homeless man in front of a Starbucks," he said. "I have sponsored many bills to protect the homeless," and there he was, launching into it, H.R.-number *this*, H.J.Res *that*, about to practically pin a campaign button to my sweater, but in sanity's self-interest I cut in: "Dad, I'm too young to vote, and I'm not in your district anyways," and that launched his famous laugh, head flying back, table slaps, wounded crow squawks, haha, ha-de-haha. He laughs like someone's filming it, like someone films whatever tiny thing he does. Probably sleeps like someone's filming that. That time, when he stopped with the laugh, when he didn't see me laughing, he went, "Remember what I said about not calling me 'dad.'"

His district's in North Carolina. That's where his other family lives, the real one, the newest one, with the cute twin babies and their matchy-matchy names. The chubbiest cheeks! You just want to pinch them! Even my stupid mother coos crap when they're on TV, hauled in for some special event like the Easter Egg Roll, which is a bajillion bawling kids uniformed in tiny suits and itchy dresses, shrieking, "Mommy! Daddy!" and messing up the White House lawn, muddles of parents fraught with self-importance, pushing in for photos they'll slap on Instagram and their office wall.

I could dig up my phone and see why he's late this time, but I'm de-gridding, trying to push past grabbing Daddy Apple every nanosecond. I mean, I love my phone, obviously, but this other way is super interesting, very olden days not knowing the temperature unless you're standing outside or remembering things with *my mind*, not a photo. No Channel of Me, broadcasting where I am, what I'm thinking. If I had more than one friend, two *maybe*, my current phone abstinence might be a thing, but my friend or *maybe* friends are so fuck-it, it's like they're forgiving.

There's a man across the hallway, standing at the bar-bar, one foot on a stool rung instead of, hello, *sitting* on the stool, and he's putting the eye on me. Yes, he is! I jolt straighter, give the bracelets a cute jingle. Toss my hair, trying not to be horsey. If my school was normal, I'd learn the right moves from those gorgeous bitch-girls, but I've been dumped into the school for black-sheep rich kids. The guy who started it ran a normal rich-kid school until he noticed how like all those kids had a brother or sister not "working out" so he started this whole other school specifically for those kids. He jacked up tuition and plugged in the code words, starting with the "-ives"—alternative, creative, progressive, supportive—and moving into the real salivators—group projects, common areas, independent thinkers, their own imagination, self-expression, and discovery—all topped with the code-word daddy of them all: EXCLUSIVE. Your kid will be a fuck-up alongside *only* the best fuck-ups. My dad pays my tuition—money I won't add to that number of how much he loves me because private school and college tuition are in the court papers. Tuition is *business*.

The man eyeing me does one of those itty-bitty head nods with a half-smile. He's got wavy long hair down to his shoulders, so I like that, but he's ancient and boring to look at. T-shirt and Brooksy blue blazer and old man gum-sole shoes, like LA meets DC meets capital-F fugly. He should be over with the plastic trays. He shouldn't be looking at me. He should know better, dirty old man. I'm like half his age, even if he's buying I'm twenty-one, or pretending to buy it. Another stupid half-nod, and his foot drops off the rung, an on-the-move move.

Riding the Metro, I overheard a soccer-mom lady go into her phone, "Nothing stabs deeper than the eye roll of a teenage girl," so I inflict that pain on him, flicking my lip in scorn, doubling down with a sneer, and giving him the heave-ho.

He laughs! He laughs *at me* and sucks on his cheap-brand beer bottle, swigging the backwash sloshing the bottom before lifting a finger for another.

I will *not* grab my phone for cover though my face burns as hot as it gets, like a bonfire is raging over my cheeks. Everyone saw. Everyone heard. I'm *so* stupid.

The waiter stops by, blocking my view of the stupid man, which is excellent for me. "Anything while you wait?" he asks like it's a line he's memorized for somewhere else, and I say, "Tuna tartare," kinda in the same way. If I eat it all before my dad gets here, he'll pay for another. It's appetizer size, so not like I'm hogging the trough, which is one of my father's big sayings from the olden days. Then I say, "Pinot grigio," pronouncing it I hope properly, and he cuts me a look, but then goes, "Yeah. Okay."

Like they'll shut down the world-famous John F. Kennedy Center for the Performing Arts and arrest everyone in it for serving me!

This is an exciting development. I hope grigio is the white pinot, not the red, because the stained teeth thing sounds logically real.

What happens when my father pulls in and I'm sipping wine? It's possible he'll be proud. Why, when he was my age—he says in that deep-blue, rolling ocean voice—he was driving tractors into town and smoking a pack a day and his grandmother sold "hooch" out behind the tobacco barn. I never met those people, so they're basically a dream. There's another family, by the way, the first family my father made, which didn't stick, so he made another one, then another. Maybe another one I'm forgetting right now. Trying to get it right. Those first-family kids are grown-ups now, busy hating me and my mom. The cute matchy-named twins are too little to hate us, but they will the minute they're old enough to know what hate is, how to do it. I mean not like how I hate grapefruit, but the kind of hate that bends your life. Hate that coils around and through your every breath, until it is your every breath. Hate like that is getting beamed right at me and my mom from North Carolina *every single second*.

I try not to feel it, but my mom does. Sometimes she says things like, "If I'd've known it'd be this, I'd've thrown myself off that bridge like they all wanted." I don't know what bridge, but I guess some bridge, some moment, some fulcrum. Then she'll look at me and go, "Only thing he ever loved was his own reflection smiling back every morning in the mirror." She'll go, "He doesn't love you any." She'll go, "We're lucky like hell that lawyer's got teeth." She'll go, "If he loved you, would he leave you here with me? You know I'm right, Madison," and it's like the words jumped from my head to hers, and that's when it's shut-her-up time and I cram in earbuds or slam a door running outside or wrestle her to bed, trying for face-up, leaving behind ice in a washcloth for the headache coming on later, if I feel like it.

Finally here's my wine, and finally here's my father, tornadoing in with left and right hand waves, and the smile and *the* voice going "howareyou" one word, not a question, grip-n-grinning as people cluster, even touching the awful man at the bar who steps in for his share. "He's in love with a crowd," says my mom. Sometimes he's solo, which is *whew*, but tonight a couple shadows trail my dad like vapor. Those guys with their earpieces and sunglasses think they're better than god with their glower. My dad said once he doesn't like them knowing "too much" so it's not his idea dragging them along. They never laugh.

He's got on a gray suit, like always; a flag pin, like always; and a lavender tie, a new color I think, with its big, important knot pressed tight up into his collar. The silk looks extra-glossy, thick as tapestry, and just by that glance I know the tie's super-hideously expensive. There's a lady whose job is shopping. He hasn't been inside a store since forever, since I bet before I was born. She buys the presents for me, and she's got good taste, or good enough anyway, and certainly she's got her calendar all set up right because gifts arrive on the dot, wrapped in store paper, brought by messenger. It's dismal imagining that little ding on her phone yipping and her thinking, "Shit. Time to pick out a sweater for the unwanted kid."

The waiter steps backward, adding a second hand to balance the tray holding my wine, edging himself out of the way so my father can sit down, which he does, sinking onto the couch next to me. He's no fan of the leather cubes, not my dad who likes "vertebral support." The shadows melt back. "Hello, sir," the waiter says, even though he's supposed to say—and at the Kennedy Center there'd be a job requirement to know, plus about everyone in Washington knows—he's supposed to say "Mr. Speaker" . . . "Hello, Mr. Speaker," like that, tack on a "sir" to nail it in, "hello, Mr. Speaker, *sir*." Plenty of people don't like my father, maybe hate him a little bit, since some blogger and then the news found out he all of a sudden doesn't recite the Pledge of Allegiance, which, oh boy, is actually really how they start every day of Congress, like it's kindergarten. Sometimes he mouths the words, but he goes tight-lipped and perfectly still at "under God." C-SPAN got a close-up. Suddenly, he's America's atheist. On Opening Day for the Nats, his butt was welded in the seat when everyone else leapt like sheep at "God Bless America," and a fake video went viral with him gobbling down corn dogs while the chorus goes on behind him. "I don't have to believe in God to love my country," he booms on TV, talking about the video, "and whose god do you suggest I choose?" My mom is really into this, with her witch cackles, saying he's fast-tracking to oblivion now, with a political death wish and it's "suicide by voter," and she knows there's an "end game" somewhere. I don't know what to think. Good for him maybe? Some campaign manager quit, which everyone suddenly cared about.

The waiter's sliding in the wine (the white one; I was right), and I'm reaching, but my father says, "This girl is fifteen," and he grabs for the glass and I kind of keep holding the stem though I don't think I mean to and the waiter's trying to pull his arm out of the tangle, and anyway, the wine ends up dumped all over my dad's pant leg and that's so awkward and embarrassing and everyone in the alcove knows my dad after that grand entrance of his so he can't yell at me or the waiter and he has to laugh a fake laugh like everything's super-insanely hilarious and paste on a grim smile showing his white, unstained, politician teeth, and now he'll have to sit in Symphony Hall with a wet leg like he peed himself. And no wine for me!

The waiter races over with a whole huge stack of clean white cloths. His face is too red, kinda scary like all his blood is right *there,* about to burn off, but my dad won't pick up even one cloth, just leaves them tumbled on the table, while he hisses me a lecture, the whole waltz about how embarrassing this all is and I should know better and how people with cameras are *everywhere* and how YouTube and Twitter are Satan's tools (which is dramatic effect, unless an atheist's allowed to believe in the devil? Does it work that way?). Anyway, who's so lame and bored they're going to watch wine spilling on YouTube? Really, is anyone? No one knows I'm his daughter unless I make a big fuss saying so. It's not like my lip or any part of *my* body touched even one tiny drop of that tasty-looking pinot grigio. It's not like he ever even says my name: Mad-i-son.

Now the bad-luck waiter's got my plate of tuna tartare in his hand and he's over to the side, stupidly tall and towering up there, like he knows not to interrupt but like some chef was hollering in the back to *pick up, pick up*, so now he's just planted there clutching that poor plate. Plus the jumble of towels fills up the table. I'm mumbling, "Sorry, sorry, I'm sorry," thinking I can quicken things, and the man who eyed me is at it again, the turd, but eyeing my father this time, with that rustling and clothes-tugging like he's about to slither on over for "just a few words," and it's a 7:30 *curtain* so it's not like we've got all the time in the universe or anything, and why these people think my dad even pays one iota of attention to what they're spitting at him, or what makes these people think he *cares*—well, it's ridiculous. Shoot him an email, dude—now is not when you want your political "coffee klatch," with my dad busily whisper-yelling up a froth at his unwanted daughter, the girl who helped turn him into "not-president," into "never-president," unless a line of people die first. So half the country hates him again, now that he's gone atheist. How can he stand being so hated? How can he *stand* it? Maybe I'll shoot him an email and ask.

Finally he stops his "filibuster." Haha, ha-de-haha.

The waiter pounces to scoop away the million wasted cloths and squeeze in my plate of tuna, the polished pink cubes resting on scalloped rows of see-through-thin cucumber slices, each with a bright dot of sriracha sauce. So pretty! I want two. My father says for him, saladnodressing, one word, and I say, "And I'll also take an order of french fries," (they come in a paper cone), and my dad puffs a sigh, but then he looks right into my eyes and winks. I love when he does that. I like to imagine him and the president both way tense and jumpy at a long shiny table of people wearing suits and army medals, going all cats and dogs about something stupid, and then there's my dad winking. Make that video, you guys. My dad orders icedteaextralemon. I could mention how tea is *staining* to the teeth. But he's not into people telling him things. He's more of the permanent teller. The waiter goes. My dad could get him fired!

The wine smells razor-sharp. That part of his pants is darker gray, the stain as big as cabbage leaves and the same shape. "Sorry," I say again. We're alone, the shadows stiff, dark-suited boards somewhere. It must be so boring being them.

My dad's so quiet, but not quiet because he's thinking. Not quiet because something important's happening on his phone. Quiet like, show's over, folks. My shoulders tighten. I'm way tensed up. I eat my tuna tartare very, very quietly, not clinking my fork against the plate or my teeth. It's yum. I wouldn't mind a Diet Coke since there won't be pinot grigio. The whole rest of the place is noisy as can be, the swinging alcove, people hugging and jostling around the host stand, even that guy at the bar bending to speak close to a red-haired waitress. But our tiny table is its own orb of quiet. He never knows what to say to me. I'm not so hard to talk to, am I? We're both fans of the french fry.

These visits are in court papers too. An order. He is ordered to see me. But they can't order him to talk. He picks the Kennedy Center. He picks being late. I don't care. Nobody has to love anyone for the show of it all to work, right? I'm swiveling so he won't catch my frozen-shut face, hunting the waiter because I'm *so* getting more of this tuna which I've practically finished.

The red-haired waitress moves on, lucky for her, so the man eyeing us eyes us again, and yanks a sleeve, glides into the crowd, coming over to bore us to *death* with his "concerns" as my dad pulls up his plastic smile and gets ready, and there's a knife tucked in the man's hand that no one sees. I'm the only one seeing. The shadows don't see but I do, the winking glint, the thin glimmer of slivery steel.

Time's a crawl so I'm thinking a whole bunch of things strung one after the other, even if they don't make sense, like it's a stage knife from the props department, or it's a joke and this man is from the same fraternity as my father back in their college days, and I want to stare into the man's evil face so I can describe him but his face is pure blank, like there's not even one single feature on this face, and all that's in my head is the photo of John Wilkes Booth from my history textbook and his puffy flop of hair and wild mustache, and I'm not screaming or going "look out, look out, look out" because I'm plunged underwater, off a bridge, into that bad dream where you can't move, chest crushed into a deflated ball and legs heavy like the sandbags I helped pile down by the waterfront when that hurricane blew up from the Outer Banks a million years ago and basements and stores flooded in Old Town and there are all these thoughts, and I can't decide if I love my father, and I do, I have to, because he's the only father I'll ever have, and when my father stands up, and the shadows are pushing and shoving, and the bad-luck waiter comes barreling in, tackling the shadows, and everyone's screaming their heads off now, even me, and I jump up and fling myself on top of my father's body, crashing him to the hard floor, protecting his chest—protecting him—and the knife slides carefully into my body, like I'm butter, "like I'm butter," is exactly what I think I'll tell the cops and TV people, and it doesn't hurt, nothing hurts right now, and I feel brave and also so stupid, and I'll tell that to the cops too, tell everyone because that's who will be listening to me, everyone, and I will tell them, *This is what love looks like, right?*

WEALTH MANAGEMENT

The husband of this couple sitting on the opposite side of the booth is Drew's wife's work friend, more or less, probably more. For sure more. Drew doesn't want to be here at this Saturday night dinner. But his wife Chloe had informed him, "It'll be good for you." "Good how?" he'd asked. She'd repeated, louder, "Good," as if increased volume were significant. So here he is.

It's a fish restaurant, in one of the fancy suburbs, though why here, Drew wonders, after the husband's wife announces she's allergic to shellfish. There's a long story about discovering this allergy while eating oysters two years ago in Nantucket. "My body betrayed me," she says solemnly, and in unison everyone sips their oversize, ice-chippy martinis. Right when they sat down, she conducted a long conversation with the waiter about which menu items were safe for her to order. "The seafood tower is out," he'd said, going for a joke. No smile: "Once there was clam juice in a sauce," she said. "Such a nightmare." Broiled salmon for her, well-done. The husband picked crab cakes, maybe grabbing his chance to live large. Drew can't remember his own choice. Some nonfishy fish.

Chloe sits on the outer edge of the booth bench, shunting Drew to the interior, which feels vaguely unmanly to him. He's opposite the wife who has nicked his shin with her pointy-toed shoe twice, an accident he presumes; "Oops," she murmurs after each incident. He's been told their names but is refusing to use them, even to think them. This is the tiny rebellion he allows himself.

Everyone's fortyish, living in suburban DC. Everyone drives an upscale foreign car and bitches about the price of oil changes. Everyone loathes their commute, exaggerating its length. Everyone's white. *Interchangeable* is the word settling in Drew's head. This wife nags about the same things Chloe does, like his not wanting to go out on a Saturday night, and this wife probably earns as much in her job, votes for the same candidates, uses the same perfume. Chloe's on track for a shellfish allergy, he concludes. (She orders tuna.) Chloe and the wife go with vodka martinis, Drew and the husband with gin.

There's some long story the husband's telling, about waiting in line for something, bringing fold-up chairs and umbrellas. Apple, Black Friday. Drew won't wait in any line deeper than two people. One of the things Chloe natters about, how he sits in a molded chair until right before the airline gate closes. Or lingers in the theater lobby, ambling in as the show starts, bumping through a row of knees to his seat. Goes to Starbucks at off-hours or bolts if it gets crowded. "You know what this says about you?" Chloe says, and he shakes his head no; how can this be meaningful? "That you're selfish," she says, a judgment he can accept. They've been married five years, together seven. Such secret relief to find a woman who didn't want children. He could have been talked into one, possibly two—but he's not someone who needs to reproduce. The husband has a child from a previous marriage, according to Chloe, a teenage daughter who lives in Providence. The husband is from Rhode Island. Chloe knows it all. When Rhode Island comes up in conversation, Drew mentions it's one of six states he's never been to, but instead of the husband saying something ordinary like, you should go, he stares silently, absorbing this piece of information, his eyes edged with glassy rage.

The wife's laughing at something Chloe has said. Everyone's laughing except Drew, so he catches up. Equally quickly, it's silence and back to gulping martinis. What an uncomfortable fit for a dinner, when he could be home watching baseball or golf, gently numbed by green grass on a giant TV screen. "Who's winning?" Chloe might ask, startling him with an irritating question. "Home team," he'll answer.

Chloe goes on about this guy, on and on, uttering his name a hundred times a day, calling him her work husband, which is a thing. Drew looked it up online. Your special guy friend at the office. The one who knows how you want your coffee, the one you give the gossip to first. Intimate. Platonic. Work husband.

The repetition of this name is a shovel digging deeper and deeper. He's embarrassed to watch the two of them, sitting opposite each other, how carefully they don't let their eyes linger and lock, their hands tightly folded, about as virtuous as praying at a pew. He imagines this posture at meetings, over lunches, in front of vendors, at office happy hours amid the swirling crowd. The whole office has to see. Also the wife here, with her pointy shoes. The waiter probably pegs those two as the married couple, figuring Drew and the wife are a misguided fix-up.

It's not physical, he wants to whisper to the wife, just a crush. Harmless, implies Urban Dictionary. The wife looks like one of those tense, determined women, frantic to see bad things with her own eyes.

"Another martini?" Chloe asks. "Are you having another?" The question is directed nowhere and dangles until the husband jumps in, "We took an Uber, so . . ."

Drew circles his finger "another round" to the waiter, deciding for everyone. He's already planning to pick up dinner, to be grand that way while testing the husband. How hard will he protest? Chloe and the husband work in a do-gooder, low-paying field, while Drew is in wealth management. The wife does something with the government.

The waiter clears the dirty glassware, and there they all are, no alcohol. The wife sips water, accidentally kicks Drew under the table, says, "Oops. Sorry. Again." The wife's lips are extra-glossy, so shiny Drew swears he sees his own reflection.

The husband says, "Do you need to trade places with me?"

"I'm fine," she says.

"You keep kicking the poor guy," he says.

She laughs, fast and rabbity.

"No, for real," the husband says. "What is that, like the sixth time?"

The wife sets her glass of water back into its pool of condensation. Just a small tap, but oddly loud.

Chloe says to the husband, "I'll kick you six times, make it even." He studiously not-smiles. His face is perpetually pinched, with those ridiculous jutting cheekbones women like Chloe sigh over. Drew's face is pumpkin-fat, or so it feels. You'd need two of this guy's face to drape over his.

Drew says, "It was only twice. No need to knock yourself out, Chloe."

The wife says, "Give me a break."

The husband says, "I'm just saying." He leans back hard in the booth, a combination of triumph and dissociation. So does the wife. Her lower jaw juts forward. One of them makes a tongue-click.

Chloe's hand is on the table, and she nudges it over to envelop Drew's, pressing into a long, luxurious squeeze. Look how we're a happy couple, that pose chides, look at me. Her fingers are cold from too much AC, though Drew's back is clammy with sweat. Chloe's not a cheater. In her early thirties she was a week away from marrying a man who turned out to be leading a double life, with a year-old kid and a girlfriend in a nearby suburb. That's when she moved from Louisiana to DC, desperate to start over where no one knew what she called her "pathetic story." "I had a Toyota Corolla, two suitcases, and a box of Waterford from his relatives I wasn't about to return," she'd confided to Drew when they met at a rooftop

Fourth of July party a month after she'd arrived. "I'm from here," he'd said, and she'd glared as if his story were ludicrous. "Really," he'd added. "Sibley Hospital. First baby of the new year." And strangely that detail made her smile and uncross her arms. Now she tells people she's an army brat who grew up all over, never mentioning Louisiana. Chloe is the new name she chose for what she calls her "storybook ending."

The wife leans forward and asks, "Have you ever saved someone's life?" Clearly she craves chatter. Her smile is toothy and high-watt, but also brittle.

The husband closes his eyes and says, "This again?" It's a low, muttery growl, though not low enough, and the words are quite clear to Drew, and likely to Chloe too. Poor wife, hooked up with this steaming albatross turd. Drew shouldn't be happy the guy's a douche, but obviously he's thrilled. He places his other hand on top of Chloe's, playing her happy couple game, but the instant he does, the husband's eyes pop open, and Chloe messily disentangles from Drew, creating the excuse of flicking a crumb on the table to hunch her shoulders and lean forward, purposely offering up—he swears—a titty flash down the V-neck of her new dress. But then she grabs Drew's hand, leans against his shoulder, her head a sudden, ten-ton weight. The husband gets fluttery and pissy. Happy couple!

The wife says, "I'm asking them. Not you."

The husband's face pinches tighter but he's silent.

Chloe stares at her fingernails, which are shellacked turquoise. She suddenly sighs, as if this scene is as excruciating as she expected. "Where are those ever-loving drinks?" she says, and she and the husband laugh together, and she explains, "It's just something someone says at work."

So. "What happened?" Drew asks the wife. "I never saved anyone's life. Must be amazing."

Out comes a long story about CPR in a CVS aisle when she was fourteen, the day after the Red Cross babysitting course where they practiced on dummies. There's a rhythm to the story, with certain words emphasized and dramatic pauses; it's clear she tells it often. The husband must feel guilty because he laughs when they're supposed to and supplies a key detail: "What about your strawberry lip gloss that smeared the guy's face and what his wife said?"

Throughout, Chloe leans against Drew. She's barely breathing, very still, like something barely contained. Is it just plain crazy or is it audacious to push him into this date? Like she's expecting something from Drew? He's not a guy who punches guys. The only grand gesture he envisions tonight is when the check comes. The husband's already finished a couple of Chloe's sentences for her, and she his; he said, "Grey Goose? You saw there's Belvedere, right?" showing off that he, too, knows Chloe's preferred brand of vodka.

Maybe he and the wife *are* a fix-up, Drew thinks. Maybe those three are all in on it, everyone except him, hoping for a swap like some Netflix rom-com.

This new V-neck dress is for the work husband, Drew already knows, as are the happy couple games. But it smacks his gut deep to understand suddenly that it's the husband who Chloe's expecting, or demanding the grand gesture from tonight, and that's why this dinner and this set of games he's barely a player in. Drew and the wife are incidental fodder, nowhere close to the center of this story. Right then the second set of drinks arrives, and everyone grabs for their drinks nervously and greedily. The waiter lingers, apologizing for a delay on the main courses—someone's food fell on the floor, so they're making everything over again, fresh. "Dessert is on the house," the waiter says. He stands there a moment, as if waiting to be thanked—which he isn't; don't drop our fucking food, Drew thinks, sensing the husband also thinking exactly that. Finally the waiter steps away. This dinner will stretch beyond the end of time. Right now, Drew couldn't say why he married Chloe. Because they'd been dating two years, and like an alarm clock, time was up? Because he thought that someone who'd been cheated on wouldn't cheat on him? Because he was afraid not to?

"They never hand out free liquor," the husband says. He speaks with authority, as if this is an important observation, then tilts his glass for a different view of his olive.

"Actually, they do sometimes," the wife says.

"Jesus, just agree," the husband says. Pouts, he pouts the stupid sentence.

Chloe twists to kiss Drew on the cheek. Her lips are chilled and ghostly, the skin slightly chapped. He smells the faint undertone of the Chanel No. 5 he gave her last Valentine's Day . . . or, he assumes, because he couldn't pick Chanel No. 5 out of a line-up, though a work husband surely could.

The wife says, "You know what Dorothy Parker said about martinis, right?"

The husband says, "Yes. We all know."

"Not me," Chloe says, pressing up against Drew's arm. "I don't know."

"Yes, you do," the husband says. "We were talking about it in the staff meeting on Thursday."

"I don't remember," Chloe says.

"For fuck's sake," Drew says. "'A martini is fine, two at the most. Give me three and I'm under the host.' That's pretty much what she said."

"So funny," Chloe says, not laughing, not smiling. "I know I would have remembered that."

The wife says, "Actually, she didn't say it. I don't know why I said she did because I read online that actually she drank scotch and actually this is one of those urban myths. Like the things Mark Twain didn't say. She should have said it, I guess."

Drew says, "Here's to urban myths," and he lifts his glass and everyone copycats. "Who gives a shit who said what if it's funny, right?" he says. "To being fucking funny!" and up go the glasses again. Chloe and the work husband finally lock eyes, send their secret messages: "my drunk husband," "my annoying wife."

The wife says, "Do you mind with the swearing? I mean . . ."

The husband says, "Once a Southern Baptist, always a damn Southern Baptist. We've got a cuss jar, if you can believe that."

"Interesting," Chloe says with a cruel smile.

The wife's face flushes pink. "Hon," she warns.

"Dollar a word." The husband laughs, as does Chloe.

"Sorry," Drew lies. "My potty mouth fucks me up constantly." Somehow, this second martini is half gone already. He wiggles his wallet from his back pocket and dredges out a five that he lets drift onto the table. "Guess I'm good for two more," he says. "Unless you've got change?"

"I do," she says, grabbing her purse.

"I'm kidding," Drew says. "Keep the extra. And I'll watch the cursing." She folds the bill and drops it into her purse, which is badass or embarrassing or both. He doesn't need the five bucks, but that she took it.

"Curse away," the husband says. "It's not like she controls you."

"Hey, I'll pay for his 'damn Southern Baptist,'" Drew says. "And spot him one more."

"Drew curses too much anyway," Chloe says. "He'll survive. He's a big boy." There's a moment where he feels everyone focused on him, assessing his bulk. Then Chloe says, "Anyway, I grew up with a cuss jar down in Louisiana. I'd've lost my whole allowance at a dollar a word." Drew is disoriented, unsure why, unless it's the gin, but it's not, it's Louisiana. That the work husband knows about that.

Chloe concludes abruptly, as if sensing a screw-up: "Ours was only a nickel. But really. Who cares? I'm just going on. I don't think about back then because it was so long ago. It's goodbye to all that. I mean, as much as anyone can say goodbye to all that. Can we wipe away the past completely?"

"I didn't know you were from the south," the wife says. "So interesting." She sounds interested.

"Chloe doesn't like talking about her past," the husband mansplains. The wife "hmmms," as apparently something clicks into place, and the husband jumps back in, as if keeping up with PowerPoint slides: "I was going to say, people predict coins are going to be obsolete in the next ten years."

"Probably more like money in general," Chloe says. "We're all going to pay with our phones. Or a chip embedded in our wrist." She flips her left wrist, exposing her pale, hairless skin, the narrow blue vein shooting directly up to her beating heart. Not like being naked—but, also, it is. Drew is certain the husband has kissed her there, on the underside of her delicate wrist. Chloe's smile is faint, shadowy, secret. The husband's too, in a mirrored reflection.

The wife leans in and presses her shiny lips onto her husband's cheek. "It's pennies that are going to be obsolete," she says. "Not all coins." His turn to flush pink, not daring to swipe his face clean of that indistinct lip print seared onto him.

Chloe folds her arms around her chest.

"Isn't that what you do, manage money?" the husband says to Drew. "Manage wealth?" He makes *wealth* sound like something requiring a buck in a cuss jar. "What's the difference between wealth and money? Is that a specific figure?"

Drew sighs. "Is this the part where we drone about jobs?" he asks. Chloe huffs a protest, and the wife says, "Work talk is so DC. Let's don't do it." He and the husband eye each other. The guy's hairline has receded to about the center of his head.

Drew thinks of a plastic headband, like his little sister wore. This guy? *This guy?*

"People spend more hours of their lives at work than anywhere else," the husband says. He clutches his butter knife like he's threatened. Then the prick smiles at Drew, showing off his coffee-stained teeth, or tea-stained.

"Drew hates his job," Chloe says. "But I have a funny story not about work."

"About saving someone's life?" Drew asks. The wife titters in her rabbity way, then clamps a hand over her mouth for a quick moment.

Chloe ignores him: "So, this happened the other night, when I was downstairs looking for my reading glasses."

"I've heard this," the husband says. "About the cereal."

Drew's muscles tighten, rising along his body in a hard, ready ridge. He instantly knows the story, knows exactly what's coming—it's not about cereal; who tells stories about cereal?—but he says anyway, "Go on."

Chloe shakes her head. "Not that one about the cereal, though that's funny. So anyway, I'm in the kitchen and hear this thumping outside on our deck, and when I turn on the light, there at the sliding glass door is this coon with a fish—"

"Raccoon," the husband says.

"Yeah, right. This coon holding a fish in its little hands, and the guiltiest look on its face. So the coon—"

"Raccoon," the husband repeats, louder.

"Racoon, coon," Chloe says. "Same thing."

"Well, up here we say raccoon."

"The animal, of course," Chloe says. "You know exactly what I mean." She tosses her napkin toward him. "Anyway, there's lipstick on your face."

He rubs barehanded, wipes his hand on his pants. Slides the napkin back to her. "I'm just saying, say raccoon. Not coon."

"I know what a raccoon is," she says. "Where I'm from, it's coon. The smelly, stripy furball dripping rabies is a coon." Her fingers and thumbs form into two goggle-circles that she presses up against her eyes, like a mask. She speaks slowly: "Coon. A dumb old coon, like my brothers shoot in Louisiana. The animal. Nothing more than that. Just a simple word." She lets her hands drop away from her face, sets them palms down on the table. "Coon."

"People can hear you," the husband says.

"People can hear *you*," she says.

The husband stretches one hand toward the breadbasket that's just beyond his grasp, but no one nudges it closer. So he reaches across the table, almost a lunge, and grabs it himself, roots for the jalapeño bread, which he doesn't butter. He chews with his mouth flapping open. Almost unfair, Drew thinks, all the things to dislike about the guy.

"Then what happened?" the wife asks. "When you saw it?" Her words are as delicate as corn silk, seemingly as innocent. Drew could tack on, *go on*, but holds off.

"When I saw the *coon*?" Chloe says, defiant emphasis on the last word.

"Just stop," the husband says. "We're not allowed to say that. White people just aren't. So never say it again, and everyone feels better." He looks at Drew, appealing to him with a man-to-man vibe, as if his next words will be, *control your woman*. Drew half-hopes they are, escalating the scene. Instead, the husband speaks through tightened lips: "Maybe you don't know what that word means, Chloe?"

"I know you're calling me a racist because I grew up in a backward place where we all call a furry animal a coon."

"Maybe I am," he says.

"I mean the animal," she says. "It's my story, and it's just a word."

"That we are not allowed to say, goddamn it!" He bangs his fists on the table, making the silverware bounce.

That's when a team of waiters arrives armed with ridiculously oversize plates they place on the table elaborately, but incorrectly, each plate in front of the wrong person. There's a shuffling, shifting the plates to their proper places, and the drama of the announcement that the plates are very, very hot. (Not true; Drew taps his with the tips of his fingers.)

It's all sorted out, and the team is turning to leave when Drew says, "Let's ask what he thinks," as he points to one of the waiters, not theirs, but the Black one, with the shaved head, perfectly domed and almost glowing in the restaurant light. The man pauses, balanced on the balls of his feet, arms folded cricket-like behind his back in classic waiter pose. Ready to serve. Doing his job for an hourly wage plus tips. If he's apprehensive, he's concealing those feelings. Drew knows the man doesn't deserve being used as a prop, but, well. All's fair, right? Everyone at this table is already hateful.

"What do you need?" Their official waiter butts in, waving for the busboy to fetch the water pitcher.

"Go on, Chloe. Ask," Drew says. He speaks evenly, and stares at the husband's cheekbony face. The wife's shoe bangs his shin yet again, but he doesn't flinch, and there's no murmured apology. Drew's motivations feel as unclear as they are powerful: Punish Chloe? Impress the wife? Show off to the pompous ass? Prove to himself he's whatever a "man" is?

"Everything looks great," Chloe says. "Thank you." Her taut smile is possibly causing muscle pain. She sucks in a deep breath, and Drew is half-terrified, half-hoping that she will, in fact, say the word again, shriek it, but she simply puffs out all the air in a noisy gust as the husband acts absorbed in the task of aggressively shaking salt across his food. The wife flicks a dismissive glance at Chloe, then tells the waiter she'll take a glass of sauvignon blanc, and Drew says that sounds good to him too.

The water glasses clink with ice and water, and the team of waiters disperses. Likely the Black waiter didn't notice Drew pointing at him as if at a museum exhibit, didn't hear that barked out *ask him;* likely the waiter's focus was on his job. Likely he heard nothing.

Silverware clatters as they eat.

Then Drew says, "The word isn't from the animal." Unclear if anyone's listening. They're shoveling in the food (which isn't very good, at least his isn't; overcooked). He continues, but instead of speaking more loudly, he lowers his voice, a trick he knows to force people to pay attention: "There was a class in college. We learned about the slave trade, and 'coon' is most likely from 'barracoon,' a Catalan word for the sheds or barracks where they stored the Africans they captured until they could be packed up on the ships and bundled off to America to be auctioned off and sold." He speaks very matter-of-factly, choosing each word carefully, as if he's explaining something complicated to people who are not especially bright, which he does often in his ridiculous job, helping rich people get richer. "Tons of Africans died there, in the barracoons, as you might imagine. Conditions were brutal."

The forks and knives slow, still.

Chloe says, "Well, of course that's terrible. But it's a different thing. You know I meant the animal. You know that. You know me." She's almost pleading, though it's the husband she faces, not Drew.

Drew nods thoughtfully. "Not like it was some wired-up pen or stockade, which would be bad enough. These people were constrained, like shackles. Or a tight iron ring looping their necks to a tree. Chained like unloved dogs. They starved. Dysentery, cholera; can't remember which. Both? Smallpox?

Of course torture. Rape. Months, sometimes, before the slave ships rolled in."

"I'm not a racist," Chloe says. "I know maybe I come from a racist place, and horrible people around me were spouting racist shit, but I'm not a racist because of saying one word."

"Haven't we heard enough?" the husband commands.

Drew pretends this comment is addressed to him. "I'm just explaining," he says. "Look it up. Facts are facts." He leans back. The wine arrives, and the wife grabs at the stem of the glass, balancing it carefully on the way to her lips. "Delicious," she says, taking a second, longer sip.

"I'm not a racist," Chloe says.

"Also, that's where a lot of wealth comes from," Drew says amiably to the husband. "Remember, you were asking earlier. Those slaves."

Drew watches the husband stare down at his mauled crab cakes. Too much filler, not enough meaty chunks of crab. He can't even order well. Drew feels sorry for Chloe; probably the whole table does, pity and a nervous sort of disgust.

Yet Drew is calm, at peace. He enjoys the arrival of juncture, that sensation when things tip decidedly in one direction. That's what he works for in his job, which is more like a therapist's than one might expect, guiding people into considering their money and its role in their lives. Yes, it's been an uncomfortable dinner, but every marriage ebbs and flows, creaks and groans, because while marriage seems to start as a romance, it's a business contract. (Ask his divorced clients!) Worse things have been said, will be said, will be done. We're the ones who assign meaning to the words, Drew could explain right now, otherwise they're literally sounds and squiggles.

Instead, he says, "Honey. It's okay. I love you." He grasps Chloe's hand, his heavy wedding ring pressing against her skin. His insistence leaves her no choice but to press back.

The free desserts are the best part of the meal, they all agree. A tray of tiny crème brûlées, which the Black waiter brings to them, and which they spoon up quickly, debating the best flavor.

He's also the one who brings the check, and Drew reaches for the vinyl folder. "Let me," he says, and Chloe says, "Thank you," and the husband says, "That's not necessary," but Drew slides in his credit card and affects a bored expression, not bothering to read the bill. When this same waiter returns for the signature he stands, hovering, as Drew retrieves his card, and lingers, even as Drew says, "Thank you. Everything was great."

"Thank you," the waiter says. He continues to stand, looming, too tall and his back too straight, and suddenly Drew can't look anywhere. It's not like he said the word; in fact, he's the one who took an African American history class in college. He's not a racist. No one here is. So why does he feel so goddamn shitty, his wife wearing a new dress and flirting all night with a douche?

The waiter stands there, stands there, stands there—it couldn't possibly be for as long as it feels—so Drew examines the credit card bill, mentally calculates twenty percent, then pulls out his wallet. "I tip in cash," he says. "No credit card fee. No taxes. More to take home," and he winks in a way that feels horrifically embarrassing. He drops down bill after bill after bill, as Chloe watches, and when he's about to stop, she nudges his hand. "Remember the desserts were free," she says. "Tip on that total." And he knows exactly what she means, so he adds two more bills to the stack, and another. Signs the receipt. The waiter's hand folds up the vinyl portfolio. "Thank you, sir," he says, and he carries away Drew's cash. Immediately the group scrambles to leave, littering the air with faux promises to "do this again real soon." Chloe thanks Drew again. That prick never does, forcing the wife to play grateful: "We appreciate you treating us. Next time's on us." The waiter has disappeared to somewhere in the back, maybe telling the story of the 42 percent tip.

In the end, Drew knows he has won. What he has won, he doesn't know. Nor does he understand why he wanted to win it. Winning seems like enough, or all there is anyway, and it's these thoughts that are in his head during the drive home as Chloe stares straight ahead, eyes glittery with tears she won't dare let him see. As far as Drew is concerned, it's over. The work husband is divorced. The funny thing is, the story she wanted to tell isn't even a good one, a raccoon dropping one of the neighbor's expensive koi fish on their deck, it flopping around uncomfortably, dying a slow, hard, lonely death.

WE ALWAYS START WITH THE SEDUCTION

The Speaker claims the Wilson Bridge is his "secret place," though as a section of I-95 crossing the Potomac (or: as the nation's most crowded highway spanning the river every op-ed reader recognizes as shorthand for out-of-touch politics), the Wilson Bridge is scarcely secret. Linking Virginia to Maryland, the secret actually might be this pedestrian walkway alongside the southbound side of the bridge that is virtually unknown outside Old Town Alexandria (where the Speaker lives).

The Speaker crosses the bridge several times a week on foot, acknowledging the handful of fellow walkers and joggers with a noncommittal nod or a quick, loose flip of one hand, gestures that tend to go unreturned. He's just another middle-aged white guy getting in his ten thousand steps. Yet he's also the third most powerful man in the United States, which translates to "in the free world." Out walking. He has convinced the no-nonsense security suit-drones to jog back and forth along the walkway, looping him into safe circles, instead of directly tailing him. The men (and women!) are grateful for the exercise. And who will tell their boss?

The Speaker enjoys that he is out among the people, unrecognized, yet also he is made anxious by this fact (unrecognized!). "Do you know who I am?" pulses through his mind, the syllables creating the rhythm his feet fall into as he walks.

The word "secret" is alluring, particularly in Official DC, and catches a woman's ear, but beyond that, he's truly convinced that these anonymous walks carry him into an unfathomable, private space, peeling through exoskeleton, delayering deep to a forgotten scrap of soul, where he imagines himself capable of surprise and what he would call "intimacy." It may seem impossible that the Speaker (or any politician) is capable of surprise or intimacy or what the hell, owning a soul. He *is* capable. We all are. *We all are.*

So, at the office, eager to impress a particular twenty-three-year-old girl, he creates a reason to mention his secret place. This is the brunette he overheard a week ago talking with other girls over sad little lunches of carrots and Triscuits. New-to-Washington, trying-to-be-tough talk amuses the Speaker, so he pauses in the hallway to listen, pretending to text on his phone. One girl says, "Of course you'd F the senator, because there's only a hundred of them, and like four hundred congressmen. And kill the Supreme Court justice, especially you know who." Nervous giggles tinkle like wind chimes, and a small gasp ripples. "C'mon," someone says, "can you imagine? At least the congressmen are young, some of them." The brunette scoops up her long hair, flicking the handful like a horse tail, sends a look around the circle, silently inviting them to lean in closer. He has the sense she knows he's listening. And why not? They are instructed that their job is simple, to be aware of him each second of every working hour, what he might need or request or want. A pen. Coffee. A folder. Without lowering her voice, she says, "Well, if we're talking about *that*, let's all remember there's only one Speaker of the House." She drops her hair so it drapes her shoulder. Another girl wearing a tiny pair of clear plastic glasses says, "That's your goal?" and the brunette laughs and says, "Like playing Powerball. Someone's going to win, so why not me?"

He likes her cocky little laugh. He likes her ambition. He likes the way her hair is draped along her shoulder. He doesn't—EVER (thanks to our tricky modern times)—EVER fuck these young girls or accept blow jobs or request sexts: the phone trail, sure, the upwardly ticking price of the barest tinge of scandal—but perhaps also he is embarrassed, now, to imagine experiencing pleasure from demeaning others, embarrassed that he must acknowledge that it's his title not him, that any pleasure for them is in the title, which, well, demeans him.

But a dose of old-fashioned flirting seems to harm no one, tiptoeing up to and along a defined line everyone agrees won't be crossed. These girls, trained in hookups and dance floor grinding, don't find enough joy in meaningful glances across the sea of navy blue at a tedious reception or the pleasure of clinging longer than necessary to a handshake at a conference table or fingers lightly grazing a jacketed shoulder (never bare skin!) to emphasize a point. He's married, perpetually married, always with one wife or another. So the Speaker flirts, and everyone on the Hill knows this. Flirting is an art, a game to play where, for once, the objective isn't winning. Possibly this is the only game like that the Speaker knows.

The brunette lives in nearby Arlington and why yes, she says, she's a runner, loves running, would love to meet up for a run. Campaign photos show the Speaker midstride, but at the last minute the Speaker invents an injury for himself, navigating the promised group run into a walk instead. She's actually not a runner, not at all, so walking instead is a relief, and she overenthuses her love of walking, how super-fun it will be to walk across the Wilson Bridge. She's thinking about Instagram, how she's already done all the major monuments and the highlights of the Capitol tour the interns lead. (She is not an intern! She has a business card! And a desk!) Maybe a selfie with him, she calculates, something casual that's not the usual grope-line photo fuckery that other people display on their office brag walls. It continues to amaze the Speaker that elements so often fall into place as if preordained.

She's waiting in the park at the foot of the Wilson Bridge, amid the web of asphalt paths crowded with joggers, people pushing strollers or walking dogs, maniacal cyclists. She perches on a bench near the bathrooms, and it annoys him that he can't determine which car in the lot is hers. Not that it matters. But the Speaker believes in gathering information. Information isn't power: information is information, and power is power. But pop your information in the bank, and it becomes currency, and currency "buys that cuppa coffee," as the Speaker likes to drawl.

She wears a short, black athletic skirt—the Speaker doesn't know the word "skort"—and a not-overly-form-fitting red tank. A perky ponytail swings through her UNC cap, and she clutches a Tar Heel blue water bottle. She, like everyone in the office, knows the Speaker graduated from the University of North Carolina. She looks ready for a walk with an uncle. He looks like an uncle. He makes a big show of starting his running watch, grumbling about how cautious his doctor is about the imaginary injury. The security drones are distant, dressed down, looking like any very fit weekend runner equipped with an earpiece.

He has done this the proper way: A group invitation to *all* the DC newcomers, offering to show them this "secret place" on Saturday morning, yet it turns out that only she is able to join him. How is that? #blessed, the Speaker thinks.

According to the Speaker's watch, the walk to the bridge entrance takes six minutes and thirty-one seconds, and they fill that time with lazy clichés about weather because today is a classic August morning in DC: hot, humid, hazy. She asks questions—"It's usually this humid?"—and he makes pronouncements—"Last summer was worse, so imagine that."

Then they're on the walkway, St. Mary's Cemetery below to the left (who are the Fannons, she wonders, eyeing a towering mausoleum carved with that single name, and he could have answered her—"donors"—but she's too nervous to ask). Highway traffic flies by on the right. Speed limit's fifty-five, but Washingtonians are in a rush, so the average runs seventy or more. A high glass wall separates walkers from the road for fifty yards or so, not to protect the people, as she's thinking, but for noise abatement, a concession to the nearby Alexandria houses during the endless negotiations between city, state, county, and federal governments back when the bridge was rebuilt and reconfigured in the last decade.

The glass abruptly ends, leaving only a low cement Jersey barrier between them and the speeding cars. Sound whips up; a dull, racing roar. Like hurtling forward into space, the Speaker always thinks, like moving into the thing where you're not wanted.

"No one walking's been hit by a car?" the girl asks.

"Not yet," the Speaker says.

She better think about something that's not getting mowed down by rampant SUVs. Like, she's walking side by side with the Speaker of the US House of Representatives! The runners looping large circles around them are security. She's never seen him standing alone, being alone. Even in her imagination, when last night she mentally role-played the morning ahead because she couldn't sleep, even then he was surrounded by people. There's a thrill to proximity, though why, she wonders, when it's just a walk.

The cemetery has fallen aside on the left, shifting into the park and a playground below, the jungle of a community garden in the distance (wholesome projects, the Speaker instinctively notes, good government at work) and now—as the bridge rises higher—the river itself is below, the Potomac, a wide ribbon of muddied water, pocked with algae bloom so thick a white egret balances on top.

They've run out of weather clichés, so silence masses between them. The Speaker knows people are nervous around him. "Relax," he'll often urge with faux gusto; but he prefers anxiety. Anxiety gets things done. That's a motto of his. He once told a shrink that anxiety makes him his best self. She suggested that anxiety doesn't foster successful personal relationships. "The only true friend in politics is your dog," he said. "Surprising how many times I've heard that," she said, not that the Speaker was surprised, and not that she was either.

There's a place they stop roughly halfway across, seemingly neither Virginia nor Maryland, a short distance before the drawbridge that rises several times a year allowing historic tall ships to dock at Alexandria and attract tourists and their money. A plaque offers facts about Alexandria's colonial days, but neither the girl nor the Speaker reads it. Instead, they gaze at the cityscape before them—the low townhouses of Alexandria; the zigzag of runways at Reagan National; the District, where the Washington Monument is the size of the Speaker's thumb; the Capitol dome like a thumbtack; the Kennedy Center, the white rectangle of a business card. Government and its grinding bureaucracy a mere clutter, tiny gray blocks easily swept aside. He can't love the city, not the way the girl presumably does, not as newcomers and visitors can, but he admires it as a worthy foe. Admires that it's inanimate and cares nothing for him. "This is the greatest achievement," he once wrote on a piece of paper that he immediately ripped up. Here, he's not that man blustering on C-SPAN or the man stockpiling death threats, endlessly grubbing for money and votes. Here he's no one, he's himself, he's only that boy born long ago.

He needs to say something important right now, something memorable: quotable words. He always needs that, wants always that. It's reflex, not even a desire he knows to express; but the emptiness of silence is a terror and his primary job as a leader, as the Speaker, is to fill emptiness with words and plans, with movement and action. He starts: "I come here to gaze out over the river at this vast sprawl, seeking distance. To view this everythingness." That's why? The question fills his mind, and he pushes out an answer, *this everythingness*, regurgitating until he is satisfied. The words are nonsensical.

She seems attentive, her liquid brown eyes studying his face. And she hasn't pulled out her phone yet; promising, he thinks, not knowing what she's thinking.

She's pondering "everythingness," a word her immediate boss, the speechwriter, would x out with scorn; pondering that the third most powerful man in the nation dreams of distance; pondering what she imagined might be in his head, what should be in there. Legislation?

A plane passes overhead. They watch that, then he points to a nearby spiderweb situated midair, spanning the iron railing and the edge of the historical plaque. A dark spider the size of a quarter poses in the center, as if placed by staff members preparing for this exact moment. Behind the web is a large light to illuminate the bridge at night. One wouldn't have to get nature other than observing moths circling a porch light to understand this superb example of location, location, location. Admirable, how nature is so comfortable with its ruthlessness.

The Dealmaker, new in town, is despised for tornadoing through custom and norms to get what he thinks he wants, attracting sycophants and voters with his big man impression. Power requires discipline: this clown's a blunt tool, serving the backroom maestros. (Try telling him that!) The Speaker still remembers DC's true model for effective ruthlessness, a political operative the whole town knew, a brainy guy who cut his teeth into razors down in the muck of South Carolina politics, a man who "just had to drive in one more stake," as people put it. Hated and feared, admired and loved, wreaking havoc to pull the vote for his guy, his head crammed with glittering political brilliance: no one, *no one* wouldn't want to be in the room this guy filled to capacity. Yet by forty, Beau was dead of brain cancer. Boom. That's how heartless nature is, creating vast potential to squander. He longs to explain to the girl how he could care about such a man years later, care about this loss, but the only words he's got are "politics makes for strange bedfellows." At least he knows the phrase originates with Shakespeare. That's something.

The Speaker inhales, gathers his wits and his memorable words and plunges forward: "Yet here's this spider, reminding us that in the midst of the great vastness is home. That's what we see, where we focus. These few, familiar strands." A comfortable, affable lesson.

"So beautiful," the girl breathes, willing the moment to feel so.

He's relieved: he has created a story for her friends, possibly a story she'll tell often, the "famous person" story. Eventually, maybe soon, she'll mock him and the pompous cliché of his words, centering herself into the story. Yes, the Speaker knows how pretentious he sounds, sermonizing on spiders. But he also knows this: he delivered. Maybe she doesn't get to fuck the Speaker (not this one anyway) but what has happened here is greater. The unspoken promise has been fulfilled, he has done what he has been put on God's earth to do: Create a story. Create a legend. Offer proximity. That, that is his secret place, this rare moment of glimpsing the certainty of his existence. As poets do, as Shakespeare surely did.

The girl props her elbows on the railing and leans, gazing straight down at the river below. "A boat!" she cries. It's filled with tourists taking a scenic trip from Alexandria to Mount Vernon, George Washington's estate. Used to be everyone loved George Washington. She says, "Wave and see if they wave back."

What he thinks right then startles him: one shove puts her over the edge. The bigger surprise: how easy for him to follow. To disappear. To achieve clarity in the fall downward, that flash of seeing what little matters. Beau's final interview was a scandal, a dying man renouncing the life he crafted for himself: "Seventy percent of the things I was frantically pursuing didn't matter anyhow. Forget power and money. I had no idea how wonderful people are." Eyebrows shot to the ceiling. Insiders claimed it was spin, that the man hadn't even torn the cellophane off the new Bible he was all up about and quoting from. "Oh fucking hell, own your evil," his most senior staffer Mary-Grace said, waving the newspaper that contained the damning interview. "No god's buying your precious deathbed confession." But to know in one excruciating instant *what matters*. . . if anything does. Would that be something, everything? "You can acquire all you want and still feel empty," Beau was (mis?)quoted as saying. What might it mean to view with one's own eyes the reckoning to come? To see—too late—in gentle, snowflake swirls, the regrets of one's life? The temptation is here, so to break off these disquieting thoughts, the Speaker takes a brief, calming moment to wonder how the headline reporting his death would read, the size of the font.

Then the girl says, "They're waving back! They see us," and she gestures wildly. "Some guy's taking our picture."

Probably unnecessary, but also powerful instinct, and the Speaker steps back, turns his head, invents an itch on his forehead, shielding his face with one hand.

She's observant and instantly halts the childish waving, moves away from the railing. "I'm sorry," she says. "For not thinking." A swelling burn of tears tells her she's stupid, and being stupid makes her angry. She's always stupid, so stupid.

Him luring her to this so-called secret place, which by the way was written up in the recent *Washingtonian* magazine with the Cheap Eats cover, this is the logical extension of his scandal-filled past, his power, of her essence: cute-not-pretty, smart-not-brilliant, sweet-not-savvy. Easily duped, bought off, or discarded. He sniffed her out, he knows. Her ridiculous talk over lunch. Everyone in DC knows and knows her. The security, trained not to think and judge, silently thinking and judging *right now*. Her plan has been to sleep with him yet tell no one, holding this powerful secret within herself for years and years and years. But now this. Crying. She could be in North Carolina, working for her dad in the family bank. But she didn't want that, she wanted this. "DC is super exciting," she writes in her texts. "I'm meeting so many important people. I'm making a difference in our country."

He feels caught out by something, embarrassed by what's been revealed—his vanity and his paranoia, his mind viewing her as a sexual conquest, *this everythingness*, those unnerving and unnecessary thoughts of regrets—so he talks aside the feelings: "We're tiny figures on a bridge," the Speaker says. "We're nothing, no one." Which is exactly why people jump off bridges like this, he thinks, then, no, no, no: the reason people jump off bridges like this is a lack of government funding for mental-health services. "We're each as vulnerable as this spider," and he chops his hand down the perimeter of the web, watching the spider scuttle upward onto the iron railing and slip deep into a crevice. "We could have killed it dead," he says. "That's the universe we live in. The difference is that the spider is blissfully unaware, and we are willfully unaware."

The girl might email the *Washington Post* or *Politico*, tell them something like, "The guy's losing his mind." Might go straight to Twitter. No one would believe her, of course; she's just a girl. His chief of staff warns: an avalanche is only one flake too many. Over and over he says this, until around the office they call him "Flake," sometimes forgetting he's in the room. "Not cool," the chief of staff says when he catches this nickname being used on him. "Hoping to the motherfucking gods of hell you won't see I'm right, but trust me you will. I'm so right on this." *An avalanche is one flake too many.*

God is dead, the Speaker thinks, then whispers: "God is dead." It's the bone-deep chant of his four AMs, the rhythm reverberating through his skull as he lurches out of bed on sleepless nights to lift weights, hauling them up, easing them down, up, down, regaining his calm.

The girl knows she should have been listening, she admires the Speaker SO MUCH, and wants to learn tons from his wisdom and vast experience, wants him to be impressed by her, wants to *be* impressive herself, and so she can't cry, can't cry, can't cry, can't cry, and there's the first stupid tear, another, another. Better to wipe them away fast? Or to look down, hoping he doesn't notice, which is what she does, mesmerizing herself with the glittering cement, blinking out the tears until they drop to the pavement. She scuffs her shoe over their tiny splotches.

But he is a man who notices, not that he cites this essential skill when asked, "What qualities are important for success?" His answer: "Luck," and he waits for the startled faces, the wonder at such a simple (and truthful) response. Tears do not move him. He won't cry. Lost elections? Abandoned dreams? Simply the flotsam and jetsam of any long political life. Deaths? The collateral damage of living. There is nothing to cry about over here, and he says this now to the girl: "There's nothing to cry about over here," murmuring the words as he lets her sob herself silly onto his shoulder, as he holds her close on the bridge where no one knows who he is.

He's lying, of course. Of course he is. He fucks them, every time.

STAY THERE

The unyielding concrete of the parking garage pushes dampl through my black cocktail dress, chill seeping along my spine, along the backs of my bare arms. His big, puppy-dog hands cup my ass; my legs vise round his waist; a tangle of bracelets tickle my fists. Sure, call me lost—in level P-3, in him, in the sex—lost with my muffled moans, biting my lips into silence, lost amid the compressed fury that defines a twenty-four-year-old boy fucking. "Jesus," one of us whispers, in the quiet of this shadowy corner on level P-3. A car door slams, a lock beeps, clickety high-heel footsteps recede. He hears because he snickers.

But I'm not lost. Not ever. A part of me stands back, always the observer, evaluating and assessing, aloof as my forty-years-old-tomorrow body responds and writhes, begs for more, begs for no end, begs for the end, gets what it wants. Even now, I'm leaning into the cliché, examining why I'm here. Maybe if I'd been happier with boys when I was twenty-four, instead of yearning for men and their once-exotic weariness, which I mistook for complexity. Maybe if I'd wanted this, only back then.

He relaxes, rummaging his face into my shoulder. I open my eyes, and he rears his head as if he understands I'm watching, and his eyes—truly turquoise—dive through mine. I blink—his face too close, eyes too blue—and scramble to focus, and his smile slides sweet and sleepy, like a baby's. Innocent. Beautiful. The word is *addicted*. I'm addicted to him. I whisper, "Jesus."

"Je*sus*." His face flops to my shoulder, his body limp, the angle of leaning deepening, sandwiching me harder against the concrete—his sleepiness wallops that fast. Like getting knocked out. I'm uncomfortable as hell but still I want to stay forever in this never-never land of between.

Two car doors slam in quick succession. Another. Laughter, a drifting echo of conversation: "So, I went to that new place by the Harris Teeter, the one where they say the soup is so amazing . . ." Maybe I'll catch my friends disparaging me and the art I'm dragging them to see, or worse, pitying me, the poor forty-at-midnight, unmarried me. I think I would welcome knowing what they really think.

"Hey," I whisper, "I can't be more late than this." He rouses himself and I untwine my legs from around his waist, planting my feet in their spiky high heels. He fidgets and pulls out of me, clasping the open side of the condom with both hands. He's always careful, but I wouldn't mind if he wasn't, if we made a baby with turquoise eyes. There's no simple way to suggest such a thing. But I think it every time. He shifts and zips and jams his fingers through the cascade of blond hair and is good to go. What a pro. I'm thinking about a comb, wiggling into my shapewear, sleeking up, though he gallantly says, "I don't know why you think you need that torture. You've got to know you're smoking hot." Tay is smart enough to avoid "still": *still* smoking hot.

I imagine he'll toss the condom into the clutter of Big Gulp cups, McDonald's bags, and candy wrappers washed up in this distant corner. The pang of waste. But he discreetly carries the condom as we walk to the stairs, plunking it into a garbage can. Conscientious, which I noticed right off, how that first night of class he lunged forward to pull open the studio door for me, stepping back to allow me through. I paused. "You're doing this because I'm the teacher?" I said, a surprising flush of power tripping on my part. "No, ma'am. Because apparently I'm raised right," he said, the words pulsing with an almost sexual glow, then a follow-up smirk as apology, as if he simply couldn't stop himself. I swept through the door, forcing myself not to look back.

I stop to balance my purse on the garage's iron railing, rooting inside for my mirror and lipstick. I also dig out a mini bottle of Purell, squeeze a dab into my hand, then say, "It's not an insult," tilting the bottle toward him. He laughs but accepts, rubs his hands together briskly. The sound always feels ugly, clinical.

"Be there in a sec," he says, swishing his fingertips against my bare arm. My skin prickles, abruptly alert. He could go again, and I long to reach for his crotch, just one lingering caress, just to know for sure, to prove something to myself, though that's needy. Or is it wrong? I'm not his teacher now. But I was when I started sleeping with him.

"It's okay," I say. "People walk in public places side by side all the time. It's called coincidence. No one will think anything." I sound desperate, afraid of my own party, my own art show. Pitifully unwilling to plunge into the crowd alone.

He often knows what I'm thinking, or maybe I imagine that. "You're the hottest-looking forty-year-old I've met."

"Not forty until tomorrow." I'm quick and light so I don't say the other thing: How many forty-year-olds do you know, besides your mother?

"Got to get something out of my car," he says. Meaning a cigarette.

I nod. He leans in to snag another kiss, to tempt me, but I jerk back at the glare of headlights on the wall, about to turn the corner and illuminate us. "No presents," I say, though I know there aren't any, that what's in the car is a pack of American Spirits. The car sweeps by: two women from yoga class. I wave effusively. They probably assume Tay's my son, since they don't know me well. I push away that thought, letting my eyes follow Tay as he leaves He moves easily, slipping place to place as if he's liquid.

When I can't see him, I glance into the tiny mirror I've found in my purse. A network of lines etches the corners of my eyes and lips; I see crevices. Another thought to push away, and I start up the stairs, heels clacking. I think of when I was growing up, watching my father practice his smile in the bathroom mirror, smiling over and over, tilting his head this way and that, as I timed him with the second hand on his wristwatch. Ten seconds, twenty, a minute. "Smiling's hard work," he would say, "and takes muscle. You've got to build muscle if you want anything in life." I thought he knew everything. It was exciting that his picture was everywhere, the smile I knew from the mirror, his famous smile. Now he's dead to me. I rouse the muscles of my own face, forming a smile. And I stride up the stairs to this party.

The gallery is a buzz of people swarming my photographs, winding through tables set with flickering tea lights, glassware flashing and clinking, the whisper of the string trio's music. My photos pop against Chita's newly painted walls ("You're forty, baby, and by golly, you deserve a fresh coat of color," she said in her drawl), and I'm greeted by hugs and kisses, a surge of applause, Chita calling, "There she is!" I let the crowd carry me forward, and I watch myself work. Conversations on a loop: "Thank you for coming," "So happy you like the show" (offer humble namaste head bow), exclamations of "You shouldn't have!" at impersonal gifts tucked into decorative bags (soap, wine, scarves). I'm gentle with those nervous around art, patient with their need to condense it to pap: "How long to make that?" "How do you decide the price?"

Deviation from the litany keeps me alert, the former students staring at me or pretending not to, unsure if there might yet be some scrap of power I wield, though grades have been posted and my judgment complete and I'm not their teacher anymore. I shouldn't waste time with them—

they're neither friends nor buyers—but what a relief to shift loops, asking what they're up to, not that I care, but to hear the bounce of their chatter: new studios, gallery visits, redesigned websites, so-and-so who ditched Durham for Brooklyn. I'm not listening close enough to get the name, and asking young people to repeat is too old-person. But who's pulling out for real? Who's the bold one? I'm bothered not to know.

Fuck it, and I'm about to ask, but I sense Tay's arrival, finally, and I maintain my breath in a calm, measured in and out, even as my skin ignites and a sharpness tightens my posture. His is a splash landing into the cluster of students, and they fuss and hug, creating excuses to touch him, the tap of fingertips, a complimentary pluck at the rolled-up sleeve of his coral button-down. I'm edged to the perimeter. These girls are in love with him, especially the redhead; the boys too. Jealousy is also very old-person, as is not understanding that this, that everything, will unfold eventually.

Chita eyes me, nudging with urgent glances, which means business and someone to meet—it's a party, but it's work. No part of my life is ever its own self. Before walking away, I indulge my glance at Tay, towering over these girls. They're nodding in unison, such a serious conversation, a line of furrowed brows, but he laughs, and even in the party din that's as clear as morning birdsong. My child would get that laugh, I think, knowing laughter doesn't run in families, isn't a heritable trait.

I dredge up a smile. Like that, my father camps in my head again, and that pang. Not remorse, not sorrow, because I wouldn't expect him to show. Maybe anger that I sent the invitation, or rather, that Chita did? "He's your father," she said, extending the word into a landscape of vowels and many syllables. "Maybe he'll buy something," with *buy* getting the same stretched-out verbal treatment along with her trademark wink. "No," I said, which to her means she can—and should—do what she wants. I also say no to her plan in which I buy into her gallery and become a partner for a couple of years before she retires to Eureka Springs, Arkansas, where her daughter ended up. Not that I have a better plan. I've lost the will for reinvention. This might be my last show.

Chita doesn't look sixty. She wears bejeweled cat-eye glasses attached to a chain she made with healing crystals and beads, a shimmery lavender three-quarter sleeve dress that looks straight from Jackie Kennedy's closet, and her signature red cowboy boots. She's not five feet even in the boots, which makes people underestimate her, which she uses to her advantage, because she uses everything to her advantage. She's the only one who knows about Tay, because she caught us in the unisex bathroom of a highway dive bar we thought was safe but wasn't: Chita would drive anywhere on a wispy rumor of great fried chicken, and I should have known that. The next day she said, "Honey, whatever y'all. Like what I read at Jewel and Cath's wedding, some mystic poet Rumi, not that I know Rumi from rummy from Bacardi, I just read what they gave me. But it was, 'Close your eyes. Fall in love. Stay there.'" I didn't wreck her moment with an "It's not love" announcement. Now, she's talking with Shannon, my old high school best friend, who drove down from Richmond, which is sweet since we're basically just Facebook close nowadays, and with Shannon's boyfriend, who apparently is her *new* boyfriend, who must be a collector or rich, because Chita's chatting him up, laughing like he's busting her gut, and now she's tag teaming me. I'm up. Time with the artist, Chita taught me, that's what they're buying, what they want. An experience to brag at friends. So I flash my smile, and Shannon leans in for a hug, too long, too loopy. Drunk already. Her Facebook scroll is cartoons about wine o'clock.

Chita says, "So, y'all are friends from way back?" The master chatter. She gets people talking about themselves, staying attentive through their monologues, but it's a data sweep, collecting and retaining information. Her memory is frightening. Right now she's honing in, certain this guy collects something—art, people, experiences. Or maybe it's simple: a house needs decorating. When she brought up the gallery deal, Chita promised I'd learn these skills. "It's in your blood," she said, meaning my politician father, and like that, the muscles of my face hardened, so she amended herself: "Selling art is about relationships, that's all. Selling anything is." There was my father's famous voice, drilling us at the dinner table: "What is politics about?" and it would be me, dutiful daughter, piping in, because if no one did, he'd ask until he got the answer: "Politics is about relationships, Daddy."

Astonishingly, this drumbeat was pounded so relentlessly into my soul that not until college did I realize politics is about power. Likely art is too.

I shake my head, back to the world, back to where I'm supposed to be, glad-handing Shannon's silver-haired boyfriend. Peter Robbins, though I think, Peter *Rabbit*, which is impossible to forget. Shannon leans forward on her tiptoes; she's wearing silvery ballet flats that look like they could be folded up to be stuffed into her purse, and I wonder if she forgot her real shoes or if she didn't think my party was good enough for real shoes. Peter Rabbit announces that he's a lawyer, giving the firm name, then takes over the conversation (negating the necessity of announcing he's a lawyer, ha-ha). He's talking about value and investment, things no one would say about art in Durham, North Carolina. I'm desperate to cut in with, You do understand you're not in New York, right?—which Chita knows, because she opens her mouth to speak first, but suddenly Shannon says, "You're so tall!" She's drunk, but we do party laughs, and I jab one foot forward to show the high spike of my shoes. "My little secret," I say, and Chita catches me glancing at Tay, who's leaning both elbows on the bar.

Shannon blathers about Peter's new beach house in Duck—they're driving there tomorrow, they want to fill those blank walls, wouldn't something from here be perfect—and Chita's eyes hint that we've hit the business part. So I ask, "What part of Duck?" and Chita jumps in with, "Who do y'all collect?" which I quickly understand is the right question. Her face is directive.

"I'm exclusively into political art," Peter Rabbit says, which makes Chita cock her head, as if the computer in her mind has stumbled into bad code. I tell students that the creation of any work of art is, at its core, a political act, but I can't imagine Peter Rabbit seeing beyond color splotches on canvas.

"Interesting." Chita's murmur is always artful encouragement, and I sense she's fascinated by this bit of information, while also regretting knowing it.

He puffs and talks on, as predictable as a clock: "I bought a George W. Bush at a charity auction and a Winston Churchill" —pausing here, letting the significance settle, and if it's possible to do a double cock of the head, that's what Chita does, because he's talking some real money now—"and of course Shepard Fairey's Obama print. I started with campaign memorabilia, like everyone, like any amateur, then branched out. My first was a Jimmy Carter. Right now I'm hot for Ulysses S. Grant."

Chita is nodding fast, faster, that way she does when she's not allowed to show her fury, and she grabs hold of my arm, presses in. That's the signal, that she'll handle it, that a sale is a sale, but I say, "You know *I'm* the artist, not my father."

Peter Rabbit says, "My parameters are wide," and Shannon chortles. Always a stupid drunk, even in high school.

Shannon paws at me, clutching my arm, which makes Chita let go. I feel like a wishbone. "You're so brave to be here," she says, abruptly serious. She downs her glass then blows her wine breath at me as she says, "Considering."

"Yes, it's very brave to walk around being a forty-year-old woman," I say, almost adding, You're doing it, too, before deciding that, drunk or not, she's an old pal and it's likely this guy isn't getting the truth about her age. When they first walked in and gave me the quickie greeting, she over-explained that "we *went* to the same high school." Which is not the same as saying we were in the same graduating class.

"Your father," she says, which are not the words I expect, nor ones I ever like hearing. Around here, I go by my middle name and the last name's common enough. But she knows, this drunk girl-woman and her too-much cleavage.

Tension crackles up like a fire coming to life.

Chita murmurs, "So, Peter. Ulysses S. Grant? Fascinating."

I say, "We don't see each other anymore. It's been years." A deep breath: "Basically, he's dead to me."

Shannon gasps and tightens her fingers around my arm. "You haven't heard?" she says, then glances at Peter Rabbit whose face abruptly turns unreadable. "She hasn't heard," she repeats. "It was on the hotel TV right before we came over." Her eyelashes are caked with mascara, and tiny lines radiate from the corners of her eyes. She looks old right now, old and tired and no longer drunk. "It's unlucky to pass along bad news," she says.

"Then don't," I say, irrationally. My heart thumps, maybe loud enough to muffle her words. Once I hear what she says, something will change. It's one of those before/after moments that life whacks you with. Shannon is the one who drove through a hurricane to rescue me from the bad boyfriend's apartment, who picked me to coedit the yearbook with her instead of Lisa Long, who taught me quadratic equations and dragged my ass through algebra. The one who, a long time ago, knew everything about me and loved me anyway. Why did she turn into this stranger?

"Oh, Lexie," she starts, dropping into my childhood nickname, the one I now hear only from my sister and brothers, only when they're sloppy drunk. "You know I hate being the one doing this, but he was knife stabbed up in Washington, and they don't know if he's going to make it."

"Critical condition," Peter Rabbit adds. "We weren't sure you'd be here."

Chita opens her mouth and seems to forget to close it. I rarely speak of my father, and only last year did she learn who he is. Speaker of the House. So fucking important.

Knife stabbed. A strange phrase, maybe not real.

"Lexie was never a girl to miss a party," Shannon says. "Not when I knew her." There's an encouraging smile, an invitation to laugh all this off, to avoid the unpleasant. That was what she did back then, too, handing over money or arranging things. "Oh, Lexie," she sighed when I told her I was pregnant, "which kind of phone calls you want me to make for you?"

"I assume his new wife did it," I say. "The, what is it, fourth one?" but only Shannon is kind enough to force a laugh, which I would love her for if I didn't despise her right now. Peter Rabbit shifts his weight. Sweat dots his forehead. I imagine this being the story he'll tell about the photograph he buys.

Shannon says, "Some nutcase at the Kennedy Center, apparently. Not many details."

Chita says, "It's really okay if y'all . . ." Leaving the sentence for me to fill in. Okay if I go. If I don't.

"I'm fine," I say.

Shannon whispers, "He was with that kid of his. She's hurt, too." I'm tired of her hand clutching me, keeping me from saying what I want to, from thinking it. "Also in the hospital," she says, as if to make me feel guilty.

I need Tay. But scanning the room, he's nowhere, not with the clique of students, not at the bar, not admiring my work, and I'm about to scream my frustration and fear when he bounds around the back wall, from the bathroom, and he catches my eye and threads the crowd expertly, one quick pause to lean a whisper into a redhead's ear. I gave her a B minus. She'll be the one to end up with Tay after he's done with me, after I'm done with him, after we're done together.

When he reaches me, I sidestep so he can nudge into the group. I say, "This is Tay, one of my star students. He's creating some intimate, contrasting narratives with found materials." He does a namaste bow, complete with hands, as if the motion is natural. A sharp intake of air from Shannon, presumably jolted by the same electrical current I feel. Peter Rabbit scowls. Chita knows my praise is biased, but she tugs the headscarf taming the frizz of her curls and says politely, "I'll have to visit your studio sometime. Let's be in touch," and Tay nods and tosses a noncommittal, "Lovely," which will certainly build Chita's interest, which Tay certainly understands.

My voice is wooden as I recite the names of everyone standing in our circle, and Chita excuses herself, her assistant drawing her away with one delicate finger sliding onto the crook of an elbow, as if the young woman had been signaled in to execute the rescue. There's an awkward few minutes where we talk about art and restaurants and the Outer Banks. There's a silence. Peter Rabbit coughs. The last time I saw my father in person was ten or so years ago, at my sister's second wedding in Charlotte. He was invited but no one thought he'd show. So him. My sister asked how I'd feel if he gave the toast instead of me, that her husband (now ex) thought it would be more appropriate. "Furious," I said, but I applauded with everyone when he came up with something so moving the whole ballroom overflowed in tears. I look at Tay's turquoise eyes and say, "Get me the hell out of here," and he grabs my hand and parts the crowd, leading me with such purpose that no one squawks or stops us or registers that we're holding hands.

We're silent all the way to my car, but once there, I say, "Want to drive with me to DC right now?" and he says, "Sure." We get in and Sirius blares on, the Lithium channel, the old-person grunge I grew up on, and I punch over to Spectrum, which I pretend is modern enough for him. I take the corners carefully and exit the garage into traffic, heading generally toward I-85, but after the first big intersection I swerve into a bank parking lot and chunk the gearshift to park, my hands gripping the top of the wheel so tight my knuckles go white. All I have is whatever's in my purse. All he has is whatever's in his pockets; his car's still in the garage. I think about my friends who traveled from all those cities. The photos Chita needs to sell. My father and the mess of his life. The reckless, restless mess of my own life lately, sleeping with a student, my creative block. A line of a dozen black and gray birds balance on a wire. I wonder if they sleep there, in a row like that. Twilight is settling in; soon streetlights will flick on. Tomorrow I would make a different decision.

I say, "This is crazy," and Tay lifts a strand of hair off my face, tucks it behind my ear. "I think you want to keep driving," he says, and I do.

My parents' marriage officially blew up when I was twelve, leaving me trying to fathom him running away to marry this crazy child bride not even ten years older than me, that there was a baby on the way, that he wasn't even divorced yet from my mother, that my mother had agreed to the whole thing and wasn't suing his ass. Impossible that all he left behind was an office phone number. Impossible to fathom a father forsaking a daughter with such shameful finality.

The child bride dumping him a year later made everything on the public side worse. She kept as quiet as a crazy person could, but no way he'd ever be president back then, no way his golden-boy name would ever top those not-so-secret, here's-our-man, savior-of-the-party lists again. All those volunteers, all those phone calls and neighborhoods canvassed, all that money and those voters who believed in him, all that hope, all of all that swirling round and round, flushed down the crapper.

Didn't stop wife number three. Or number four. How did he manage to find those women, all those women and girls, who flocked to him, who happily ate his shit? Did he find them or did he somehow create us?

Eighty-five up to Petersburg is empty and dark. I tell Tay that my father's been rushed to the hospital without telling him my father's name. "I need to see him," I say, letting the cliché work its magic. If Tay thinks it's strange that my phone's not buzzing with calls from family, he doesn't say so. I dread the merge onto 95, with its East Coast megalopolis traffic and long lines of trucks rumbling and shuddering their way north, but now, right now, I'm flying. The car, a Lexus SUV I bought off an old boyfriend who upgraded his car before he upgraded me, is beautiful for road trips, like lolling in an armchair while a kaleidoscope spins. Tay plays with the satellite radio, finding some specialty station the specialty of which, apparently, is to play every song I've ever loved. The sunroof is open—it may be chilly for that, but I like the scrape and race of the whipping wind. The art I left behind on Chita's walls is distant, an old, tired thing. I could let go. That I hopped into this car with only my purse must mean something, and I thrill at the colliding possibilities, that 95 ribbons on to New York, to Boston, lands deep in the wilderness of Maine. Or I could reverse and charge south, to Florida and the Keys, to the end of the world. Time and place are worn out, wrung dry; they are concepts from the old world. We're nowhere but here, now. It doesn't matter that I'm forty, tangled in an inappropriate and out-of-control relationship with this boy, this savvy sweetheart of a boy with turquoise eyes. I lost my job over this, whatever this is. I don't know who told the dean. Tay doesn't either. The redhead? I don't care anymore.

This journey is animal instinct, and it occurs to me that my only motive might be to watch my father die, which startles me into speaking: "I think I'm going there to watch him die."

He seems disconcerted, as if he'd planned on silence the entire distance. "He'll pull through," he says. "Our bodies perform a thousand daily miracles we don't even know about."

"How do you know that if we don't know about them?" I ask.

"Excellent question." Then he says, "Anyway, no one's dying. Be positive."

He glances at his phone, buzzing a text. "My buddy in Adams Morgan is good with us staying at his place and he'll jump over to his girlfriend's."

It's deflating somehow that there's already a plan, someone in charge, but I smile. I imagine my teeth shining in the dark.

"He's not far from the zoo," he adds, like he's reading an Airbnb listing.

"The zoo," I repeat as if thinking it over.

I should explain to Tay who my father is. People Tay's age are awed by very little; he won't care. But my father is a political legend. People sobbed when his life exploded into rubble. My father could have changed the world, people say, if he had had the chance. He *had* had the chance, I counter, but fucked it all away. I should U-turn over the median and tear back to Durham, back to my party, which is catered and costing a fortune. I went with prosecco instead of the cheap pinot grigio. Everyone is getting drunk on my prosecco.

It occurs to me that no one has contacted me. I ask Tay to grab my phone out of my purse and read off my missed calls and texts: Chita, Chita, Shannon, some other friends. My father's staff tracks me down every year to check my contact information. I imagine a file somewhere, a plan that includes my number, a phone tree or whatever they're called now. I should be part of a chain of events. I haven't seen him for ten years, but he's my father. Is he allowed to pretend he's not?

A few minutes later I say, "I haven't cried."

"Maybe you're not sad," he says. And a minute later, he asks, "Are you?"

"Hell, no." But I feel bad for saying that, so I add, "Maybe I'm numb. Or in denial."

He says, "Families are complicated." It seems like a polite response.

"Is yours?"

He laughs. "Actually, not really. I was raised by a wolf pack, so you know. Survival of the fittest. It's all pretty simple."

I say, "I think maybe I'm angry."

He says, "What's making you angry?"

It's unexpected, but I start sobbing, shaking and heaving. The car drifts, and he grabs the wheel one-handed and says, "Look, there's a truck stop right after the Virginia line. Let's pull in and grab some beef jerky and cigarettes. We'll talk. It's just another couple of miles." He murmurs and soothes like I'm a wounded animal. All this kindness is making me angrier. Peter Rabbit would never say these things to Shannon.

I focus on steering. Focus on hating my father. Focus on these two easy, comfortable things.

It's a real-deal truck stop, with a sign advertising showers and Wi-Fi. There's a vast parking lot and an off-chain, all-night restaurant you'd have to roll the dice on—it's either a stack of amazing pancakes or salmonella. There's also a 24-7 shop for snacks, and Tay says, "I'll run in for beef jerky," and I laugh through the tears, but he says, "Seriously. They've got a great selection," and I shake my head at him. It's meant to be fond, but it feels like a tired shake, like at a bad joke.

I park under an overhead light in a gravelly corner, over by the air hose, so no one can see me sitting in the front seat crying. I click off the car. The interior lights flare then fade out. I never want to leave this car. The sliver of a moon peeps through the open sunroof.

When he unbuckles his seat belt, I grab at the neck of the coral button-down. "Hang on," I say, pulling so he can't leave.

He wraps both arms around me, nuzzles his face into my hair, smooches my head.

"Do you love me?" I ask. I never ask. I never say it back if they say it. I like to think of myself as hard, but right now, I don't remember why.

"Of course," he says. "You know I do."

Too fast. He doesn't. That's fine. Plus, the words. He didn't say them.

So I say, "How crazy is this, walking out of a party and driving north with no luggage, no nothing?"

"Whatever shit we need, we'll buy," he says. "That's how America works."

"What's a father anyway?" I say. "One sperm hitting the right place at the right time. It's simple luck more than anything." I take in a deep breath and hold it for a long time. Then I say, "I decided. We're going back home. This is stupid."

"Look," he says, "we're already in Virginia." He pushes open the door as if to show me the ground of this different state.

"I decided," I say. But in the silence I think, *I love you. I love you.*

"Huh," he says. The silence is different, tight. He draws the door closed.

I ignore his disappointment because I feel relief. I feel a flood of sanity. My father will die and I'll read about it online. That's fine. This is fine. This boy was raised well, raised to appreciate an older woman. He's great in bed. His art is thoughtful enough, shows enough promise without, I'll admit it, threatening my art. Roman numerals follow his name, which shouldn't matter but does. It does. He's everything I want without being anything I want. I want a baby.

I say it: "I want a baby."

He shifts backward in the leather seat. I feel his mind travel a million miles away.

I say, "Honestly, that's not what this is about, but I do. I just really do."

He grunts in some noncommittal way that's animallike without being an actual no.

I talk fast: "You don't have to know. I don't have to tell you. You don't have to have any responsibility. I'll do everything by myself. My mother was practically a single mother. I know it's not the same, but I know how it works."

That same strangled sound. But still not no.

"This is what I've waited for my whole life," I say. "I lied in class. All the art in the world means nothing without a baby."

He still has not said no.

"Your beautiful eyes." I reach to touch his cheekbone, but he pushes my hand away, which is still not the word no.

"I'll die if I don't have a child," I say. "My father is dying, maybe he's dead already, and I want a child."

Still no no.

"We'll get a lawyer," I say. "I'll pay. I'll pay for the lawyer and a lawyer for you, and I'll pay you, if that's what you want." I have no idea how this money will materialize.

"What I want is so simple," I say. "A baby. To be a mother."

He says, "I'm HIV positive. AIDS. You're not getting your baby from me." And he jumps out of the car, the interior light glaring an accusation before fading down into darkness. I listen to his footsteps walking away, then I sit in silence. Enough time passes that I know he's not picking out beef jerky. Enough time passes that I think maybe he won't return. Trucks pull in and out of the parking lot, their rumbles like a distant summer storm. He might have already hitched a ride on one of them. He is gone.

I should have followed him. Generally I am enlightened and calm about AIDS, but at this exact minute, I'm not. My thoughts are ugly. I'm thinking that this is why he chose me, because I'm old and half-dead anyway. I know enough to know he's not going to drop dead, that there are drugs, that Magic Johnson has been alive for years and years, and good for him. Good for everyone living with HIV. I am ugly, ugly, ugly right now. I should find Tay and apologize and talk and understand. I should thank him for finding us a place to stay by the zoo in DC and tell him I love pandas.

There's a double rap on the window, but instead of Tay it's a thirtyish man wearing jeans ripped at the knee and a light blue Carolina Panthers T-shirt. He's waving a phone side to side like a metronome. "You Crystal?" he squawks. He presses his phone up against the window, showing me a picture of a girl with a pompadour of black hair. "You Crystal?" he asks again, shouting.

I shake my head, ignoring the prickles of fear while chastising myself for not closing the sunroof, for not locking the passenger door after Tay got out.

"Sure?" he says. He is tall and wiry, either a dark-skinned white man or a light-skinned Black man. His shaved head gleams as if polished.

"God, no," I say. "My boyfriend will be back in a minute."

He says, "I sent a hundred bucks to her PayPal. Jesus Christ."

"Maybe she's late," I suggest.

"Fuck," he says, shoving the phone into his back pocket. "That's money I ain't getting back. Am I right?"

I shrug-nod. "My night's pretty shitty, too," I say. "My father's dying in some DC hospital." The man's eyes glisten. There will be a story. There will be sympathy. I can bear neither right now, so I pound ahead, desperate to shut him the fuck up: "And I just found out my boyfriend's got AIDS," I say. I can't believe I say these words. Suddenly they're real. Maybe that's why I say them. I hope I only thought them.

He stands there, I don't know why. Like he's growing roots. Finally he says, "Tough about your dad." His face knots with more concern than I'd expect from a horny dude whose hooker bailed. I have an image of his father's face, worrying over some screw-up, his father calling him "son" at a Panthers tailgate, on a fishing trip.

I harden my voice. "He's basically been dead to me for most of my life. I mean, he was never much of a father. I haven't seen him for at least ten years. So, you know. Fuck him." I grip the steering wheel. The muscles in my forearms are taut. My knuckles feel as big as walnuts.

"Honor thy father," the man announces. "Like the Bible says."

I want to ask if the Bible mentions paying for sex with a stranger, but instead I roll my eyes and stare straight ahead, waiting for him to walk away. Waiting, waiting.

The man still stands there, so I say, "Okay, thanks!"

"It's a fucking commandment," he says.

"Thanks," I say again.

He presses his hand up onto the window, palm flat and wide, sideways, fingers splayed. His eyes settle and fix on a point in the distance. Even so, my heart jumps across my chest. I'm statue still, though I want to grab for my purse or my phone. With one hand up against the window, he can't pull a gun—or that's my irrational assumption. I think about

Crystal and her hundred dollars. She's probably some guy in Nigeria. She probably doesn't exist at all. I think about a man, this man, lonely enough to send money to a girl who doesn't exist, though surely part of his brain had been warning him not to.

I cautiously rest my own hand up against the window where the man's palm is, spreading my fingers to meet his. I'm startled to hit smooth glass, expecting his rough, warm skin, and I wonder how his rough, warm skin might press against mine, might push into the deep me of me. I'll never see this sad man again.

All these years it was so easy, saying, "My father's dead to me," because he wasn't dead.

Feelings explode across my mind, flaring like fireworks. Why we persist in loving things that don't exist.

The man's face is wreathed in shadowy angles, a contrast to the smooth shine of his head. I am one second away from pushing the button that unlocks all the car doors, one second away from saying, I'll do you for free, one second away from making a baby with eyes the color of this dark night. A baby doesn't need turquoise eyes to be loved.

I hope—no, I pray—that Tay doesn't decide to come back right now, but of course I hear footsteps and as my eyes flick to the rearview mirror I see him. A cigarette glows between his lips, and he's carrying a plastic bag. After what we said, he actually bought beef jerky, and it's ridiculous that I know a boy who would do that. Maybe that plastic bag is oddly hopeful.

The man's eyes snap over to Tay. "That kid the fag boyfriend with AIDS?" he shouts.

Tay freezes, and I expect him to crumple and drop to the pavement, struck dead by these words, by my casual and rapid and utter and real betrayal. This is what over will look like, this late night at a truck stop at the Virginia border, this shrieking stranger. How will Tay get back to Durham, I half wonder, half care. Is our betrayal equal? I half wonder, half care about that for a minute, too, until I hurt too much.

"Choose me," I say to the man. Can he hear me? I press the button that unlocks the doors.

The man shakes his head, sadly, slowly; his sorrow looks to me immense and heavy, a burden he assumes I'll never understand. His hand drops off the glass, and he steps away from the car, sliding back into the shadows. Not even a fingerprint on the window. As if he had never been here at all.

Tay, too.

I am alone, left with the same ache of nothing I started with, as if anything in the world can change in a single instant except that.

I BELIEVE IN MARY WORTH

If vampires can't see their reflections in mirrors, can ghosts?

And: Would a ghost see her tattered, haunted self? Or the hearty, vigorous contours of her face, alive again? Bright eyes, glossy hair: the girl who came to DC to make a "difference," to preserve democracy, to *matter*?

No woman from my small town in North Carolina had ever *mattered*. I'll show those fucks what the word means. Not that I would have even whispered "fucks" back then.

Things change. Now I work for the Speaker of the House.

I'm looking at Mia, fidgeting in the hard-on-purpose guest chair in my office (subtle signs of power my specialty), watching her tug at her black pencil skirt, at the sleeves of her dry clean-crisp white blouse, at the gold David Yurman bracelet identical to mine that I immediately donated to Goodwill after she showed up wearing hers. She's here for the spring semester to save and serve democracy, to parlay her Hill experience into . . . what? A bullet point on a law school app? Grad school letter of rec? Run for office? Lucrative lobbying job? A husband? Was she told this experience would be good for her?

Is it, I wonder, good for her?

Elsewhere in the office, people yell on phones, whisper gossip, spout off-color jokes about the famous actor who died over the weekend; the hiss of the printer continuously spits out emails to be tossed into the secret "if I'm fired" file everyone learns is essential. But silence collects here in this insignificant cranny tucked at the back of a winding hallway. I chose this crummy room. Let the others squabble over territory. Learning to live unnoticed is a talent.

Mia's fidgeting stops abruptly.

I wait. I can wait forever. I have waited forever—for less.

I recross my legs under my desk, and she mirrors my action, though she couldn't possibly have seen me. I've trained myself to move with secret precision, to slide one booted leg atop the other without shifting my upper torso. Trained myself not to reveal discomfort, a necessary skill in this life, though not one overtly valued.

Mia wears short booties, as the young girls do. Not me. Full boots, black. I like knees covered by expanses of leather and I'm enough of someone now that my days of toeing the line in sensible pumps are behind me.

She speaks first, as I expected. "I'm not sure where to start."

"The beginning," I say, offering a plastic smile. "I have all the time in the world. Let's get things straightened out."

"It's just . . ."

In the pause that follows, we both eye the tissue box situated at the far corner of my desk. I'm sure she'll grab it within five minutes, mascara smearing her pretty face.

She crosses her arms against her chest. "I mean," she says, "I'm a total professional. This outfit's from Nordstrom, where some lady picked it. She said—exact words—it's a polished, professional look."

Nice to know she read the employee handbook, those two words, underlined and italicized: *polished, professional*.

"The complaint that's been filed against you doesn't concern your clothing," I say.

I'm staring at the orange on her desk, staring, staring, because I absolutely cannot bust into tears, that way I do—to my chagrin; *chagrin* being a word from SAT prep, making my dad's two thousand dollar expenditure so worth it—which could be a perspicacious observation—another SAT word—except that's one I maybe confuse, like how I want *sanguine* to mean its opposite.

So . . . the orange. The orange!

Why would the She-Beast of the office, star of intern nightmares, this wicked-witch bitch, why would she allow a lone orange untethered, unmoored, at the edge of her desk, where it might roll off, hitting the Pottery Barn Persian rug—continuing on under the credenza (a word learned here on day two—"get the red folder on my credenza" coming at me over the phone—"the what?"—her sharp sigh and acid snarl: "You're googling it right now, aren't you?"—which I was—*dining room sideboard??*—"God help us all," because she knows everything and can't understand that someone else might not—or not *yet*, anyway) here must be a reason this exact orange specifically—organic, no doubt—is on her desk at *this* moment for *this* meeting for *this* conversation that's going exactly as she has planned and why, why, why, an orange versus an apple versus a banana?

It's stressing me out.

Can I imagine her sorting through a bin of oranges, muttering "nope," rejecting dozens, holding out for the perfect orange to become the necessary, if mysterious, prop for this meeting?

Mesmerizing: her confidence, her orange, her. I confess to no one my longing to be her, to be *powerful She-Beast* instead of *me*, endlessly quivering along the verge of tears.

She says, "Mia. Did you hear me?"

My head bobs yes like a covered wagon bouncing through prairie landscape; I tack on a verbal yes for emphasis, then channel my father—always, always bursting with insistent advice to *speak up*—and I add more, maybe too much: "Okay, yes, ma'am. Then I guess this all started with that maybe inappropriate kiss you caught me in at the end of last week's office happy hour at Capitol Lounge, which, yes, I shouldn't have attended, but which, well, I did." Spilled out in one long continuous breath—minty-fresh breath, given that I spray Binaca resolutely before encounters, so resolutely that friends call me Binaca maybe as signs of resentful affection, affectionate resentment.

She says, "This office has neither control of nor jurisdiction over nor responsibility for what may or may not go on between staff at office happy hour or anywhere outside the workplace. I can't speak to kisses in public or private places. Only within the bounds of the workplace." Her stiff voice is extra flinty. She rolls the orange an inch to the left, lets her fingertips rest against it.

Mysterious! I vow to acquire one perfect orange for my desk (cubby, actually) that I share with Garth. He's malleable, easily trained to fear an orange.

I say, "But honestly, I think maybe I'm pretty sure that's where things started, when you saw me at the bar, you know, and this kiss that I guess wasn't appropriate. At happy hour. After we chatted in the bathroom?"

"I don't"—OMG! she's going to finish with, *go to the bathroom*, but, no, it's—"chat in bathrooms."

"You did, maybe only this one time?"

It's an eye-to-eye stand-off, though sitting down.

Without breaking her gaze, she picks up the orange and moves it to the credenza. Which means . . . ?

I say, "I know he's not my boss, but I'm aware he's the boss of other people. I know maybe I wasn't thinking. You specified 'bounds of the workplace,' but it seems like maybe right after this kiss is when suddenly there's a report filed that's not about my clothing like Cassidy's tank tops, because you agreed I'm polished and professional. I think maybe you saw that he actually kissed me, not the other way around—but not like I'm saying he attacked me. I mean, I guess we kissed each other. Maybe, maybe also the Speaker saw. We shouldn't have, or maybe he shouldn't have, or maybe you're saying I shouldn't have?"

"I see." Her eyes drill down into me like she really does see something. It's a terrifying moment, waiting for what's next.

Several months ago, also in my office, I'm asking, "Mia, do you believe in spirits?"

"That's maybe an unusual question for a job interview."

I could respond, *Though not an illegal one*. I do not. Silence stretches, turns awkward.

Finally she says, "Well, I believe in Mister Jack Daniels. Does that maybe count?"

What a clumsy laugh. Awful to witness: exactly why I asked this unusual question, to gauge this young girl's reaction. To understand who she is, who—with my help, time, patience; *my investment*—she might become. She tugs at her too-short skirt. Why no pantsuit, I wonder, like the other female college intern applicants—which, actually, is an illegal question.

I decide to make things worse: "Is that a relative?" I can keep my face neutral during moments more challenging than this. Watch me.

She thinks I'm joking and waves her hand in fluttery dismissal, then shifts the gesture into swatting an imaginary fly. That swift reading of the situation, I respect. That I like.

She says, "Sorry. I maybe have a lame sense of humor."

I scribble on my legal pad, as if this information is noteworthy. It's not.

She sucks in a deep breath, causing her breasts to lift suggestively. I imagine her sucking in deep breaths in the office, in dive bars across the Hill, downing shots of JD with boys and men. Jack Daniels is a curious choice for a young, underage girl—did she think it a reference I, an "old person," would follow?

I say, "I don't understand." This is fun. I blare the Polite Smile typically reserved for those paying $50K at the Speaker's fundraisers.

Out poofs her breath. She says, "Look. I'm pretty sure maybe you know that Jack Daniels isn't my relative, that Jack Daniels is the country's leading seller of American hard liquor. And"—she leans in—"I bet maybe you know that Jack Daniels has been a major corporate donor to the Speaker's campaigns since the mid-90s. I'm pretty sure you maybe know all this already, and . . ." She trails off—enticing, menacing; I'm charmed and amused—and she leans closer, too close, assaulting me with perfume far too obtrusive for an office, but I like it, this watered-down Gen Z version of the Chanel I used to dab religiously, hopefully, on the insides of my wrists, imagining myself all grown up. There's promise here. Anyway, I'm not bored.

Unable to sustain this faux-intimidating posture, she slumps against her chairback, then views me through half-lidded eyes. Picks at her thumbnail. Bounces the leg dangling atop the other. Her voice is miserable. "Do I maybe get the job or what?"

"Yes," I say, and I slide a thick folder across the desk. Her name's already printed on a label on the tab. When she sees that, her eyebrows rise and she smirks, though not unattractively.

Her father donated the max last year and commits to every host committee request. Holds fundraisers at his mountain house whenever we ask. I smirk back, pleased we're fluent in the same language.

That dive bar "ladies' room" is intensely deep pink, exactly the color Georgia O'Keeffe would use to paint you-know-what, and I love this suggestive pink but fear it, which is maybe why I remember standing there, squirting breath spray hard into my open mouth. Never an attractive look, but how else do those droplets get in there and clean me up? I'm addicted to the flavor but mostly, right now, I'm basically sort of a lot drunk, so it's a firm squirt, then another, and music bleeds in from the jukebox—a country song about the glory of trucks—so also I remember for sure thinking, why's country music always about trucks, like there's a law. That spray's burning exquisite polka dots of pin-prickly pain into the skin inside my mouth, and if something hurts that means I'm not too drunk. That I know I know enough to know what I'm getting into—which is why girls jab needles into arms and slide razors across bellies. It's all perfect sense.

The door flings open.

I'm hoping it's him. I'm ready. That cute man with his own nameplate on his desk, a desk in a room, a room with a door and two windows and couch seating for three, and a brag wall of photos where he's with people who were or should have been presidents, that man who's so smart and deliciously tall. That man who's not the Speaker but right-hand close, who said, "Tell me about yourself," at the bar, and I did, because anyone would! "I was wishing maybe you'd be here," I said (kind of drunk already), which is true, because I'm always wishing for a night where something inevitable happens, where once more there's that chance I don't gleefully hate myself the morning after like usual.

It's not him. It's the She-Beast! For whatever reason, I aim my breath spray at her like it's a teeny-tiny gun, which stops her, and I say, "Need some?" and I spray into the empty air, getting the pink bathroom minty. "I love your boots," I enthuse with a ton of gusto. "Where'dja get 'em? I wantssome."

She steps around me, to the other sink. "Go sit down and hydrate," she says, full-blasting the water.

"I'm soooo happy to see you," I say.

"And why's that?" she asks.

I don't know. I don't know. I spray breath spray into my mouth, watching myself in the mirror. "Maybe you'll fix me, stop me from doing sssomething awful," I say.

"Here you are, so likely too late for that," she says. It's her She-Beast stare into the mirror, her demon eyes seizing mine: like she's Mary Worth, from stories my mother tells about her childhood sleepovers, her friends summoning Mary Worth by chanting, "I believe in Mary Worth," at midnight, and how one time IT REALLY WORKED, with a woman's horrible face popping up smack-center of the mirror, and everyone clutching everyone else while falling over shrieking until the dad bounded down the stairs two at a time, hauling a rifle, shouting, "What's wrong?" and when they described Mary Worth's "wolf face" and "fangy smile" and "crushed-rose-red eyes," he scolded: "You silly girls. Stop scaring yourself," and my mother swears Mary Worth rasped out a giggle right then. My mother only sleeps when every door's all the way closed. She drilled into me: "No one believes girls." So here's the She-Beast with Mary Worth's bloodshot eyes burning mine across the bendy angles of a mirror, me wobbly-kneed, going faint.

"I'm maybe atta bar every night," I say, because right now there's no lying.

"Then I doubt I'll be able to stop you," she says. "Now get out so I can pee, and *stay out* until at least three minutes after I exit this bathroom."

And I stand there because she's joking, but no she isn't, so I have to slink out, our conversation maybe complete.

At the bar, he says, "You're different, aren't you? Not like the others, right?" and I agree and parrot the words back to him, though my face blazes with recognition and superiority. His hand slides up my thigh, higher, and this is maybe what I like, and I'm remembering why the breath spray: getting ready for now, this.

I always shut my eyes as a guy's face narrows in, but even eyes closed, even amid that roiling kiss with the important man who's boss of so many people, even with all that: cold wind pierces icy and abrupt like that scary spot your bare legs find in a lake, that strangely frigid deep current, where my mother says you immediately know someone drowned right there, a long time ago. My eyes crack open, and yes but also no: it's not the She-Beast walking by right then, watching. It's the Speaker.

I close my eyes to all of it and kiss that man anyway. I kiss and kiss, then take him to the condo my dad bought me for my new life in DC. I hand the man a scarf like always, and I'm on the floor, tied to the radiator, and I maybe like this fine like usual, but maybe I don't like this one thing he likes, and then I really, really maybe don't like what he's doing, but I do it anyway, and finally when he's done he hocks a loogie, landing it steaming hot on my ass cheek. Every time I see him at work, I'll feel his gob of spit hitting my bare ass, balancing there, the warm slime of it all, the slime of him. Every day. He won't quit. I always quit, so I can't quit. My dad bought this condo, because I'm his smart and accomplished little girl, his favorite, who's *going places,* who's *on fire*. And it's a good investment, he said. I remind myself that he said that also.

I cry and cry. Awful to cry in front of someone, but, you know, maybe more awful when no one hears.

In the condo bathroom, it's my own demon eyes checking me out in the mirror, my voice chanting one familiar word: *fuck-fuck-fuck*. Damn it, again I'm that girl who should have known better. I want to be the She-Beast. Let her armor wrap around me. Let it suffocate me.

I bring quality tissues from home. No one enjoys watching young people cry, and crummy tissues make it worse, those shreds clinging to their upper lips. It's compassionate to spring for the Puffs Plus, not that I'm appreciated for this kindness.

Finally, amid her sobs, Mia chokes out, "I'm just going through all this shit right now."

Can we admit that witnessed distress is numbing? I say, "Do you need a moment?"

She shakes her head, but I give her one anyway and pretend to review important papers. It's a folder that holds a birthday card that circulated the office today: the Speaker's birthday. Everyone, even each intern, has signed, even people I don't like. Though this event's on his schedule, he'll fake surprise when we gather to present the card to him around sheet cake at a ten-minute party later this afternoon. Ten minutes is a lot for such a busy man, I remind everyone, we should be grateful. I set down the folder. My birthday's the same as the Speaker's. Not that I want a card and sheet cake; public approval is unnecessary to me.

Finally Mia says, "You don't remember talking in the bathroom? Why would I make that up? I know maybe I talked to someone."

I raise an eyebrow. "Mia," I begin. "I've been made aware that your behavior in the office may be creating a hostile work environment for some of your coworkers."

"I liked your boots," she says. "That's what we talked about."

"Here's some advice for DC," I say. "Conversations in bathrooms don't exist afterward." I lift one hand, anticipating her protest. "That's something for you to think about on your own time. Right now, focus. What I'm saying is important."

She says, "Have you ever had anything get out of hand?"

I glance at the birthday card. Any birthday may be one's last. I skim the obits in the paper *Post* each morning, perpetually surprised to observe that many people die shortly after their birthday. "No," I say.

She says, "Me neither." The garish smile on her face looks left over from something else.

I say, "It's been brought to my attention that you stand too close to people when you talk to them."

She wads and kneads the tissue in her hand. "How's this a complaint? What's 'too close' even mean?" She tosses the tissue at the garbage can, but it sails wide. "How far should I stand from people? Did I miss something in the employee handbook? Also, see how terrible I am at judging distance, which maybe is an ADA thing, right? It's all ADA-this, ADA-that in the handbook."

"We're not about to abuse the Americans with Disabilities Act," I say.

"All I did was kiss one dumb guy in a bar," she says. She lifts then releases her long hair, redraping it down her back.

"This is a matter of your workplace performance," I say, longing to tell her the world isn't entirely and only complicated: all she needs to do is feign listening to my rote speech, then sign her name on a form. Though—all she truly needs to do is sign. I pick up the folder underneath the birthday-card folder, grab a pen. "I'll need you to sign here to indicate we had this discussion."

"This was a discussion?"

I click open the pen. "Sign," I say.

I've always considered my job elegant in its simplicity: make one man happy, keep one man out of trouble, acquire power for one man. Here I am, accomplishing all three tasks with this single signature. I shouldn't have hired her. But what? Never hire girls? Never give young girls their shot?

"I'm reported for standing too close to people?" Her voice is insistent, nagging, a tinny buzz. "For real? Do I maybe need a lawyer? Is this because you caught me kissing? Is this maybe all you?"

I click the pen again. The tiny sound reverberates. Surely she sees she's not unique, that women all across the Hill know of this man she kissed. I recommended that the Speaker pass on this hire, but the man dazzles in an interview, when he senses power up for grabs. Consider the hungry way he looked over my crummy office, studied me, studied me harder, smiled razors at me. "We'll be in touch," I said, my firm handshake the real message, but the Speaker overruled: "People gave me chances," he said, "and if nothing's illegal . . ."

Now I say to Mia, "Additionally I'll remind you that the employee handbook states that office romances must be reported. Merely a matter of paperwork, to protect both parties. We'll start that process as well."

We eye each other. This is fun, I remind myself.

"There's no romance to report," she says, speaking stiffly.

"Ahh," I say, presenting surprise on my face. I set the pen on the form, nudge both closer to her.

"I mean," she says, "what if I want to report someone for something. Can I?"

The silence turns so heavy I might weigh it in two cupped hands. I say, "Of course. The employee handbook offers protocol for and protection from everything that could arise in a workplace. But do you want to?" I cock my head. "You're smart." That sits, then I add, "Aren't you?" I rearrange the surprise on my face into something that I hope comes off as sympathy, or close.

Such a joy people always telling me how goddamn smart I am, like no other compliment applies, just smart, smart, smart, smart, smart. Wait a sec while I throw up in my mouth hearing this word right now, and for a dangerous moment that's what almost happens. I drank too much last night which, yeah, isn't SMART, and I understand abruptly that she's not saying "smart" as something good. Oh.

Still, I nod, afraid not to. Watch my head move like a dog's watching its master eat bacon. Woof.

She says, "Maybe you want to think over that approach for a day or two. These things aren't always as simple as this," and she taps a finger on her precious form, "a conversation, a signature on a piece of paper that's easily misfiled."

"No." My words careen loosely. "This can't wait. I'm so uncomfortable in the office around this man. I feel threatened. He's creating a hostile workplace. I have a grievance."

She purses her thin lips until they disappear. "Would you like my advice?"

No, I think, because your advice will be something maybe I *should* hear that I *should* follow . . . but won't—and it'll leave me feeling shittier than usual, knowing the smartest and scariest woman on earth, the power behind the power of a powerful man, suggested one thing, but I still—still, still, still—did what little, puny ole me wanted to do. "I know your advice," I say. "Like you said, wait. Sit back. Be nice. Don't take things personally."

She stares at me, eyes unvarnished, unblinking: no mirror between us. I can't decide what she's thinking, so that keeps me going:

"I could call a reporter," I say. "Or lawyer. I should be maybe taping all this, and you can bet next time I will. This isn't your world anymore, and women don't have to put up with anything. You don't get it. I googled and know exactly how old you are, when you were born and everything. I think you're afraid of me."

"Maybe you're afraid of yourself," she says.

"Thanks for the psychoanalysis," I say. I'm so bold! Bold and smart, so smart that I've just about almost forgotten that technically I don't have a legitimate complaint, that whatever I claim I'll have to supplement with exaggeration and lies, that no one wants the headache of believing me. My heart thinks I'm right (and I bet so does she, because she saw that kiss, she was there, and why was she in the bathroom talking if not to maybe warn me?). But because I'm nothing and no one, I'll never get another job on the Hill or K Street or maybe anywhere because this town is tiny, which my father explained, saying, "Politics is a funny business, with its own rulebook, and that's either the best thing about it or the worst, depending on what kind of person you are." I said, "What kind of person am I?" and he said, "Guess we'll see."

Now, she says, "There's always a bigger picture, and can we agree that a smart girl like you wants to stay relevant to it?"

Do I?

It's like I've been let suddenly loose, maybe soaring, or is it crashing? Everything here, now, moves fast. I'm a speck on the desk, an orange rolling over me. "What about the employee handbook?" I ask.

She laughs. "Oh, that. What about it?"

"Mary-Grace, do you believe in spirits?" he asks, looking up from his desk. His eyes are magnets, drawing mine in, locking them into place with scientific force.

It's 1988, one day after I've turned eighteen, and all I want is this man elected to something. Congress first, president someday. The talk is this man's a miracle. Sinful to imagine a man, not Jesus, walking on water, but in my dreams, this man crosses a calm pond carrying one white rose, like girls descending the staircase at their debuts at the country club we can't belong to. I've never been given a rose, but this man sitting at his heavy desk—the cadence of his voice, his eyes seeing only me—is that rose.

"The Holy Spirit?" I ask. I'm Catholic, raised in the Trinity: Father, Son, Holy Spirit. My great-grandma stowed away on a ship from Ireland. I'm named after her, expected to be the nun that ensures my family's protected place in Heaven.

"It's an inkblot test," this man says. "I can tell things, everything I need, by your answer."

I'm scarcely eighteen. The adult world is mystery and thrills. I'm ready for anything to come next, for getting out of the dank house on the creek where my grandma lives, where I landed. My grandma says she's old and very tired of taking care of people, but also she wouldn't let the state whisk me away like they did my brother last year. The army stole my other brother, which is differently gone, "gone for good," my grandma warns, feeling it in her bones.

The man leans closer. I smell mint covering cigarettes and an undertone of onion, but this aroma, too, thrills me. I skipped lunch. I barely eat. What's the point of doing something once, then doing it all over again? My body's tight, thin like a nail.

He says, "For example, I can tell you're intelligent. That you want to please."

These things are true!

"That you really, truly want this job."

I've read every article mentioning him in every newspaper in the public library, watched him on TV. He's not even thirty-five, with people saying, *charisma* and *all the smarts* and *going the distance*. He sees beyond the me the others see, sees through into the me I truly am. And I see him: Our Country's Future. I'll stuff his envelopes and tongue-lick each flap closed; I'll handwrite addresses, arrange stamps slightly askew so voters picking up mail touch his letter and think, *A real man sent this*, and these details (I'll later learn) will ensure 23 percent higher donations to the campaign. I'll stand on any corner anywhere holding printer-fresh brochures and a clipboard;

I'll call phone books A to Z and insist that whoever answers must love this man's policies; I'll knock on all the doors; pick up pizza for the volunteers, letting them eat first, never complaining when nothing's left for me. No words convey the longing I feel. Maybe my face shows it.

"Is it only this job," he asks, "or something else you want? Where do you want to be in five years, ten? Next year? When I'm a congressman, when I'm president, where do you want to be? What do you want? What, my dear, do *you* want? What do you *want*?"

This kaleidoscope of questions. I smile. My grandma says to smile if I don't know what to say. He bounces back his own smile: grand in real life, like a flower opening in slo-mo, like an umbrella shooting out wide and bright across rain. I've been alive for eighteen years, and now's the first time I feel smiled at.

"You're pretty when you smile," he says.

My face glows ember-hot as my mind anxiously churns through how to answer all his questions, not that I remember most of them. All I can do is smile. Be pretty. Oh, can that please be enough?

"I believe in you," I say.

"That's how come you want this job?" He tilts back in his chair, balances on two legs, lets his eyes drift all the way down my body and then slowly right back up. I watch their slow, hungry path. For one spare second I imagine—but banish that. I'm not special. The outer office overflowed with beautiful women and girls—all equally in love—who eyed me, unthreatened, as I passed through. "Can you think a little harder? Maybe there's more."

Sweat rises in my armpits. Here's the most important moment of my life.

"Do you think . . . ?" His chair slams forward onto four legs. "That you want to be powerful?"

"Me? Powerful? Oh, my, no. No." I laugh teeny-tiny, tittering hiccups of nervous laughter.

He laughs back: belly rolls of, well, power and confidence. "You might be surprised," he whispers, then says, "Being patient, for example, is a kind of power."

I'm so patient! I nod. In fact, I nod *patiently*.

"Outlasting all the others," he says. "Not easy, is it?" He glances at his chunky gold watch. He's busy and important yet talking to me, ME, understanding my ache to matter, to answer phones for his campaign. I want to be "office helper" and earn credit at my community college; to brew coffee in a real pot and clean up foam cups and sugar packets after a strategy session; to decide if the pens we order are blue ink or black.

I say, "I pulled the flyer off the bulletin board at school so no one else could apply. I've never stolen anything before, ever. That's how much I want this job."

My face scorches hot to reveal this secret.

He says, "Bet you don't understand how pretty you are. Even when you're not smiling."

No, here's the greatest moment of my life. He'll sweep the papers off the desk with one arm, like in the movies, and it's goodbye to this virginity I've been pointlessly guarding. In the office, he and I will secretly link pinkies at the copy machine. He'll recognize my perfume out of all perfumes, and his wife will like me enough to say, "If I die, you should marry that nice girl down at campaign headquarters."

He says, "We could talk more about this job over dinner," which stops my heart from beating. My head nods, my face says, *yes yes yes*. Then he says: "But I'm not going to do that. You're different. Not like the others. You're patient. And—" He pauses.

I listen to my dulled heart toll seven times.

"I'll be honest here," he says. "This world's got two choices for girls like you. One: there's the power God gave you."

He peers in at me. I nod. He sighs, because it's that clear I'm confused. He stands and walks round the desk to where I'm sitting, legs neatly crossed at the ankle, and taps his pointer finger right there, yes, *there*, exactly between my two legs. I gasp. Like a butterfly pinned down. "A woman might think *that*"—the finger taps, lingers—"gives you something. Maybe makes a woman feel powerful around a man. Thinking you'll corner him, get what you want. It's biology, after all."

That finger travels up to his own forehead and rubs tiny, mesmerizing circles into his temple. He speaks slowly, deliberately: "Contrast that with the power you seize when the time's right. Pardon my French here, but convincing a man he *wants* to slide his precious dick right on into your mouth, slip himself between your sharp teeth, the hinge of your jaw maybe snapping down any moment. Getting him belly-up and vulnerable. That there's power to envy. That there's what anyone should want." He crosses his arms against his chest, towers over me.

I'm a cluster of nerve-ending feelings. Did I get the job? Are we having dinner? Is it sex on the desk? Or I'm supposed to . . . ? Should I . . . ? I'm not yet clear on the swallowing. Worry heats my face. "You want a . . . ?" I whisper, embarrassed of the words.

That rolling laugh. "I get plenty of those," he says. "What I want is for you to be that one woman who knows exactly what she's doing each and every time she opens her mouth. So to speak. Is that what you also want? Or are you afraid?"

I know that I know nothing. But I stand up so fast he's forced to step back, out of my way.

"Do I get the job?" I ask at the exact same time that he says, "Job's yours." He jabs that finger straight at me, hitting each syllable as he says. "Don't you forget to register to vote."

"Yes, sir," I say. "Of course. Thank you." Shouldn't there be something more to say—but since he isn't saying it, maybe not.

"Leave the door open," he says. "Closed doors mean someone's in trouble."

He and I never talked about this job interview again. Likely he wouldn't remember it, and likely he understood I'd never forget it. That's the man I work for. That's the woman I became.

I'm at the sheet cake party. It's maybe almost like it's my own time, so I'm thinking, thinking. I'm sitting in a conference-room chair because I came stupidly early, and he showed up exactly one second before the Speaker, so he's standing for all to admire, artfully propped within the door frame. Who else's birthday would he appear for? He's, of course, the one charged with saying a "few words" after everyone insists, and damn it, they're perfect words, with the room knowing when to laugh and when to look thoughtful. Thought bubbles rise above everyone's head: Such a natural leader!

Not one glance at me. I don't exist. My fingernails are clamped into my palms, digging sharp lines of pain.

Okay, how am I different from the others, is maybe what I could have asked that night. Or, simply, Others? Accompanied by that withering raised eyebrow the She-Beast unleashes.

I don't have to be loved.

Me inviting him in, I think, is not rape. *Not* the workplace, like Cassidy, calling him "dickbreath" in covert whispers.

Look in the mirror, I think, that's not Mary Worth, campy haunt of sleepovers: that's you.

He's perfectly wrapping up his perfect toast, and we raise Solo cups of sparkling water or prosecco. The She-Beast poured water, so I did too. She won't fix me, but I want to still trust her. Because who else is there? The Speaker smiles his heart-crushingly beautiful smile, messaging to us that we're each important. People say he practiced smiling to get it exactly right. We laugh at his dopey, self-deprecating joke. Practice, or muscle memory?

I want so, so, so much for this to maybe be the moment when I go, fuck it, and file a burn-it-down complaint. Instead, I finally remember something else she had said in the bathroom that night: Ask why they reward you for being different, not for being yourself.

Cheers! I slug it all down, feeling slightly queasy.

They're all late nights. I don't mind. The real work gets done alone. An orange for dinner is fine.

I photocopied the birthday card, of course, and now I'm forging her signature onto the form acknowledging that yes, we had the conversation we didn't actually have.

Tomorrow, I'll make some calls. Rustle up options for Mia. A better job. People listen when I whisper, Hire this one. Better for her to start fresh.

I'm patient. I can wait them all out, this young guy, whoever's the next one eyeing my office. He's only been here eighteen months, hired with great fanfare, Our Own Wunderkind, with his Twitter followers and choice of Sunday morning roundtable guest spots. Oh, he can do anything!

A danger to all of us.

Doesn't take long to put together the complaint I scared Mia away from and forge her signature again. This document goes inside my "if I'm fired" file, ensuring Our Own Wunderkind will steer clear of me in the future, ensuring no one's replacing me anytime soon. My job description is: Think of *everything*.

That's exactly what the Speaker values about me. I mean, look: I'm working till midnight on my birthday, and Mia's the one off to find a better way, maybe. Oh, I'm not about to save her, not in the simplistic way she hopes. She'll endure, and learn patience, and as people do, assume she saved herself. In the end, she's no different than the rest of us old gals, and eventually she'll figure out who filed that original report that started our conversation, who safely got her out of the office.

PEOPLE LOVE A VIEW

Jillian and Patrick met at a mutual friend's after-work happy hour ten days ago, and today was their first date though not a real date. "More like a thing," they agreed. "Meeting up, Saturday exercise, two friends." Lots of words describing this nothing that might lead to coffee or beer, or dinner, or a rom-com weekend of inside jokes and lingering sex, or to the extravagant story of "how we met" splashed into the feature piece in the "Vows" column of the Sunday *New York Times*. They had planned on a short run, but Patrick had pulled his calf muscle on the treadmill and wanted to rest it. Rather than reschedule, they decided to walk instead. Jillian worried the sore muscle was an excuse, but friends talked her out of this paranoia, and Patrick showed up at the park underneath the foot of the Wilson Bridge on Saturday morning wearing a Pacers 5K shirt, so his story felt legit.

This location was Patrick's idea, his favorite quirky spot for "not a date" dates. The Wilson Bridge linked both sides of the Potomac River, Virginia and Maryland, as part of I-95, the East Coast's busiest, most dreaded interstate. Recent reconstruction created this park along with a protected pedestrian walkway the length of the bridge, roughly a mile, adjacent to the southbound traffic lanes. Something immediately noticeable but rarely mentioned was that the walkers and joggers starting on the Virginia side, Alexandria, tended to be white, and the people starting from the Maryland side, Prince George's County, were virtually all Black. Just an observation, Patrick tried to convince himself, and noticing that disparity didn't mean he was racist. Noticing that didn't mean anything.

This place wasn't any great secret—sign at the entrance, googleable park website, inclusion on "Fun Spots in DC" listicles, mention in the *Washingtonian*—but Jillian didn't know about the walkway. "Because I'm way out in Springfield, right?" she texted after the happy hour. "Where nobody tells us anything?" Patrick lived in Old Town Alexandria, another reason he set dates that weren't dates here: his ten-minute drive. Also, whatever happened after was up to him, coffee at the place with the fancy machine from Italy, the Irish bar where they started pouring his Guinness pint as he sat down. A well-planned day evolved as if it had not been planned. At the happy hour, they'd talked about Alexandria. She didn't much like Springfield, what were rents in Alexandria? He spoke generally, not admitting that he owned his condo. Maybe she thought he was younger than he was (thirty-five). He figured her for midtwenties though she acted older; maybe they both looked younger than their ages. A walk (coffee? beer?) would sort it out.

Jillian purposefully arrived early, first, and she loitered at the basketball court in the shadows under the bridge, watching two teenagers practice elaborate shots. "Mofo," they cat-called each other with brash fondness. Highway traffic thumped above, and she felt dropped into a postapocalyptic pocket. Towering cement Vs supported the bridge, creating angled shadows, sliced by shafts of sun; scrappy weeds sprouted through the gravel fill; security cameras robotically scanned the landscape, unsubtly hinting not to plant bombs. She had moved to DC from North Dakota two years ago, and her mother still ended every phone conversation with "be careful, sweetie."

The day was hot and humid, typical for August, and even the dank shade was oppressive. The teenagers had tossed their shirts into a heap, their smooth chests slicked with sweat. How ghastly she'd look after walking, she thought, why had she bothered to shower? The boys ramped up, joyful, enjoying the audience she provided. She half-wished they'd toss her the ball; she'd played shooting guard in high school. They could tell their friends stories later about the crazy white girl's three-pointers.

But she returned to the bench by the parking lot where she and Patrick were to meet. According to her phone, he was four and a half minutes late, which felt as calculated as her excessive promptness. "Sorry I'm late," he said when he arrived.

"Are you?" she said. "Doesn't matter."

He made a show of setting his excessively fancy running watch, the dial about as big as a saucer. She braced, afraid he'd explain its every last function to her, but he said, "My dad gave it to me for my birthday, and I don't know half of what it does. Maybe space travel? He likes to think he's this tech guy."

He led her across the park, which abruptly no longer felt postapocalyptic; they crisscrossed bike paths scattered with parents pushing strollers, dog walkers, joggers, the zip of bikes; walked past the basketball court where the teenagers had been joined by several more, a game starting, threats flying: "Wipe that ass on this, motherfucker!" They veered to a different sidewalk, alongside patches of tall, summer-dry grasses—dragonflies darting and hovering, a steady, unseen buzz, flies swarming a thin strip of shit—then up an incline to street level and the entrance to the walkway across the bridge.

"Six and a half minutes," he said, glancing at his watch. He pointed out sights along Washington Street—a once-forgotten slave cemetery that until several years ago had been paved over by a Sunoco station, historic Old Town up that way, and George Washington's house down the other way. He was interesting enough but talked too fast. He'd been like that at the happy hour, from the three-dollar margaritas, she'd thought. "We're both fizzy," she'd said then, explaining, "My mom won't say *drunk*."

Definitely prettier than he remembered. Plus, he was a sucker for girls in athletic wear, girls with glossy, dark ponytails swinging side to side. Better than shorts, she wore a flippy little skirt that clung sweetly to her ass. That skirt made him nervous, and he reminded himself to shut the fuck up and let her talk, to ask some questions: "What's North Dakota like?"

"Never as hot as all this," she said, then talked about snowmobiling as they started along the walkway of the bridge, St. Mary's Cemetery below on the left, jammed with mausoleums and stone angels, while on the right streamed a steady line of cars and trucks barreling by at seventy or more, mostly more. A twenty-foot glass barrier for noise abatement protected walkers for about thirty yards, then abruptly ended, leaving a line of Jersey barriers between them and the oncoming traffic.

This was his favorite part, beyond the glass and alongside the full blitz of roaring traffic, exhaust fumes, eddies of road dust, that unnatural, constant hot wind bull-whipping the air. He couldn't describe the moment nicely, or explain why he craved these sensations, feeling only a four-foot-high cement wall shielding the blurry onslaught of rushing cars. If one semi lost control, if one SUV careened off course, people on the walkway would be carnage, then headlines—the subjects of ratings-grubbing stories splashed across local news, giving rise to another round of cautionary tales about texting while driving. Yet it wasn't a death wish in Patrick, more like an animal longing to feel danger without experiencing it.

She paused, maybe assessing the swirl of emotion surging through Patrick, then fiddled with the metal disk dangling off her runner's ID necklace. "It's my mom's phone number," she explained. "Like she could do anything from North Dakota."

"Are you okay?" he asked. "People get nervous being close to traffic. Or they're afraid of heights." He pointed to the river on the left, far below them, explaining that when the bridge span was rebuilt in the last decade, it had been raised to accommodate ships that might come up from the Chesapeake Bay. "And it's a drawbridge," he said, "which is crazy for an interstate."

Jillian knew these facts but nodded as if she didn't. "Heights don't get to me, it's snakes." She wrinkled her nose as a child would. An impossibly cute reaction.

"Me too," he said. "Especially any snake who finds itself all the way up here."

They walked for a few moments, their gait fairly matched. The river below was brown, the water pocked with large, depressing blobs of algae, thick enough to support plastic bottles and logs. Fringing the left side of the Potomac was Alexandria's waterfront, a low line of townhouses, restaurants, and shops—glittery skyscrapers banned—and the airport beyond. Above, planes descended along the curve of the river, landing one after the other, in a steady, gentle stream. The Maryland side was a mass of trees interrupted by the dull bureaucracy of the regional water treatment plant. Up river, off in the distance, DC's icons were tiny but immediately recognizable: the Capitol dome, Washington Monument, the grassy Mall. On the opposite side of the bridge was a land-grabbing, soul-sucking hotel and entertainment complex that he joked was "Disney meets Kafka meets capitalism"; her laugh in response was gratifying.

"Still," she said, "I liked riding that huge Ferris wheel they've got." She gave him a sly smile before adding, "With my mom, who was visiting."

Damn it, he *had* wondered. He spoke casually: "People love a view."

"True."

Jutting off the walkway was a semicircular promontory with historical plaques. There was a brief, uncomfortable back and forth as they debated whether to pause to read the panels about Alexandria's colonial history, would it be fun to peer through the industrial binoculars—"if you want to," each said. They stopped. She swigged from her water bottle. Side by side they gazed toward the tiny monuments of DC. "I should take a picture, but this is one of those things that never ends up looking like it does," she said. She wrapped her fingers around the prison-bar iron railing, stared at the water below. It would be hard to jump with this railing here, she thought, but not impossible. They never made these things impossible. She suddenly felt anxious. Did she like Patrick? Did she want to like Patrick? Another swig of water, and because he had no water bottle, she held out hers, but he shook his head no. Showing off by toughing it out? Not thirsty?

"Not many people out today," he said. "For a Saturday."

"Too hot," she said. They watched a tour boat trundle toward them and then on under the bridge, avoiding the algae bloom. She felt like half of a boring old married couple living in slow motion.

Precisely then, a car crunches onto the shoulder, jostling and grinding to a slow stop, and Jillian's startled shriek wrenches Patrick out of his fantasy about captaining an old-time Maryland clipper ship. He turns to see a battered, white Corolla rolling in, followed by a silver highway patrol cop car and its swirl of blue-and-red lights. The driver of the Corolla is a Black man with salt-and-pepper stubble along his jaw and up through his scalp. His T-shirt is faded burgundy. A dog's head bounces into view at the passenger-side back-seat window, then rebounds to the driver side and on back to stare closely at them through the passenger window, as if deciding something. It's a largish dog, maybe part border collie, part German shepherd, and part many other things. There's an intelligence to the dog's eyes, the cocked head, and excitement at landing in this new place. The window is cracked open several inches, enough for the dog to push its snout through.

Patrick scans the length of the walkway ahead, the Maryland side, aching to see someone. There's no one. How can it be Saturday without bikers and runners? Behind them, Virginia is equally empty. The sun notches immediately hotter, the humidity thickens, the air feels like pudding. He's afraid to look at Jillian but he does, hoping she'll say something like, "Let's keep walking," so he can respond, "If you want to," and shrug.

She says, "Wait. Shouldn't I film this?" Either he doesn't hear or he's pretending not to, so she feels weaseled into dredging up her phone, which balances limply in her hand.

Cars whiz by. The driver rolls down the front window, switches off the engine. He slaps both hands at the top of the steering wheel, at eleven and one. His forearms are thick. Almost immediately he shifts, lacing his hands tightly behind his head, leaning back and angling his elbows into a wider stance, ensuring they're more clearly visible in silhouette.

The cop is the Hollywood stereotype, bristling with importance and authority. Thick-chested, thickheaded. A bulletproof vest implies that his business is always to assume the worst. Sunglasses. That fixation on their sunglasses, Patrick thinks, before trying not to think, At least the cop's Black, too—which has to be better. Right? Though he knows the cases, the situations, the litany of names, the possibilities of the equation *Black man + cop* x *gun*. "Probably a speeding ticket," he remarks, steadying his voice. His stomach feels knotted. "Asshole highway patrol."

"I think we have to do this." Jillian taps numbers into her phone, swipes, taps again. "Just in case. I mean?"

He imagines footage of right now, this not-date, looping on YouTube, tweeted, retweeted, hashtagged, Facebooked, Instagrammed, and all the rest; angry protests, marches, and clashes; the cop's cell number ferreted out and forwarded; teary-eyed family members pleading for calm at some press conferences, for justice at others, lots and lots of lawyers; a haunting photo of this Black man but in a suit, a woman telling and retelling the story of how much he loved his kids. The nauseating formula. "It'll be a speeding ticket," he says. "But yeah, just in case."

"Maybe it's our chance to make a difference or something," Jillian says. She points her camera at the car, and calls, "We're filming you!" She narrates into her phone, giving the location, date, and time, and, Patrick notices, omitting his name, though she has mentioned her own, clarifying, "Jillian with a J." He doesn't feel anger exactly, but something squirmy and unpleasant. It's like the bulletproof vest, assuming always the worst thing will happen. Like if it is just a speeding ticket, she'll be disappointed. But maybe so will he.

He yells at the cop, "Turn on your body cam," which seems stupid, since he doesn't know if that really is the technical term, if it is or isn't already on, but Jillian says, "Oh, good thinking."

No visible response from the cop. Perhaps he can't hear them over the rush of traffic. "I'm watching you," Jillian shouts louder, cupping one hand at the side of her mouth. Her face is flushed pink, maybe heat, maybe the drama of the moment. She trains her phone on the Corolla then glides it, capturing the cop's purposeful strides. At this point, the dog charges to the far side of the car, shoving its head through the cracked window, barking out deep and rapid anger, then it lunges into the front, fully thrusting its head out the driver-side window, and the barking intensifies, joined by the man's shouts: "No! Down!" He clutches at the dog's neck, wrestling it to the back, but the dog surges forward.

At the trunk of the car, the cop stops, commanding in a clipped and professional voice: "Restrain the dog, sir."

The driver shouts: "Trying to, sir! This's a good dog."

"I'm filming!" Jillian shouts, but no one looks her way. We could not be here, Patrick thinks, except that we are.

"Restrain that dog," shouts the cop. "Hands so I can see them." There is no logic to these competing instructions, which everyone recognizes, just as everyone recognizes what is about to happen, which happens: the dog plunges through the open front window, its feet hitting the pavement with a scratchy scramble, and the cop pulls his gun and steadies his stance, again shouting as the man pushes open the car door, "Hands so I can see them! Do not exit the car, sir," and the driver leans forward, elbows up and jutting alongside his head, calling, "Bella! Bella! No! Get back here!" but the dog turns not to the cop but to Jillian, who has rushed the Jersey barrier, shouting, "Here, boy, good doggie," filming forgotten as she dangles both hands over the edge of the wall because one thing she knows is that she's very good with dogs.

The driver's voice rises: "I gotta get my dog. Sir. Bella!"

The dog seems confused, overwhelmed with options and grand ideas, and it stands alert, only barely still. It's a tiny moment where everyone thinks maybe they can draw in a deep breath, but a semi rattles by, boxed in its lane, pulling its horn long and hard—presumably a warning—which startles the dog into action, into making the wrong choice as Patrick sensed it would, as if there were no choice at all, and the man or maybe Jillian or maybe the cop shouts, "Fucking shit," as the dog runs at the traffic, skirting the road's edge as cars skid over a lane, and maybe, maybe it will be okay, but the dog dodges onto the road itself, immediately getting clipped by a swerving taxi that hurtles on. A thud, a howl, and the dog's body careens onto the shoulder, sending up shudders of dust. Patrick's fingertips are suddenly, bloodlessly, icy cold.

"Fucking shit!" the man shouts, flopping his head onto the steering wheel, elbows still akimbo. "Jesus fucking Christ!"

Finally, the cop holsters his gun, his hand fumbling. Other than that single motion, his body appears very still.

Jillian shrieks, "Oh my god," and lifts her phone, sweeping it across the scene, her fingers zooming and expanding. "The dog got run over," she narrates. "That effing cop stood there while a taxi plowed this guy's poor dog."

And then the dog yelps. Lifts its head, pokes its snout upward, feebly falls back.

"He's not dead," Jillian says, and she clambers a leg at the Jersey barrier, ready to heave over it, but Patrick grabs her arm, and she stops. Later, he'll wonder why he did this, tried to stop her. Maybe because he didn't want to follow.

"This makes me sick," she says, squirming free of his grasp. "My god. I'm shaking." She extends one quivering hand, palm down.

The driver flings back against the seat, his face locked in a taut grimace. The cop straightens his impossibly straight shoulders, resumes his resolute strides to the driver-side window. The exchange is easily interpreted: the cop requests a driver's license, car registration; both are carefully relinquished. A brief conversation, some nodding, no eye contact. The cop does not remove his sunglasses. Patrick imagines the words: *unfortunate, regrettable, beyond our control, tough break, given the circumstances.* Unspoken words echo: train your dog to obey, loose dogs in cars are hazards, if you weren't speeding. *If only. You should have.* If you left the dog at home today, if you took a different route, if you weren't late. *If you cared a fuck about your dog.* Words even the cop won't say. Patrick doesn't want to think these things, hates them in his head. He wonders if Jillian is like him, powerless to stop their maddening buzz.

The cop returns to the cop car, license in hand, to check the records, and finally, finally, the man gets out, running and half-stumbling to the whimpering dog up ahead. The hind legs are mangled, splayed perpendicular to the front legs.

The dog struggles to scratch out some footing but sinks back down. The man squats, then drops to cradle the dog's head in his lap; he strokes its fur and kisses the dog's snout. Another yelp, softer, almost gentle.

Jillian is over the wall, jogging to the man and the dog. She kneels down to let the dog sniff her hand, but just as quickly, she jumps back up, photographing the dog, the man, the cop car behind them. Patrick tries to remember if she has a dog, talked about a dog. Did she say anything about pets? He doesn't even know her.

The heat bores deeper as Patrick waits for the man to scoop up the dog, the cop to release the man, the dog to be raced to the vet, the vet to fix the dog. Jillian is waving him over, and he's afraid she'll photograph him if he doesn't join her, so he scales the wall and hurries to the group. The dog's eyes are bleary, filming over, its breath coming in sharp rasps. "What's his name?" Jillian asks, and he blocks the answer from his mind. Traffic slows into a procession of gaping faces that kaleidoscope past. He flashes the middle finger to several cars, a flare of anger that feels childish.

The cop sidles into the group. His voice is professional: "Everything checks out here."

Jillian says, "What about his dog?"

The cop remains standing, studying the dog through his sunglasses. He says, "I can siren-escort you to the emergency vet off Telegraph Road, no more than four minutes away. I wouldn't say cheap, but they know their business."

The man says, "Like I got cash for your fancy emergency vet. Sir."

Jillian says, "I can pay, we'll pay for everything," neatly looping Patrick and his almost maxed-out credit card into her offer, as if they're a couple. "Right, Patrick? The least we can do," and she glares not at the cop but in his direction, wanting to guilt him into volunteering to chip in, but his face is impassive, like a piece of armor. He takes a step back and pivots to gaze toward the river, though with those sunglasses, he could be looking anywhere.

"Those legs are about smashed flat," the man says. "Nobody's fixing legs looking like that."

"Vets work miracles," Jillian says. "You'd be amazed. They'll set him up in those carts, where it's wheels in the back. You've seen those, right? Dogs running around like it's nothing." She's rambling, words spilling out so fast she sounds slurred and drunk. "Let's get going. The vet will figure it out for us."

"A dog in a cart?" the man asks.

She explains the dog-wheelchair concept, waving her hands and talking quickly, how the hindquarters are propped up, how the wheels work as hind legs, then expands into a story about a three-legged dog in her neighborhood.

The man's eyes are fixed on his dog, and he keeps shaking his head. "No way to live," he says, "dumping a dog in a cart."

"Think like a wheelchair," she says. "Plenty of people have very happy lives in wheelchairs, right?"

"Don't see you in one," he says. "So you know?"

She babbles about volunteer work her sorority did in college where they coached a basketball league of kids in wheelchairs. Patrick has been nodding at her every word like a bobblehead, as if he has heard these stories many times, as if he knows all about this time in her life. He can't remember what they talked about at happy hour. Why he's with this stranger.

The man shifts the dog's head in his lap, gazes into its filmy eyes, massaging tiny circles into a spot on top of the dog's head. Just now, Patrick notices that the dog wears a red plaid collar. "Nah," the man says, shaking his head. "This is a good dog, she's the best I ever had." He gently slides the dog's head from his lap, like transferring a droplet of water, and scrambles himself up to standing, rubbing briskly at his knees and thighs. The cop's posture ratchets tighter and he steps closer. Side by side, the two men are the same height.

"Shoot. Her." The two words are precisely spoken.

"Excuse me, sir?" the cop says.

"No," Jillian commands. "The vet will—"

"Shoot my dog," the man says.

"Sir, I can't—"

"She's suffering." The man shades his eyes and looks back at his car. They all look at the car. No one looks at the dog.

Jillian grabs Patrick's hand. "This can't happen," she murmurs.

His watch lets off a series of three soft beeps, a timer reaching zero—meaning he pressed the wrong button back in the parking lot. He lets go of Jillian's clammy, wet-towel hand and pokes at his watch, desperate to stop the noise, which he finally does.

"Shoot her," the man says. "Shoot my damn dog."

"But . . ." The word trails off. Neither man shifts his weight.

"Can't afford that vet," the man says. "And my dog's not wanting any doggie-wheelchair life."

"I'll take the dog," Jillian says. "Please. I'll bring him to the vet, get him good as new. I love dogs. My brother lives in the country, if you want lots of outdoors for him to run in. We'll take super-good care. You'll visit."

The man is eye-to-eye with those sunglasses. "My dog, my decision. She's my dog," he says. "*Mine*."

The cop's mouth moves like maybe there's something to say. He doesn't say it.

This moment feels infinite. The dog whines and tries to lift its head but can't. There's so much blood. There's some rubbery something worse than blood. The dog will be dead soon anyway, with that much blood on the road, on the man's pants. Flies have targeted the blood and the dog. This is a matter of fifteen, twenty minutes. No one needs to shoot a dog today, Patrick thinks. Jillian wraps her arms round her body in a hug.

"Shoot the dog," the man says. His voice is calm and even and slow, a metronome.

The cop breaks the staring match and looks back to the cars, the cop car and the white Corolla. He looks at the stream of oncoming traffic. Patrick follows his gaze: the blue-and-red lights seem surreally slower than before, as if they will drift to a stop if someone doesn't do something.

"I'll wrap her in a blanket outta my car trunk. Take her on home, bury her in the backyard," the man says.

"It's not legal to—" starts the cop before shaking his head the tiniest bit.

Jillian says, "This has to be wrong."

Patrick's body feels sticky and hot and pale, a burden to haul around. He can't imagine coffee or a beer afterward. He can't imagine afterward with Jillian or without. Or ever getting off this bridge.

"Bella's a good dog," the man says. "And seeing her suffer. I can't bear it."

A semi pushes by, another. Cars keep coming and faces peer out windows. People want to see what's going on, commenting to people in the car, "Oh no, it's a dead dog." Seconds later saying: Are we there yet? Did you hear what the president said yesterday? Have you seen that movie where they blow up the Eiffel Tower? The noise of conversation.

"This is one you owe me," the man says.

"Fuck you," the cop says. But he makes a practiced and professional motion like *stand back, everybody*, herding them carefully backward, beyond and behind the cars, and they huddle at the Jersey barrier. Jillian's face contorts, and her tears look aggressive and angry as she aims her phone at the dog, flicking finger and thumb on the screen to zoom close.

Her ponytail has gone limp, her skirt too. Patrick smears the sweat on his forehead, leans against the wall, tries to think about if he will watch or look away, if Jillian will watch or look away. Right now, she's looking. The cop says, "This won't be pretty."

The man faces the river, hands braced on the Jersey barrier. He throws back his head, maybe watching the Southwest airplane above. Everybody buckled in, Patrick thinks, safe in their seats, staring down at the ribbon of water.

The cop says, "I shouldn't be doing this." Then he says, "The vet is only—"

"My dog's not deserving to live like this."

"The angle's tricky, so might be easier to—"

"Shoot the dog."

The cop uses those same professional, purposeful strides to get himself back to where the dog lies and there's barely a second before the shot and Jillian throws her arm up over her eyes. "Oh my god!" she cries over and over. Patrick has looked away but then he forces himself to see, knowing—goddamn it—he will want to tell this story, and in his quick, cowardly glance, the only image is "shredded." The dog is absolutely *shredded.* And the red plaid collar. The collar.

The man's eyes are fixed on the sludgy river. He seems to be concentrating. There's a faint something that could be the quick twist of an angry smile.

The cop walks fast, faster. "That's what he said he wanted, you heard the man!" he calls. "None of that's on me. None of it." His car door opens, shuts.

"I'll help you," Patrick says because Jillian doesn't. He hopes to God the man's got a shovel in that car trunk, that the blanket is big and thick. A metallic, retching taste coats his tongue.

The man shakes his head. "Nah, not giving that mother-fucking cop the satisfaction," he says, and trudges to his car, getting in, fiddling with something on the dashboard before shutting the door.

"Oh my god!" Jillian keeps saying, "Oh my god," and, "That poor dog, that poor, sad dog," words that feel extraneous. Patrick is somehow surprised to see her still standing there.

She points her camera yet again at the dog. "He should sue," she says. "Sue that damn cop for killing his dog." It's the glimmer of justice, the scraps of hashtags and importance. He understands: she wants the story, wants to be in the story. A story means an answer, a solution, redemption. Makes her a hero, Jillian with a J. "Can't we sue someone? I'm emailing this to the Humane Society, to PETA."

Why does he say this hateful thing, when he knows it's not true? But he does: "It's just a dog."

Her ragged gasp radiates pure disgust. Maybe that's why: he's pushing for reaction. He's lost nothing today and needs to, even if it's only this happy-hour hookup North Dakota girl he barely knows. All of his thoughts right now are sickening.

The Corolla noses into traffic, a cautious wobble, and disappears into the stream moving south. The cop car waits, lights flashing.

"He's just leaving the dog here?" she says. "On the road? For god's sake. Everybody's fucked up. This world sucks so goddamn much."

"It will be fine," Patrick says, pushing, pushing. It's virtuous pain. "He'll get another dog."

"Another! Dog!" Her outrage is palpable. "Oh my god. Who are you?" She slumps in that way people do when they want to be hugged but of course he won't touch her. Maybe she's crying.

But the words circle Patrick's head: Who am I? Who am I?

He watches the cop in his car as Jillian rails on about injustice and the poor dog and this sucky world. The funny thing is, he agrees with her. But he's watching the cop, hunched over his steering wheel, shoulders shaking, sobbing. He wants to feel sorry for the cop, wants to hate him, wants to hate someone. It's easiest to hate Jillian right now. But really he hates himself.

Later, he tells the story that night to his friends at the Irish bar. He tries not to make himself sound braver, tries not to make Jillian sound bitchy, tries not to think about the flies swarming the body left behind, the body on the side of the road in the dark, the man somewhere, telling the same story, but starting from that other side of the bridge.

THIS ISN'T WHO WE ARE

Everyone in your Northern Virginia neighborhood belongs to the neighborhood e-list because everyone's mission is to find a reasonably priced plumber willing to replace a busted garbage disposal at five-thirty p.m. the Wednesday before Thanksgiving. Also on the e-list will be requests from people seeking vacation plant-waterers and cat-feeders and mail-fetchers that start, "Looking for college student/recent grad home for the summer . . ." Also: requests from neighbors with dandelions and pokeweed crowding their mulched flower beds: "Any high school students available for light weeding?" Pretend not to understand that those requests written in that exact way are code calling for white people to do the work. And pretend that you didn't tweak the front curtain aside to glance out the window after seeing the e-list warning, "Aggressive door-to-door solicitor @ W Maple; black man selling candy bars from cardboard box but was nervous that my (big!) dog was barking. Reported him to the nonemergency police #. Where's his permit!!?"

When you're riding the Metro and land a double-seat to yourself because you board at the beginning of the line, watch the car fill up as you approach the city. But pretend you don't see how the white-collar Black men stand instead of slide next to you, sharing your seat. Pretend you think that's because they'll be sitting at a desk all day or because they're riding only a couple of stops. Pretend not to see the blue-collar Black man alone on a double-seat, how no one sits next to him, until the train packs so full that commuters can't breathe. Pretend you aren't imagining yourself "brave" when you sit next to him, especially if the train is only slightly crowded. On the way back home, at Gallery Place, when you're descending on the escalator, pretend you don't look to see if the people waiting on the platform are Black, because if they are, you'll know immediately that it's the Green Line arriving next. Pretend you're not hoping to see white people waiting because that means the incoming train will be the Yellow Line to suburban Virginia. Pretend you're the only one pretending not to notice this. Pretend that Black people notice too so it's okay. Pretend that sometimes you don't walk a few extra blocks after nine p.m. to the Archives station because fewer "rowdy" and "noisy" teenagers wait there to catch trains. Pretend not to notice how many Latino riders catch the last train at night, after late shifts. Pretend they'll be walking to their houses after exiting the Metro, not sitting at a desolate bus stop.

Pretend you aren't thinking you're also "brave" when you pass through a sprawl of Black teenage boys clad in hoodies (winter) or tank tops (summer) or T-shirts imprinted with the face of a dead Black man or boy (any season) on the street where you walk daily in your historic suburban town's shopping district. Pretend that they bother noticing a drab, middle-aged white woman wearing lavender running shoes purchased with a coupon at a strip-mall DSW. Pretend they're examining you closely with the male gaze. Pretend you're fine with that. Pretend your breathing doesn't race just a tiny, tiny bit. Pretend you wanted to walk this fast for cardio.

Next time you're in DC, notice a young, striking Black woman's natural hair as she stands next to you at a red light at McPherson Square, her paisley-patterned maxi dress billowing like she's in a photo shoot. Pretend that your desire to compliment her hair isn't about you. Pretend she'd be happy to hear how pretty you think she and her hair are, you in your schlumpy clothing because you're headed to a cut-and-color appointment. Pretend you're not practicing the exact phrasing of this compliment in your head to get it right. The light turns green and off she goes, swift in her platform sandals, and now you can pretend that *you* changed your mind. At the hair appointment, pretend you're not overtipping the bad shampoo girl who splashes soap in your eyes and grinds her knuckles into your temples, though you ask her to stop; pretend you "asked" when really it was "told." Pretend to understand it's okay to maybe be a little tiny bit demanding if you are physically in pain; nevertheless, tuck a ten into her tip envelope.

Pretend you've forgotten a certain conversation from fifteen years ago when you were a sweet, young thing at a happy hour of up-and-coming lawyers with first mortgages and first babies, all complaining that their cleaning women didn't dust the ceiling fans, "not even when I pointed right at it," a woman whined. Pretend that you said—instead of merely thought—"Dust it yourself," and now pretend that it's not driving you just a little tiny bit crazy that the ceiling fan in your bedroom is layered with dust and that, honestly, just how hard would it be for her to lift the damn Swiffer up there?

In downtown DC, always have a dollar in a pocket that's easily accessible so you can quickly pass it to a panhandler without breaking stride. Pretend you're doing something principled, and explain to your friends walking with you, "I don't care what he spends it on. Food, liquor, drugs. All I know is that it would be hard to live on the streets, so whatever he needs." Pretend you're not royally pissed when you don't hear "thank you" or "god bless" immediately upon handing over your crumpled dollar. Pretend you don't save the clean, crisp bills for your wallet. Pretend you've never walked into a NJ Turnpike McDonald's and thought, "See, the Dollar Menu. So people can buy food for a dollar." You also support *Street Sense*, the newspaper about and sold by the homeless, but pretend you're not a little tiny bit pissed that they jacked the price from one dollar to two. Pretend that reading the poetry written by *Street Sense* vendors, filled with clichés and optimism and God, doesn't make you feel impotently sad. Pretend you don't imagine posting one of those poems on Facebook or Twitter and being heroically responsible for it going viral. Pretend a dollar will save someone's life.

Pretend those canned vegetables you donate to the food bank would be right at home on your dinner table, that your husband would happily say, "Hey, hon, please pass over the bowl of delicious canned corn because I would really love a second serving." Pretend that you eat beans or tuna every night for dinner because you're grateful for protein. Pretend that you prefer the store brands, and maybe even pretend that the people getting the food won't notice that nothing is Del Monte, nothing is Jif, nothing is organic, nothing is bought at full price. Pretend you would be bursting with appreciation for this bounty. Pretend that when you do eat canned black beans that you don't shake on fancy hot sauce from Miami for flavor. Pretend you're noble because you'd never grab expired crap from the back of your cabinets; you're noble to throw that shit away. Pretend not to mind dropping off a bag of (unwrapped) toys from Target to a holiday gift drive, and that it's okay to take your donation to a box in a busy realtor's office, and pretend you don't wish someone there or anywhere would thank you to your face and/or (but really and) pop a handwritten note with a real stamp into the mail. Pretend not to be pleased with yourself for imagining the smile of the Black teenage boy enchanted by your gift on Christmas Day, a regulation basketball, and then pretend you don't see the dozen or so Spalding basketballs already filling the box at the realtor's office.

Pretend that you never notice that there is maybe one Black couple at the parties you go to. Pretend not to feel instant relief when you see that couple there, clutching their glasses of Trader Joe's wine. Pretend to have no idea that everyone around you is equally relieved, that the host of the party is thinking, "Look, I have Black friends." In a different conversation at a different time, maybe over brunch with women, pretend that you've been invited to a party at a Black couple's house. Or an Asian couple's house. Or a Latinx couple's house, and pretend you have now learned how to use *Latinx* properly, without feeling nervous about screwing it up.

Pretend you're outraged at the gentrification of DC, once proudly called "Chocolate City." Pretend you don't sometimes secretly fantasize about moving out of the suburbs, into the city, scoring a nice condo or row house on U Street or H Street, or in NoMa or Petworth, or maybe even getting in early in Anacostia, which has got to be the next real estate hotspot, right? When speaking of it, which is rarely, always say "Prince George's County" so you can pretend you never think "PG County" in that dismissive way. In the end, stay put. Order an Etsy "kindness" sign for your front lawn like all your suburban neighbors, and pretend you're not a coward who's still afraid of getting your car jacked in the city. Add a #BlackLivesMatter sign when you see three others on the block. Add a Little Free Library and slip in books by Black authors during Black History Month.

Pretend that when someone mentions "a professor," the image in your mind is of a Black person wearing tweed. Pretend this of lawyers and lobbyists, of CEOs and hipster entrepreneurs, of PhD students and research librarians and all scientists. Pretend that when someone mentions "Blackperson," that athletes and musicians and Oprah and Idris Elba aren't in your mind at all, and neither are the homeless or single moms or *The Wire* or prison or a dead boy in the street or a body pressed under a cop's knee. Pretend you've always seen "Black man" when you think president or Santa Claus.

Pretend that the Washington Redskins honestly is a perfectly normal and excellent name for a professional football team worth 1.5 billion dollars, even though one simple Google search shows online dictionaries calling that word dated, offensive, derogatory, contemptuous, and a racial slur. Shout, "Go, Skins," at your large-screen TV, and pretend that's acceptable. Pretend that if your burgundy-and-gold T-shirt doesn't have the Indian's face printed on it, then it's okay to wear it in public; but pretend you don't actually want to wear that shirt in public because it's "lucky" and that's why you only wear it at home. Pretend you're not looking forward to the December 17 game against the Cardinals and your friend's season-ticket seats. Pretend you believe that one day the team's owner will magically come to his senses and change "Redskins" to "Pigskins" and that doing so will undo all the damage of rooting for a team named after a racial slur. Pretend you don't type #HTTR on Twitter during a tense overtime when the passing game has been sucking and the QB nails it. When the owner magically comes to his senses and dumps the team's name after the biggest sponsor, the corporation with stadium naming rights— and with seventy billion dollars in revenue—threatens to pull out support, pretend it's okay that money and an ownership feud are what made this name change happen.

Pretend there's nothing more to say. Pretend this is the end. Pretend you admitted to all of it.

Read this, and pretend that it's not about you.

Publish it, uneasily, as "fiction."

HAT TRICK

The date's strange to begin with—not a date-date, more of a get-together, though less a get-together than an obligation or an attempt to prove something undefined. In short, Kasey has been invited by her old college friend Ari to a hockey game, accompanied by Ari's teenage son, Ben. Kasey gets the seat that Ari's ex-fiancé should be sitting in.

"The Douche" is what Ari calls him, and Kasey's too embarrassed to admit she's forgotten his real name. She and Ari lost touch shortly after college and have only recently reconnected (thanks, LinkedIn!), though they both migrated from the Midwest to DC's Virginia suburbs.

Still—The Douche didn't have to leave behind the Caps tickets for Ari after he broke off the engagement. So, there's that. A ten-game plan, suggesting to Kasey the barest commitment compared to season tickets. Back in college, each breakup stunned Ari. Anxiety churned her social life, "What did he mean, really-really mean, when he said that, did that, looked at me that way?" If Ari wasn't plop in the center of a conversational web she'd created, her interest evaporated.

Fifteen years later, little has changed. "Cold feet" is how Ari explained away The Douche when Kasey reunited with her over coffee five weeks ago. "There's a club of them, guys getting cold feet around me." She stabbed a straw roughly into her iced latte. "This was supposed to be for real. I mean, seriously? What happened?"

"What do you think happened?" Kasey asked.

Ari sighed. "He's a douche, that's what happened."

Okay, Kasey thought, cooing and listening, sure. She reached into her purse for a mini pack of decorative tissues.

This pattern with Ari was familiar—and comfortable enough—that Kasey relished sliding back in. Her female Hill friends were übercompetitive about their competence, so finding this scrap of weakness and vulnerability was novel. How fun to win the competency contest for once.

Ben came up only at the end, when Ari said, "Plus, you know, The Douche wasn't so keen on my son. So there's that."

"That's a big thing, right?" Kasey said.

"I guess," she said. "Of course." A small hand flip like swatting away a fly. "You'll have to meet him. I'm trying to throw good, strong role models at him, especially women."

"Oh, I'm not—"

"Just say yes," she said. "I like us being friends again, don't you?"

Before contacting Ari on LinkedIn, Kasey had talked to her therapist about whether she should, outlining a few tangles of their complicated friendship, that complicated time. The therapist said, "You got something from the relationship back then," and Kasey had said, "She's my oldest friend."

Now, she produced the line again: "You're my oldest friend, Ari," and Ari nodded, saying, "Come watch hockey with us."

The plan is to drive to Ari's townhouse in Alexandria and they'll all metro downtown to the arena, but when she arrives, Ben's begging Ari to take an Uber because it's raining and he's wearing new sneakers he refuses to get wet. "Not unless you're paying," she says, and he huffs a nonresponse. Ari's not ready, though Kasey is exactly on time, so as Ari disappears, she and Ben sit opposite each other at the kitchen island, a large bowl with two oranges between them. Everywhere that Kasey sets her hand feels sticky, so she crosses her arms. Ben's a gawky teenager: skin stretched over toothpick-thin bones that seem too long, and a stiff, ravenous face. His dark eyes are enormous. An aura of discomfort manifests around him as eerie, near-perfect stillness. Kasey doesn't encounter many older children; her friends with kids have competitively adorable toddlers and babies. She isn't prepared for this reality of a fifteen-year-old boy. He's a kid, she thinks, which is how Ari introduced him: "Here's my kid, Ben." As if she knew Kasey might need reminding of that fact. Kid.

Ben's been talking about the special sneakers for several minutes, pointing out nuances: laser-etching, unique sole, how Kanye wore a pair, the Twitter feed for this line. "Just fabulous," Kasey enthuses often, working to respect the depth of Ben's knowledge of minutiae. Her job requires a suit—hell, women aren't allowed open-toed shoes in the House chamber—but if she were brave enough to move to Silicon Valley as her brother encourages, there'd be a new unspoken dress code; in DC, one glance at a woman's sparkling flag pin and she knows whether it's real Ann Hand or a rip-off. Maybe it's the same with sneakers. She imagines Ben tagging the tech titans by their shoes, ranking them by net worth, so perhaps she'll learn from him. Kasey's best or worst habit—depending on who's asked—is seeking good qualities in unlikable people, viewing a tedious conversation as an opportunity to learn. Around the office they call her LMS, short for Little Mary Sunshine. She's testing the market, looking to get off the Hill. That's why she cyberstalked Ari: she's an executive assistant at a trade association where Kasey would be a match for lobbying in the GR division. Plus, she was curious: What had Ari turned into? Her own LinkedIn profile is purposefully vague, so she doubts Ari understands how high-level she is in the Speaker's office.

Ben's also wearing a Kobe Bryant 24 shirt, apparently in honor of the basketball player's recent death by helicopter crash. Since his eyes go glassy when she says "Nice shirt," she'll overlook his wearing a basketball shirt to a hockey game: a perverse decision, not rebellious. Wear regular clothes if you don't own a Caps jersey.

Their conversation feels complete, and she tries to think of a question not about school but loses him. He yanks his phone from his back pocket and stares into its oracle. If eyes could go limp, his do. One thumb flicks upward.

Intuitively, Ari calls out, "Almost ready! I promise." A distant toilet flushes—possibly an encouraging sign, except that Kasey remembers Ari's tricks, how she created the suggestion of action without acting. The two were randomly assigned as dorm roommates, which pressed them into a quick intimacy. "Our arranged marriage," Ari called it, one of those jokes that's amusing at the time though possibly racist now. "Can you imagine me letting my *mom and dad* pick out my husband?" Ari said. "Such patriarchy." Still, Kasey's last long-term relationship was with a man she met through "Date Lab," the *Washington Post* match-making column—most people sign up to get a free dinner at a nice restaurant paid for by the *Post*, but Kasey meant business and so had the male Casey. (Yes, that name thing was embarrassing; it headlined the article written about their dinner. If he'd been named Kyle, maybe they'd still be together.)

Ben glances up. "Why do all women take forever to get ready? To do anything?"

All women. Kasey bristles, a lecture forming, which she turns into a smile and a weak laugh. "But she said, 'almost ready'!" Kasey mocks, hoping for the proper tone of detached irony.

He snickers and looks directly into her eyes. The sudden force of his attention startles Kasey, who quickly says, "She's got the tickets, so I think we need her."

A dismissive shrug. "I could hack her phone in like thirty seconds. Print them off."

"Oh, sure," she says, as if she could too. "You have her password?"

Now a grunt. "Come on," he says. "Passwords are bullshit window dressing."

"I'm not up on tech," she says. Her brother in Silicon Valley is VC, a money guy. "Tell me what you've got and why my DC sister would give a shit" is famously his opening line at meetings. "You've made me rich," he tells her.

Ben says, "You think I couldn't? Want to see how fast I can hack into your phone?" He holds out a hand. His long fingers are slender, spidery.

Though she's curious about how secure her work emails might be, she shakes her head. "Some other time."

"Why did you and my mom stop being friends?" he asks. Again, that direct look drilling into her. Like he knows this is his only superpower.

"We're friends," she says, keeping her eyes steady on his.

"Of course we are," Ari says, appearing at the end of a hallway. She's wearing black jeans and an Ovechkin jersey that Kasey suspects was a gift from The Douche. "You guys ready?" Ari speaks quickly, always has. As if there's so much to say. "What were you talking about?"

"Shoes," Kasey says, pointing at Ben's feet. "I love his."

Ari hands them each a ticket, the official paper kind, not print-at-home. "Here's some responsibility, hanging on to your own ticket," she says to Ben. "And you, sir, keep out of my phone." She smiles at Kasey, as if this is some sort of performance. Also so that Kasey knows Ari heard everything, including Ben's question.

It's like a drain stopper had been yanked loose, and water's getting sucked down.

Ben stands the entire Metro ride, spinning his body around the vertical pole like tourist children do March through August when they invade the city on school and family trips. What a relief when the train fills with hockey fans and he's forced to stand still. Ari, in the window seat, stares at the dark, opaque glass, which—as Kasey knows from her commuting days, before being promoted and getting paid parking—is how to watch what's going on in a window reflection without engaging or appearing to observe.

Kasey tries: "Are you thinking about him? Because you're better off without him."

Ari turns to face Kasey: "Ben?" Oddly, her face is placid, as if this is a reasonable assumption.

"Oh, gosh, no!" Kasey says quickly. "The Douche."

"You'd be surprised at how hard I put a person out of my mind these days," Ari says. "I mean, when there's reason to."

Kasey's face grows warm. She feels at once clunky, overweight, and zitty; the girl who doesn't fit in, included because she's Ari's roommate, because everyone likes Ari, or if they don't *like* her, they're interested in her, eager to see what she'll do next. Kasey lacks mystery. That's the other Casey's breakup line: "I want to be with someone who keeps me guessing." Such bullshit, but it stung.

"Oh, I know," Kasey says. "You're strong."

"The word you want is *survivor*," Ari says.

The train pulls into L'Enfant Plaza, and masses of hockey fans press in. For a minute Kasey can't see Ben in the crowd, and Ari says, "He'll be fine."

"The Douche?"

"Ben. He's just a cranky teenager. We should send them all off to an island."

"It's called boarding school," Kasey says.

"Trust the rich to have the answers," Ari says.

The train doors slide shut, and Kasey looks at Ari, and beyond her, she catches the reflection of Ben in the window, there all along.

Hockey playoffs loom, with the Caps on the bubble, so the atmosphere at the arena is amped, especially since the opponent is their archrival, the Pittsburgh Penguins, architect of countless season-ending heartbreaks. Kasey knows all this because Ari fills her in on the drizzly walk from the Metro to the arena. Though she's likely parroting the opinions of The Douche, Ari's voice bristles as if she, too, were devastated by the overtime loss in Game 7 in 2009.

Ben lopes a few steps ahead, fixated on his phone. "I always follow," Ari murmurs, "otherwise I'd have no idea where he is."

Inside the arena, crowds surge in waves through the concourse. The women continue following Ben—bumping, being bumped, slowly jostling their way toward Section 114. They're almost there when Ari clutches Kasey's sleeve and points to the mascot, Slapshot, an oversize eagle wearing hockey attire. He's mugging and fist-bumping as he poses with kids. "I want a picture," she says, then shouts, "Ben! Ben!"

He stops abruptly, not turning around.

"Let's get a picture," Ari says.

"With the *bird*?" Ben says.

"Come on, honey," Ari says. Ben death-rays her, then stomps over. She reaches to push aside a hank of his hair, and he recoils as if punched. Ari smiles.

"I'll take it," Kasey says, pretending to ignore the psychodrama.

"It should be all of us," Ari says.

"Her too?" Ben says. "Oh my god."

Ari's smile wrenches tighter. "Apologize, Ben."

"It's okay." A relief—not that she cares about the picture, but that Ben's rudeness confirms what Ari won't say: Ben is why The Douche left.

"It's not okay," Ari says. "You know, we can turn around and go home—right now."

Ben flips his head, sending that bit of stray hair whipping backward.

Slapshot shifts his jittery attention to the three of them, herding them close for a selfie, as he reaches a gloved hand for Ben's phone. Ari says, "Give Slapshot your phone, Ben," and the bird grabs it. But Ben holds on, and the bird tugs, and as Ben holds harder, the bird yanks. Kasey's selfie smile feels clownish.

Ben sharply calls, "Jesus fucking Christ," which snaps heads their way, and a passing dad calls, "Language, Kobe Bryant. Kids are here," and Slapshot grips the damn phone—though other kids have swarmed in, *eager* for photos rather than resistant. Surely Kasey imagines this, but Slapshot's grinning beak seems suddenly malevolent, cruel—and definitely competitive, as if this bird is so over sullen teenage boys and their endless tugs of war.

The ponytailed handler drops her conversation with a man studying a clipboard and sprints over as Slapshot releases the phone, sending Ben into a backward, off-balance stagger. He drops the phone, which Ari swoops up.

Slapshot gets steered to a family with bouncy toddlers, and the crowd swarms on, leaving Kasey to feel as if the three of them are a hard, rocky island rising out of the current.

Ari studies Ben's phone, scrolls. As Ben reaches for it, she spins, her back to him, keeping the phone from his grasp—which heightens his efforts to snatch it back. "Mom!" he whines, dancing around her as she circles again.

"What's this site?" she says. "Nine O'Clock . . . I can't even say the word," and she thrusts the phone at Kasey as Ben yells, "Jesus fucking Christ, it's my phone," and the word Ari won't say blares at Kasey: "Nazis."

Ben's face flushes a bruised pink. "Where'd that come from?" His awkward body shifts, like trying to fold a paper map.

Ari's lips press into one thin line. The phone weighs heavy in Kasey's hand, but she sneaks another peek: a line of blond men—haircuts like Ben's, buzzed low but long and slick on top—stand in the sunlight, looking attentive. She needs her glasses to read the fine print, or she needs to touch the screen to enlarge it, and she doesn't want her fingerprints here.

"You swore you were done with all that," Ari mutters.

"I am." Ben's earnest voice doesn't match his skulking eyes.

People crowd them, rushing to their seats before the puck drops. Kasey should be one of them. This is Ari's problem, not hers. Like always. Her car is at Ari's, she realizes, and the whole thing will be awkward if they leave, if she stays, if she leaves with them. She has no way out.

Ben says, "It's for school. This time for real."

"Enough lies." Ari seizes the phone, stuffs it into her clear plastic stadium purse. The screen glows, then darkens. To Kasey, she says, "It's just a phase," and she starts walking, slipping into the swift flow of the throng, carried away almost instantly. They couldn't follow even if they're supposed to—which, clearly, they aren't.

Kasey looks at Ben who stares at his special sneakers. Made in Düsseldorf, he'd told her.

The national anthem starts, and the press of hurrying people turns urgent. "*What so proudly we hailed . . .*" and there's Hitler's smug face in her mind.

Ben says, "She's going to the seats?" His voice is light but hints at anxiety, and he bites his lip.

"Sure," Kasey says, though Ari went the opposite direction. She could be confused. "Maybe the ladies' room. Let's wait here a minute for her."

"Fuck," Ben says. "We're missing everything." He slams his arms across his chest. "And what'm I supposed to do with no phone?"

"She'll be right back." Kasey stays cheerful, though she doesn't know why. She imagines Ben's face lit by a tiki torch, screaming hate into a dark night. In a different world, she might have known him his whole life, the son of her best friend in college. She might have been his godmother, or celebrated his first birthday, or vacationed in beach houses with him and Ari, or carefully selected educational presents in museum gift shops. Instead, she's known him for about an hour, this fucked-up teenager coming to her already finished: a fact, an almost-man. No chance to cozy up in front of a fireplace and read him picture books, no chance that he's influenced by "dear Aunt Kasey," who strategized for sweet liberal candidates until that churn was a hassle; who then grabbed the high-level Hill job she earned, notching experience before moving on to cash in on K Street as a lobbyist for a firm or a trade association. The familiar path everyone takes. Who makes a difference in the world, anyway?

The anthem's over, and the game starts. While the concourse isn't entirely clear, wide patches of empty space have opened, and Kasey three-sixties, desperate to spot Ari. Without a phone to stare at, Ben's ended up staring at her in that unsettling way. "I promise it's for school. A report on hate speech."

Does he think she's dumb? She pulls out her phone and texts Ari:

where RU

When there's no immediate answer, she adds:

WTF ????

Ben says, "I had a phone . . . once." An extended, dramatic sigh. He flips his head, shifting that annoying clump of hair for a moment before it falls back to the place it wants to be. He needs pomade, Kasey thinks, and imagines Ari buying a jar that Ben immediately rejects. She never wanted children; the endless exhaustion seems daunting. She hears more of that, never the exhilaration of motherhood. Maybe the good stories go to other parents, protecting the feelings of the pitiable childless, like her.

Ben says, "I'm out. I'm going to the seat."

"Wait a sec," Kasey says. "She'll text back." She reaches out an arm but isn't sure she should touch him. He's not her kid, not related to her, not even a friend. Her hand dangles midair, and Ben glares at it with disdain, so she pulls it back, running her fingers through her hair.

"She'll find me at the seat," he says. "No big deal." And off he goes, so Kasey follows. She's the adult, right? Ari really wouldn't leave, would she? Her own kid? Of course, she did this all the time in college—promise Kasey she'd stay at the party for an hour, then disappear. Promise spring break in Daytona then cancel the day before, leaving the group scrambling because the plan had been to drive Ari's car. Her excuse always was something like, "Couldn't deal."

At the portal, the usher stops them from heading to their seats, tick-tock waving a paper stop sign on a stick, and they huddle along with a man and a teenage boy, waiting for a stoppage in play. Ben stands, arms crossed, as does the other kid; they're mirror reflections, same pose, same scornful affect, same haircut. Another Nazi? Kasey peers at the father, white as white can be, wearing khakis and a pale-pink polo. Who needs a secret handshake? He flashes a toothy smile and says, "Feeling good. Hat trick for Ovi tonight." Kasey stares, startled to be addressed, and he adds, "Three goals," then raises one open palm for a high five and Kasey embarrasses herself by giving it to him with a dull smack. The man's son rolls his eyes and hunches deeper into himself. Ben's narrowed eyes stay focused ahead, either on the action on the ice or on row M, the three empty seats on the aisle: Ari not there. Kasey knows what a hat trick is; he doesn't need to explain it. But saying so now would be awkward.

Kasey looks at her phone: a phantom vibration.

The goalie gloves the puck, and the group clambers down the stairs to their seats, the father-son Nazis ending up in the very front row, which just figures, Kasey thinks.

Ben collapses into the aisle seat, jutting his folded legs out from his hips at forty-five degree angles, manspreading, leaving little room for her to squeeze next to him, so she climbs over his legs to the third seat, leaving an open space between them. "Your mom can sit there," she says.

"If she shows," he says, his voice neutral. He flips his hair yet again, perhaps the most annoying gesture invented.

"She will," Kasey says.

There's a flurry of action at the Penguins' goal. People around them whoop, but she and Ben remain silent. The father-son duo bangs the glass. The Caps score a goal, and the arena goes raucous. Ben doesn't react, so neither does she. "Goal scored by Alexander Ovechkin," the announcer intones, and the noise ratchets up: *"O-vi! O-vi!"*

Kasey watches players skate and snap the puck as she ponders the ethics of offering to go buy popcorn but not returning. Why should she get stuck babysitting a Nazi? (The word's a needle of pain jabbing deep.) Still, she knows why. She was there that night at the bar, with Ari. Whether Ari remembers or not. Whether Ari believes her or not.

She tried to stop the guy. She tried to stop Ari.

He was a basketball player—a walk-on from Slovenia, but still. That was senior year, the winter Ari had a thing for basketball players, mostly because the team had a shot at March Madness. So she had to find which bar the basketball players hung out at. She had to sashay around enough until one took a little notice. She had to win at beer pong. She had to drunk-fuck the guy in the bathroom. And she had to get pregnant.

Kasey was expected to prevent all that? "Blow job only," Ari announced as she stumbled off with the guy.

The team lost in a double OT buzzer beater and didn't make the tournament.

Looking back, it was all such a sad waste.

Over the summer Ari stopped returning Kasey's emails and calls. Birthday cards came back stamped "return to sender," then "addressee unknown." And now, fifteen years later, Kasey's facing this baby Nazi.

Ben says, "I already know why you and my mom stopped being friends." He cocks his head, smirks. Another burst at the net, but he's watching her.

"Do you even like hockey?" she asks.

He shrugs. "The guy bought the tickets like it was this big thing, so my mom made me go. She thinks hockey's violent and stupid. But I wasn't supposed to say so."

"Did you like him?"

"I don't much like anybody," he says. "I'm a misanthrope," which he mispronounces, mis-an-thrawp-ee.

"You're pretty young to have given up on the world already," she says.

"You don't know anything about me." He slouches further down his chair, knees banging the shoulders of the man seated in the row ahead, who spins and glowers at Ben until he slides his knees back. After the man turns, Ben flips him off. "Like, see?" he says. "The world pretty much sucks, especially all the people in it."

"Is that why . . . the website?" she asks.

"I don't know," he says. "Probably just to get at my mom."

Probably.

"Get at her why?" Kasey asks.

Again with the shrug and the hair. "Why not?" A moment later he adds, "Didn't you ever just hate everything about everyone?"

She speaks immediately so she won't think about the question: "No."

"Aren't you special."

There's a roughing penalty against the Caps, and the arena groans as the team goes shorthanded, four against five.

He says, "You don't have to stay with me. She'll show up. Worst case is I metro home."

"She does this a lot?"

"Let's just say I can take care of myself." His words are boastful, but Kasey doesn't know whether to believe them. Really, she just wants to watch the game. Hockey tickets are hard to come by. Like Nazi-Dad, she'd be thrilled to see a hat trick.

They're silent as the Caps kill the two-minute penalty. Again, everyone cheers, as Ben stews in a sullen fog. His fingers twist and fiddle, seeking the soothing presence of a phone.

"Want popcorn?" she asks. She *probably* won't abandon him. But she could look for Ari on the concourse. Or just get away and breathe.

"Whatever. I'd eat some or not." Then he turns toward her, his face contorted by an uncomfortable grimace. "You told my mom to get an abortion. That's why."

That hard-smack landing deep in her soft gut.

"She told you that?"

"Yeah," he says. "She got pregnant in college, and you said she should abort me. If she listened to you, I wouldn't be here, would I?"

"Let's go, Caps!" the crowd chants, and the rhythmic call of the three words buries Kasey in noise. Players slash the ice up and down, side to side; they rattle round the back of the net. She's watching this game. She's cheering mindlessly like everyone else, frantic for a goal.

But Ben says, "Well?"

Kasey says, "Okay, yes. That's advice I gave when she asked me. But it's not like I—" She breaks off. I said I'd drive her is what Kasey could tell Ben, I offered to pay so her parents wouldn't know. I begged her not to let one mistake change her life forever. "You sound just like my nagging mother would," Ari had shouted. "I never should've told you, and for sure I'm not telling her until it's too late." Then she left school. And suddenly here they are, fifteen years later. What Kasey forces herself to say is, "I'm glad she didn't listen to me. Right? I'm an idiot."

Ben nods. "In the end, I'm alive. Though I'll never have a father."

"If it helps any, that guy was a jerk."

"I'm not talking about that douchey asshole," he says. "My real father. Her college boyfriend. The musician."

Kasey's mouth hangs open as she waits for her mind to catch up. Luckily, the Caps score again, and everyone around them leaps up, and she does too, elevating herself above Ben's penetrating gaze. But he stands, asking, "Did you know him? What was he like? Where's he now? My mom said his band was awesome."

Your mom's a liar, she thinks, grinding her fingernails into the flesh of both palms to keep that statement buried. Why is Kasey so furious? She's done nothing wrong. She says, "Yeah, I knew him. He was Jewish. Exactly who your Nazi pals hate."

Ben's turn for the gaping goldfish-mouth.

"I'm getting popcorn," Kasey says. Her heart beats way too hard. She's lying. To a kid. But parents lie to their children all the time, she reminds herself, as she climbs over Ben's long legs to reach the aisle.

Out on the concourse, she almost expects that Ari will be standing right there. All she sees are clusters of fans carrying beer or whisking into the bathroom.

There's a line at the popcorn stand because the credit card reader was just fixed, and waiting's a relief: precious minutes alone. She breathes in, breathes out, inhales the greasy smell of popcorn and calms herself.

The Sunday after, Ari barely left bed. She spoke about two words all day, skipped mimosa brunch because she couldn't deal, ignored her history of Russia paper due Monday, let every call dump to voice mail, didn't turn on her computer. The only thing she did was take a long shower that hogged all the hot water, and then leave wet, crumpled towels on the floor.

Kasey knew she was supposed to ask what was wrong, was Ari sick, did Ari need anything, should she go downtown to Baskin-Robbins for a pint of Rocky Road, all the usual. But she already knew what was wrong: Ari regretted the basketball player. Ari regretted getting drunk. Ari regretted so many things lately: this college, her major, signing a lease on an apartment without parking, the too-short haircut last week. Kasey just didn't want to know about one more thing. *She didn't want to know*. Was that a sin?

"You should have stopped me," Ari had said that night as Kasey unlocked the door to their apartment on College Street.

"I tried," Kasey said.

"Next time try harder," Ari snapped. She beelined to her bedroom and slammed the door. Kasey slammed her bedroom door in response. "You're not my responsibility," she shouted through the silence, at the wall between their bedrooms. "Don't have a 'next time,' how 'bout that?"

Now, here she is, wasting nine bucks on "bottomless popcorn" for Ari's kid. Blame LinkedIn for this mess. When she reaches in her pocket for her twenty-dollar bill, her fingertips brush the rounded corners of her Metro card.

Let Ben imagine himself Jewish for a little while longer. If she goes back to the seat too soon, she's sure to say more—too much—and she feels herself getting angry, eager to blow up the sadly desperate story about the musician and his "awesome" band. Honestly! Ari scorned musicians: "Too full of themselves." Kasey was the one mooning forever over a locally famous bar-band guitarist who was an expert at stringing her (and others) along, and now she's infuriated, realizing that Ari has stolen her heartbreak, turning her guy into Ben's so-called father.

Still, she marches back to Section 114, waits behind the usher's paper stop sign. Nazi-Dad's also there, holding beer and Aquafina. He nods in recognition at Kasey and says, "Ovi's killing it out there."

She says, "Hat trick," with enthusiasm, but what she hears in her head is Ari's long-ago, shaky voice: "You're saying kill it? You want me to kill it?" Her own voice answering, "It's nothing yet. Don't think it's something. Don't do that. Don't do that. Don't throw away everything over one mistake."

Nazi-Dad jostles his drinks to offer another high five, and Kasey shifts the popcorn and slaps his palm with a satisfying, energetic whack.

At the TV timeout the usher lets them pass through, and Nazi-Dad sprints down the stairs like he's running bleachers for a high school coach. Kasey moves slowly, watching each step. When she looks up, there's Ari, sitting next to Ben, and as Kasey reaches row M, the announcer says, "And now we ask that you please stand for a moment of silence as we honor the loss of one of the NBA's greatest heroes on and off the court, Number 24, Kobe Bryant; his thirteen-year-old daughter Gianna; and the other victims of the weekend's helicopter crash." She's standing in the aisle, holding the giant bag of popcorn, and Ben leaps up, as does Ari. An arena is never exactly silent, but it's pretty damn quiet as the big screen shows a montage of Kobe in his Lakers uniform. Ben bows his head and clutches one hand over his heart, as if this is the national anthem. Ari gently reaches along his back, hooking her hand across his far shoulder, and Kasey braces for the angry shake-off, but Ben allows it. In fact, he leans closer, cocooning in, tilting his head so his cheek rests on the top of her hair. His eyes are closed, the lashes long like a baby's.

Kasey watches. Maybe he's thinking about basketball or musicians or Nazis or the scent of his mother, and maybe this is what a moment of silence does, stills the collected thoughts of twenty thousand fans as quiet builds, billows. A moment to be at once all the things we are, good and awful, vulnerable and tough, a moment to marvel at how rare it is to mesh into anything shared, even something as simple as this moment of silence—

A man's loud voice booms: "Alleged rapist!" It's Nazi-Dad, twisted backward in the front row, hands cupping his mouth for maximum amplification, his face blotching red from the exertion of that bellowing reminder. The entire length of Ben's body twitches and jerks, as if words could Taser, and Ari's hand slides down his back, rubbing away the tension.

The moment's gone; the announcer says, "Thank you," and the ice crew skates out to shovel away the snowy ice shavings. Ari wraps Ben into a real, hard hug, her arms tightening around him, tiptoeing up to kiss his gaunt cheek, and she just holds him, nudging in closer, pressing him tighter. Maybe they speak, or maybe they don't have to.

Kasey waits, clutching her ridiculous bag of popcorn. She carefully narrows her focus to Nazi-Dad, the sad goofiness of his being such a stickler for the law that he tacked on "alleged." True, the case against Kobe was dropped, but to be so legally precise when shouting into a moment of silence is . . . something. Nazi-Dad's got to be a K Street lawyer, and this must be the most "only in DC" moment Kasey has ever witnessed.

But this is the DC moment, right? Imagining that labeling something "only in DC" offers real, actual, safe distance. That distance means never letting yourself ache over the disappointment of imagining you'll save the world and seeing that the world doesn't need you or your smart advice.

Maybe there's not a DC moment. Maybe there's just, finally, silence. And maybe silence is complicated too.

The Caps win, 5–3, and yes, there's a hat trick, but it's not notched by Alexander Ovechkin, the team's superstar, but by T. J. Oshie. After the game, Ben and Ari wait as Kasey buys his number 77 jersey in the team store. Outside, the night's clear now, and she slips Oshie's shirt over her head, over her jacket, and the three of them walk to the Metro. It's silly: a simple shirt offers no skills on the ice or the court. But she's happy wearing it, feeling part of something bigger. "Let's go, Caps!" she shouts to a passing group of Ovechkins. Ben calls her a fangirl, and she and Ari laugh. As they step onto the escalator taking them down to the trains, she says to Ari, "I'm sorry," and she waits for Ari to ask what for. Instead Ari says, "Thank you," and everything feels lighter now, brighter, like fresh ice.

ANYTHING YOU WANT

A few years later

You really hammer down the nail, the man I call my boyfriend says the second he taps off his phone call. Thank you?

Not a compliment, Madison, he says.

I arrange a hurt, pouty look on my face, a look that does okay with ticket-threatening male cops. I say, What are we talking about here?

He pushes a hand through his hair, bristling it. I checked his hair products online: thirty bucks a bottle. Innnn. Sane.

He's twenty-six years older than me, grateful to have hair.

What are we talking about? he says, mocking me. Are you for real?

I pinch my arm. Smile. Appears so, I say.

Though I do guess what we're talking about. His credit card. Which I used. It's platinum. When he hauled it out at dinner when we met, I confessed platinum was my favorite color. He said, Me too.

That spiky hair of his would be platinum if he didn't color it at the place in Georgetown where his wife goes.

Goddamn it, he says now. I want to love you.

Then do, I say.

I can't trust you, he says.

We're at a baseball game, by the way, in a fancy box next to the owner's even fancier box. Shrimp on ice keep coming. I've eaten maybe fifty. He's telling everyone I'm his research assistant. No one believes him. Oh, and the Nats are winning, up by seven in the fifth inning.

I say, I want to love you too.

Not technically a lie because I do want to love someone.

Oh, his wife is in the box, too. Sure I've met her. She's pleasant. She doesn't care. Never you mind why we stay together, he said to me once, we have our reasons and our arrangement. It's spelled out, he said, in writing.

Like I don't know what "spelled out" means.

I've seen everything. I don't even care anymore.

Earlier I told someone I started at AU this fall (true), wanting to be a doctor (false).

The Nats rack up another run. Everyone in the box whoops and hollers except the two of us. Did I mention it's a playoff game? Everything—Amped Up! It's cold for October, like forty. His wife is wearing this gaudy National League leather baseball jacket with a shitload of garish patches and logos. It's unbelievably ugly, I mean unbelievably so. Guess the platinum card paid for it.

He's been spiraling out this long, whispered hiss, badgering me to do this or that instead of that or this. You know, it's not awful. I'm getting paid. Not trashy, in cash, but he takes me places and buys stuff. I grew up with a mom constantly wanting things she didn't have and couldn't possibly get, not even in a thousand lifetimes.

We met on Craigslist.

I catch the wife glancing. She gives her head this tiny shake and zips up her ugly jacket. I feel dismissed. I feel like the people here know things I'll never know, not in a thousand lifetimes.

You're the hammer here, I say, can't we watch the game?

Why'd you steal my card, he murmurs, when I buy you anything you want?

I point to his wife and say loud enough for everyone in the box to hear, I want a jacket like hers, like your wife's. I love it, I exclaim.

The game is on pause, between batters, so everyone catches this. The wife laughs and unzips the jacket with a loud, slow ratchet that grits my teeth.

Oh, honey, she says, take it. She slithers it down her torso like shedding a skin, extricates her arms, and hands over the heavy, ugly thing. All yours, she says.

In front of everyone, I have to slip on the jacket, cozy-warm inside from her body. People stare at me, sort of, or maybe just stare somewhere.

He seems confused now that I look like his wife.

Oh, god, he mutters.

There's a crack of the bat, and it's back to the game.

He pats my head like I'm a dog. I let him because that's how this goes.

Yeah, Nats! he shouts.

I stand there in this jacket then push my fists into the pockets. It's the wife who I want to love me, actually, not in a lesbian way, but in a way where she'd hand over a jacket and say something simple like, You look cold, honey. Here, take this. Take this, honey—it's all yours.

GREEN IN JUDGMENT

Every story needs a ticking clock, perhaps one that's deceptively simple. Here, the clock is ticking because the beloved, local professional football team formerly known by the racist name will kick off in half an hour.

Every story needs an inciting incident:

This isn't the grocery-store line Christine would have chosen, though she couldn't explain why not if asked. But when the line she's aiming for is cut off with a curt click of the plastic chain, she's shunted one over—to lucky lane 7, she thinks—behind a young mother who has disgorged the contents of her cart onto the black conveyor belt. Her (presumed) son—four, five, six—hovers anxiously at the cart's front edge, poking at the items piled eye-level before him. Christine is terrible at placing ages, and the boy's vibe is that of a delicate child, perpetually small for his age. It's the sag of his lean, and how his mother's uneasy glances latch onto him. Christine is too polite to stare, so she assesses the accumulation of food. Three large jugs of apple juice. Dried black beans. Peanut butter. Shell macaroni. Spaghetti sauce, the cheap brand made mostly of soybean oil and a doughnut's worth of sugar. Cans: green beans, creamed corn, peas, carrots, all vegetables and no treats, unless—she realizes—the package of store-brand hamburger, this meat so decidedly not-organic the cows probably eat petroleum byproducts, is the treat, thanks to its sale sticker's semi-alarming command to "sell today."

Sure, she's careful to think, and why isn't meat a treat? She remembers a point in her life when a burger was delicious background fantasy amid those paycheck-to-paycheck couple of years in the city, pursuing various urgent, artsy dreams that would be silly to speak of now. "Salad days" is the term, which makes sense as food was the worry ringing the mind back then, food second only to rent. On a work trip to London last spring, she dodged a day of sessions to play tourist and learned at the Globe Theatre that the phrase was Shakespeare's, found in *Anthony and Cleopatra*.

Every story needs a title taken from Shakespeare.

There's a name, she muses—Cleopatra—and as if the young mother is responding to the sound of Christine's actual voice calling across the crowded room of a party, she whips her head to gaze at Christine. Her eyes are green-gold, somehow rounder and more penetrating than other eyes, and Christine has the shivery impression that these eyes see with more clarity, though of course this can't be true; she's wishing it so because the eye color is extraordinary. Christine refocuses her mind to facts.

And the fact is, she forces herself to think, here's why she doesn't want to be in this lane. Eye contact with a young mother on food stamps or whatever the government calls them now. SNAP. The acronym lunges into her mind with force, not allowing her to pretend ignorance. A cheerful, happy pop of a word, unlike the dull, bureaucratic chill of: Food. Stamps.

Every story needs to find its unique, organic way to push characters together, especially characters who would not encounter each other in their daily lives.

Christine smiles. God knows she's not that clueless dope who goes around smiling randomly in public, unloading chitchat on people, but she can show support of the difficult challenges of modern life, can suggest that she has *no problem whatsoever* with the government—*our* government—offering financial assistance to moms and kids, to *all* kids, whether they're cute little boys in red sweater vests like this one or hulking, brooding teens tethered to phones. It's a smile to cover all that ground while also being a regular, friendly smile, or so Christine assumes.

In return, she's rewarded with a guarded half-nod from the young mother, now locked in Christine's mind as Cleopatra (that's not wrong, such thoughts concealed by the safe privacy of her very own mind?). "Careful, Marcus," Cleopatra says to the boy, redirecting his wandering hand away from the six-pack egg carton.

A sign from the universe, the coincidence of the boy's name being Marcus when Christine's got Cleopatra and Mark Antony on the brain?

Every story needs one coincidence. (Only one.)

Christine widens her smile, maybe to beaming. She has no children, but it's not as though she doesn't like kids. She's an only child and her own childlessness distresses her mother, who worries irrationally about what will happen to the family quilts when Christine dies with no one to pass them along to. And her grandmother's silver tea service. And—a thousand things that Christine prefers not to think about.

Every story needs either a silver tea service or a silver cocktail shaker.

The boy, Marcus, warbles a string of sounds under his breath, not decipherable words, but Cleopatra says to Christine, "I'm so sorry about that."

Christine says, "It's fine." Keep up that smile! She doesn't normally speak like this about people's children, but she adds, "He's a cutie."

"Who's got to learn when to keep quiet." Cleopatra says, "Right, baby?" and she tweaks his tiny earlobe gently, like pinching a bug off a lettuce leaf. "We don't say those naughty, nasty words in public."

His face stills, turns somber, and Christine wonders if he's special needs or on the spectrum. It's the babbling, and how overly erect he keeps his head. His eyes are the same arresting green-gold as his mother's, but otherwise he doesn't much resemble her: she's lithe and willowy, exuding a calm glow, while he, even for a boy, is small and compact, like a mini-adult not a child; a boy who will bloom into a man uncomfortable in his own body, desperate to prove something. The kind of man who lives his life strolling around peaceful coffee shops screaming his business into a phone, oblivious to glares around him.

Too much to project onto one little boy, and Christine erases the picture from her head. Also, she wonders how she missed the naughty, nasty words.

Cleopatra's purchases have rolled forward and now there's room for Christine's. She's always organized: heavy things first, then cold, then produce, finally fragile—it only makes *good sense*—that's her mother's voice in her head—so it's simply The Plan as she starts piling items next to Cleopatra's wall of apple juice bottles. First, her reusable shopping bags (pledge drive giveaways from NPR and PBS). Her boxes of d-CON mouse poison (mice move into everyone's houses in the fall, right, we *all* have mice). A pack of no-name scrubber sponges because she couldn't find the shape she likes in the brand she prefers. Store-brand spaghetti noodles—same brand as Cleopatra's shell macaroni, in fact. On-sale laundry detergent that who wouldn't buy at that price? Four cans of chili—for next week's food drive at the office, but not like she's never eaten canned chili. Christine leaves the ultrasoft, superplush, never-on-sale, multiroll package of toilet paper under her cart; the store has knee-high sensors to detect bulk. Christine assumes people hope to sneak out items under the cart without paying, so she's extra solicitous about dredging her large items upward for the clerk to scan. But later is okay this once.

Every story needs a long list of possibly irrelevant details.

The boy's muttering again and Christine listens, wanting to ferret out the bad word. Just idle curiosity. She hears: "Awn-wa-ney-dooort-ney-coo." Even stretching her imagination to its linguistic limits doesn't offer much. He grips both fists around the red handle of the shopping cart and aligns his fingers in a perfect row of eight, which seems to steady him. Cleopatra darts him an anxious look, maybe warning, maybe worry. He seems not to notice.

Everything's moving along. Everything's calm. She'll be home soon. Beep, beep, the steady sound of items scanning through, until Cleopatra says, "That's wrong."

The cashier twists the jug of apple juice in her hand, examining the barcode, shaking her head back and forth as if quickly trying to scrub clean a whiteboard. Or, this is what Christine is reminded of, having had to do such a thing on Friday, grab an eraser to swipe off the list of proposed layoffs from her department. Those faint green letters lingering on the board, and the narrow-eyed, curious stare of her assistant, carting in the boxed lunches. What a bad day. Too many days like that, which is why Christine is buying three containers of Talenti gelato ($5.99 each) to stress-eat. When there's room on the belt, she'll line them up, eighteen dollars' worth of gelato, practically an entire twenty-dollar bill, which would buy twenty cans of corn, maybe more, and Christine realizes she doesn't know how much a can of corn costs. The cashier says, "Nope. Not on sale. This isn't that one."

The boy stares at Christine, that open-eyed, uncomfortable gape that children have, then looks away—a relief—and stabs one forefinger against the package of violent pink sponges. He glances back at her, then at the sponges, maybe trying to communicate a question.

"Pink!" Christine pushes the word into new levels of upbeat cheerfulness, like a day care worker on steroids.

"Ney," he says. "Nyordt."

"Uh-huh," Christine agrees, bobbing her head super-enthusiastically, distressed she lacks the magical skill set bestowed on mothers and teachers of small children: How to fascinate with single-syllable words. How to entertain with few props.

Cleopatra yanks her purse from the cart seat, dredges out a worn Ziploc jammed with coupons, the kind clipped from newspapers and the register receipt coupons that clutter Christine's reusable shopping bags. She unfolds one of the advertising flyers from the racks at the front of the store. "No, no," Cleopatra says. "You pulled this last time, and it's clear here that the gallon size . . ." She trails off, peering at fine print Christine would need glasses to read.

Every story needs a villain, possibly more than one if the story is eighteen pages or longer.

"It would scan," the cashier says. "And it's not." She points to the price on the screen, and Cleopatra flurries through paper.

There's conversation back and forth, which gets the cashier studying the fine print. Marcus pinches the cellophane on the package of sponges, reveling in its crinkliness, but abruptly tires of that and starts mumbling, the sound and pitch escalating.

"You, no," Cleopatra commands out of one side of her clenched mouth. "Be still, or . . ." Christine doesn't *think*

Cleopatra would hit her son, especially not in public, but she doesn't want to witness that, so she yelps, "Hey, look!" with such enthusiasm the boy's riveted into silence and the cashier swivels her head to gawk for a blank moment before returning her focus to what Christine is secretly thinking of as The Caper of the Mysterious Apple Juice Price. The problem is she spoke before having something to show Marcus, and her first thought—popping open the package of sponges, might wreck the single distraction that's been effective, that intriguing cellophane crinkle. "Hey, look," she stage-whispers to Marcus as she slides her stack of reusable bags an inch backward, triggering the conveyor's electronic eye to start up the belt and jerk everything forward.

"Ney-awn," Marcus murmurs. "Coort."

"I know, big whoop, but check this out." Christine slides her forefinger over the sensor in the inch-high side rail of the checkout lane, and with her other forearm consolidates her groceries backward with a shove. She retracts her finger then quickly drops it back down, illustrating—voila!—the secret superpower she possesses: making the belt move.

Every story needs nostalgia disguised as relevant flashback:

A simple thing—yet a vivid memory: an afternoon with her mother at the Hy-Vee, too young to be in school so perpetually dragged along on errands just like Marcus. A benevolent female clerk with swirls of white hair piled on top of her head demonstrated this same trick, called her "sweet pea," which weren't words Iowans used. The clerk's voice was amber honey ribboning off a spoon, husky, glowing like embers, almost magical in this remembering, saying, "Y'all wanna see a secret, sweet pea?" and this laser of attention electrified Christine, the pet name, the secret, and a free red lollipop. Her mother usually shopped at Randalls, not Hy-Vee, and there was no reason to be at that particular Hy-Vee on that particular day, unless, maybe, destiny presented Christine with a misplaced southern cashier yearning for connection so that years later—in a flash of memory barely identifiable as having happened—Christine would intuitively try the same trick on this fussy boy, maybe dare to call him sweet pea. Maybe he'd recall this moment himself years from now, in his conscious mind—"that nice lady"—or in his bones, pausing at some point in adulthood to share the secret with a future child trapped with a mom in a grocery store.

His eyes are alert, and she lifts one finger so the belt slides forward, then lets her finger drop, halting movement. Perfect control. "Like that," she whispers. "I think maybe it's magic."

The boy's tiny fingers spider their way toward her hand, as if he's no longer in control of their movement, and he squeezes his warm index finger up against hers, nudging himself in. Smart kid, she thinks, picking it up like that.

The cashier says, "I get it's confusing to understand, but the one on sale"—she jabs at the store flyer with a rainbow-painted nail—"is this brand, uh-huh, but it's the one from concentrate, and this's all juice. That's different. They're two different things. Like oranges and apples," she concludes without irony. Her voice has sharpened, taken on a haughtiness that is uncomfortable to hear, like barbs repeatedly jabbing the same spot. Cleopatra's lips tighten and her eyes narrow. She shifts her purse strap higher up her shoulder. "Want me to send someone for the sale one?" the cashier says, folding her arms, making herself comfortable. "Hold up on the line for that, if you want. Happy to make everyone wait for you."

Christine pretends not to hear. She shouldn't always be in this relentless hurry, and the store's freezing with its air-conditioning in October so it's not like her Talenti will melt into a giant green Mediterranean mint puddle. Her therapist is always telling her to be mindful, to take deep breaths and r-e-l-a-x.

Every story needs an allusion to therapy, setting up characters who can be proud of their heightened self-awareness.

Cleopatra scans the tiny pictures in the sales flyer, two fingers tracing along the page.

"Or you want these right here?" the cashier presses. Each word sounds sticky and tacky, like the back of duct tape. Someone's behind Christine and someone else is lined up behind that person, and someone behind them. Sunday before the football game is always a busy shopping time. Christine's familiarity with this fact is residue from her (now ex-) boyfriend, a football fanatic who in four years of dating and six weeks of being engaged lured her into following the game, learning it, and leaving her with at least enough interest to put it on the TV while doing other things around the house. "At full price?"

Marcus retracts his finger and the belt shifts Christine's mouse poison forward until it triggers the belt to a halt. She snatches it and tosses it to the back so the boy can't reach it, and he bobs his fingers on and off the sensor. He laughs, a glittery sound, like wind chimes in the middle of the night. "Doort ney coo," he says, chuckling. He slides the fingers of his other hand into his mouth and sucks on them.

"What'll it be?" the cashier demands. "I gotta buzz someone over, if you want us to get you that sale juice."

"Stop causing trouble, Marcus," Cleopatra snaps, and as if waiting for this cue, Christine says, "Oh, he's fine, such a sweet pea, this one," and the words sounds so awful and wrong in her voice that abruptly she can't stand herself, for thinking she could pull off saying "sweet pea" and she can't stand this crap she's buying—all of it so precious, as if eating a regular carrot instead of organic will make her drop dead, or like chickens really care that they're living out their nasty, brutish, short lives in a ten square foot outdoor pen instead of jammed six to a wire box so her scrambled eggs can taste so much happier. (These are the most expensive eggs at the store, stamped with every possible buzzword: Omega-3, vegetarian-fed, cage-free, free-range, certified organic, pasture-raised, from a Maryland family farm; for Christ's sake, a photocopied note is tucked inside each carton giving names to some of these happy chickens, including an artful typo that—Christine suspects—is intentionally placed to make the whole enterprise seem that much more mom-and-pop-ish. And then? She predictably ends up throwing away the three or four eggs left over beyond the expiration date.)

It's this pressure of thinking about the chickens and her horrible appropriation of "sweet pea," and knowing the game starts in twenty minutes and having to acknowledge that, ugh, she cares more than she admits, not wanting to credit her newfound allegiance to this team and this sport to the ex-boyfriend (she can't bring herself to say *ex-fiancé*) who dumped her for an old high school flame, and her quarterback is returning from injury, and she really, really believes the team can pull off this upset—everyone does—and springboard into a winning season for the first time in about forever, and it's these thoughts, this pressure—along with the herky-jerky, moving-stopping as Marcus jumps his finger up and on; and the press of people's carts loaded with junk food and fresh produce, not canned beans like Cleopatra; and noticing everyone else's frozen food that Cleopatra doesn't have, because her cold food is small-portioned (six eggs, quart of milk), meaning Christine pictures Cleopatra's mini fridge—what Christine had long ago in her almost-Ivy college dorm for chrissakes, using it for, well, wine and beer and cream for coffee, but never "food"—beer and wine being two things also not in Cleopatra's haul—and the grating voice of the sneering clerk and suddenly Christine finds herself saying:

Every story needs one bad decision.

"I'll pay for the apple juice."

Sudden silence, sudden stillness, except for Marcus enjoying his gleeful manipulation of the conveyor belt. The cashier's fingertip balances on the white button that, if pressed, summons another employee to amble the aisles for the apple juice that's what, a quarter, forty cents, a dollar less than this apple juice?

Christine is desperate to fix her error, and does, she hopes, by saying, "I mean, I guess I'm sort of in a rush and then we'll just be done and you can pay it forward one of these days."

"Pay it forward?" Cleopatra repeats, her voice carefully neutral.

"Help out someone else," Christine explains, nagged by an undercurrent of nuance, suspecting Cleopatra already knows the cliché.

The vulture lined up behind Christine huffs a tremendously agonized sigh, and the person behind that person slings their cart to lane 6, the lane Christine originally wanted to be in, with no candy display and a dedicated bagger. Ironic it's reopening now, which is always Christine's exact bad luck. They're not even close to finished here in lucky lane 7; the cashier has to bag everything (which she could have multitasked while fighting Cleopatra over the stupid juice). More than anything, Christine's desperate to be home, slipping into her lucky shirt, watching the opening kickoff, burrowing a spoon into her Talenti. She hasn't had breakfast (for all that concern over eggs!) and abruptly she feels weak and famished. Trapped. She tries a therapist-sanctioned deep breath and says, "Some small, kind thing for someone else. Whenever you get a chance."

Another tortured sigh behind her, a shadowy, "These people," that stiffens Cleopatra's shoulders. She yanks Marcus's hand away from the belt and says, "We'll get this juice, but thanks for being so kind." A bit of heaviness on the "so kind," which may be a dig at the cashier, or, Christine realizes with discomfort, may be directed at her.

Which she deserves.

Cleopatra adds, "We like it better than concentrate." She brushes a hand across Marcus's head. "Right, baby?"

"Ney. Ney-ney-ney." He squirms free of her grip and wiggles to the cart handle, lining up his fingers on the red plastic, pressing his forehead up against them.

"I'm really sorry to get involved," Christine says. "I'm just . . ." She swoops her palm over the cluttered conveyer belt. "Invested, I guess." What does that even mean; her words are presented to fill space, and she bends to pile more crap at the end of the belt, screw organization; let Cleopatra mock her organics. At least it's not Whole Foods, Christine thinks, conveniently forgetting that's where she shops when she's grabbing something for the book club potluck, there or Trader Joe's. Not that she cares, but a couple of the women are a little judgy.

The cashier says to Cleopatra, "Sensor tagged something under your cart." Spoken in a moment of triumph at catching Cleopatra in this epic heist. A pumpkin. Thank god for one thing that's not functional, not sensible; for one lighthearted, nonpurposeful item: a ridiculously round pumpkin as big as the boy's head, shellacked and perkily painted with a smiling cartoon face. It's cute, Christine forces herself to think, not depressingly manufactured. Anyway, you don't give a little boy a sharp knife to carve his own pumpkin. Maybe there's no father to take charge the way her father did, but maybe there is a father at home, turning on the game. Don't assume!

Cleopatra says, "One of those pumpkins," and the cashier is snotty as she snaps, "Gotta scan it," and plenty of times a cashier grabs a scanner gun and walks around the bagging area to ding the twelve-roll paper towels under Christine's cart, but this mean, lazy cashier is planted in place, like a huge old tree—

Every story needs to avoid one-dimensional villains.

—or like someone whose feet are swollen at the end of this long shift, like someone impatient to head home to catch the big game against the dreaded "America's Team" rivals with their flashy, big-haired, big-boobed cheerleaders; eager to rally behind the local hero quarterback who rose from a DC high school to win Maryland's BCS bowl game with a glorious Hail Mary pass, perfectly placed, an arc like a rainbow-dream (Christine and the ex were together then, watching on the new big screen he'd hooked up earlier in the day, fire in the fireplace, shimmering Bordeaux);

—or like someone who's working a second job to pay bills.

Cleopatra heaves up the pumpkin, an awkward motion with the slim dress and heels she's wearing, as if she's come from a church where people dress up for God. After all of Marcus's back-and-forthing with the conveyer, Christine's items have crashed into one another, jamming the front of the checkout area and there's no space to plop down this large pumpkin, which Cleopatra holds as if it's a heavy, obstinate offering. The cashier takes her time finding the handheld scanner, then lazily circles two fingers so Cleopatra tips the horrible pumpkin to reveal the barcode sticker on the bottom, which mercifully dings, and finally, finally, thinks Christine, we are about done here. She's getting the kind of headache that attacks when she's going off sugar.

"Ont-ney!" Marcus shouts, pointing at the pumpkin. "Ney-ney!"

"That's right, baby, home soon," Cleopatra says. "You're being so good." As she squints at the computer display of prices, she adds, "Hang on," directed not to Marcus, but to the cashier, who also gazes at the screen.

It's not the Oracle at Delphi, Christine wants to scream. I'll buy the stupid pumpkin and every last thing in that stupid cart if we can just get the you-know-what out of here and move it the you-know-what along. She gulps in another cleansing breath, another. Grabs a magazine off the rack and flips through pages without reading the lurid headlines about plastic surgery and cheating spouses. The magazine is annoying, but she chucks it on her pile because she hates people who read magazines for free and slop up the pages. Grabs sharing-size peanut M&Ms off the candy display. Grabs batteries she thinks are the right size for her TV remote.

The cashier is not unkind but she's not kind either, as she says, "Yeah, that pumpkin's not going on the EBT card when it's painted."

"That makes no sense," Cleopatra says.

"That's what it is," the cashier says. She taps her long talon at the screen. "It's inedible is why," she says. "Only edible goes on the card."

Cleopatra is still holding the pumpkin and Marcus dances on his tiptoes, reaching his arms for it, trailing his fingers along its smooth curves . . .

Every story needs to push conflict a little deeper.

. . . and kissing the cluster of his fingertips and plopping kiss after kiss onto the pumpkin's garish lips. "Luurve ney," he murmurs. He starts kissing one finger at a time, planting each individual kiss onto the pumpkin in a different spot, alternating carefully between the finger of one hand and the finger of the other.

"That's not edible once it's painted," the cashier says. "Can't eat it."

Cleopatra stares into her Ziploc of papers and coupons. The cashier sucks in a deep breath, about to sigh, but doesn't; she gazes spacily into a distance no one else can see (instead of getting off her lazy ass to do some bagging, Christine thinks).

Christine could buy this pumpkin a thousand times over. But she supposes Cleopatra already knows that, just as Cleopatra also knows that the mouse poison is not because there are actual, literal mice streaming through Christine's house but because Christine is a paranoid freak, fearful of the thought of a mouse now that the boyfriend's an ex. Christine can smash spiders and flush stinkbugs, but imagining seeing a mouse panics her. Thus the fall ritual, sliding boxes of poison into the murky corners of her basement and attic, next to last year's poison, which Christine leaves in place because she's afraid to touch it because a mouse might have touched it. Ludicrous that luxury means forking out money for mouse poison JUST IN CASE.

Christine draws in another supposedly soothing breath, thinking she'll offer one last time to pay for the pumpkin. Or maybe she can carry off, "Look, you dropped a five"—not that she has a five or any bills because she only pays with her phone or her credit card, the one offering double points at grocery stores. She holds that breath, holds it, holds it, then blurts to the cashier, "You know, this has gone on long enough. You've been extremely rude to this poor woman from the start, making everything a hassle, and honestly. It's too much."

The cashier says, "Uh—" and Christine rants, unleashed and virtuous, relieved to take charge and get it all settled.

"I shop here all the time," Christine says, "and this is unacceptable. I think maybe I need to talk to the manager." She crosses her arms, her body feeling solid and satisfying.

The cashier jams a finger onto the call button, and the lighted aisle number flashes like a distress signal. Christine senses the rush behind her, as people flee to other lanes—what she wanted to do in the first place! Though if she had, she wouldn't be here to stand up for Cleopatra, so there's that, and she's startled to remember that she doesn't know the woman's actual name and she better *not* say, "Cleopatra."

Marcus hunches into his mother's legs, the fingers of both hands crammed into his mouth. His eyes scrunch shut, and he's rocking. Cleopatra elbows aside some of her items cluttering the bagging area and jumbles the pumpkin into that empty space. She tucks the Ziploc bag of paperwork into her purse, which she magnets shut and presses to her chest. She says, "No pumpkin, baby. Mama's sorry."

The cashier clicks buttons. Bells ding. And finally, finally, she thunks cans into plastic bags. The pumpkin rests there, an island surrounded by a sea of practical, no-nonsense edibles, enough utilitarian food to last for weeks, as if maybe getting to the store is a hardship of multiple bus transfers. The government can't buy one little boy one hideously painted pumpkin? Christine can't either?

Every story needs to flash ahead, to show off that it knows things the characters can't.

The manager will appear, wearing a red shirt embroidered with the store logo—collared, unlike the loose T-shirts worn by cashiers and baggers. His nametag provides a last name. He's come from his private, doored office where he had been adjusting a cheap clock radio, tuning into the game, fiddling the dial and jiggling the cord to set the station so he can duck in and check the score all afternoon. He'll issue the usual manager apologies without blaming his employee, and he'll smile uncomfortably and nod thoughtfully, as if listening to each word Christine sputters. "I understand that you're saying . . ." he'll say, and by mirroring her words in a trained, calm way, she'll be forced to nod in agreement. He'll repeat, "I see how hard that is . . . " At the right moment, he'll juggle the word "policy," carefully citing "the company" as if "the company" is a person everyone is the tiniest bit afraid of. When Christine says, "I shop here all the time, and I like to think my favorite grocery store treats all of its customers equally," she will emphasize "all" and "equally" in a way that dredges up the word they've been anticipating, the word they understood would present itself after enough song and dance: "exception." "In this case, we are happy to accommodate the customer and make an exception for the pumpkin," he says. "As a matter of goodwill, ma'am, we'd like you to have this pumpkin, complimentary."

The cashier will be an efficient and capable bagger, perhaps the best in the store. She'll double-bag the cans and jugs of apple juice without being asked, not making any bag overly heavy, separating eggs and white bread so they won't get crushed. She'll lift the pumpkin with both hands to delicately nestle it into its own plastic bag. She'll pull free a scroll of coupons and tuck them into a neat bundle she'll hand to Cleopatra, who will slide them into that Ziploc bag. Neither she nor Cleopatra will speak, yet if Christine weren't busy blustering, she might sense a weighty, impenetrable connection between the two women that excludes her.

"Come on, Marcus," Cleopatra will say. "Time to get us home and watch Mama's Redskins win, right, baby?" She'll wheel away, the cart shrieking, and Christine will remember hearing that squeaky-wheeled cart amid the aisles, remember how annoyed she was at its incessant screech.

Christine will feel that someone should thank her. Of course not the cashier, and the manager's obsequious gratitude doesn't count, but someone, Cleopatra or the boy (though he can't speak properly, so who'd expect him to know to say a polite thank you?). She should be thanked. Someone should recognize what she has done.

Later, she does:

On Monday morning, as her group slowly gathers for the weekly staff meeting, there's first the chitchat about the 34 to 7 victory, the massacre, and then she decides she'll tell this grocery-store story, exaggerating it to be funny. As she's about to start, she notices herself glancing around the room to see if the Black employees are in yet, and when she notices herself noticing this she understands—or imagines she does—exactly what she has done.

Every story needs an uncomfortable writer.

MY FATHER RAISED ME

My father raised me to despise neediness, yet at this moment, I'm extremely needy. "Do you also have a toothbrush?" I call down the hallway to Vaughn, an ex from another life, now safely married. In our olden days, Other Life Vaughn would've been captivated by a crazy late-night phone call from a crazy woman from the crazy past announcing she was in town and asking, could she stay? Saying she had no luggage and ended in DC impulsively, explaining neither the impulse nor the absence of luggage. Saying not quite a lie: "I've been thinking about you, and I'm eager to meet your wife." Other Life Vaughn would've said, "We'll open wine for you, Lexie." New Life Vaughn's response is more cautious: "A night or two in the guest room, Lexie," he said on the phone, repeating these exact words when he greeted me at the front door wearing pajamas and a silly striped bathrobe, and again when he led me upstairs to the guest room. As if he suspects me of settling in, as if his friends often pop up this way. "I loved your novel," I said on the phone, but he'd already hung up.

Now, he pauses in the hallway, wary that my toothbrush question's a trap. But, "hang on," he says, trudging to the last door on the right. His bedroom, where his wife's enduring a migraine. Vaughn promises my phone call isn't what triggered her, which is encouraging—that I didn't, that he knows I'd assume I had. He's aging well, with a physique that's tight, but without that whiff of someone living at the gym or jabbering about food they can or can't eat; his is casual aging, someone with confident genes. The marble-dark eyes, a solid head of hair; it was silvery-gray when I knew him, premature in his family, but he wore it assertively then, and now. I wonder how I look to him, in my rumpled black cocktail dress and stiletto heels, exhausted smudges of makeup streaking my face, a definite aroma of pink rest-stop soap and road wind clinging to my hair.

Seventeen years, eighteen, nineteen. Let's pretend I'm too tired to do the math.

His door's partially open, and lamplight knifes out across the textured carpet into the hallway. Inside, I glimpse the corner of a bed covered with an invitingly billowy duvet. I wonder about the light, because people with migraines usually beg to lie alone in the dark. It's information to tuck away, that this migraine might be fake. Information is currency, according to my father. I can't hear anything, but I imagine awkward and angular questions, cold looks exchanged as Vaughn heads to the bathroom for that extra toothbrush. It's a large house in an upscale suburb, containing a tidy guest room, complete with fresh sheets and a decorative decanter for water: even so, I suspect it's not a happy place. I want Vaughn to be happy, but not too happy. Sounds selfish, but happiness is untrustworthy. Another thing I was raised to believe.

So Vaughn's got a house like this, along with a wife faking(?) a migraine, and a sullen teenage boy who skulked past, sneering when Vaughn said, "This is Lexie, an old friend," as if "old" were the only premise the kid agreed to accept. Vaughn e-blasted me about his novel, and I send postcards for gallery openings, including this recent one, which I mailed last minute, knowing he wouldn't attend. We send up flares—lookie what I did, zowie! look at meeeeeeee!—keeping in touch through achievements. When he answered my phone call, he said, "My god, Lexie. What is this?" An angry undertone to his voice, the way you'd speak to someone who bumps you in a crowd or splashes juice on your new sweater.

I said, "Tomorrow's my birthday," sounding stupid and confused, but dissolving his anger.

"Happy birthday?" he said. "Where are you?"

"I'll hit DC in, I don't know; how long if I'm in Woodbridge right now?"

He sighed, implying a glare the wife's shooting across a room. I spoke quickly: "I wasn't sure this number still worked. I guess I could use a place to stay. Please." I was careful not to use the word "need." That word I avoided in our life together, etched in my mind as a no-no. Also, it wasn't true "need" because I had a credit card. I could find some dumb hotel.

Just that—

Just that I was tearing up 95 to DC where my despised father is dying, and the boyfriend either I loved or I was using to shake up my life or both, who was supposed to see me through this metaphorical and literal journey, instead climbed into the cab of a semi at a truck stop, kicked out of my car because he won't give me a baby. Just that I'm forty *today* and I'm still, still, still doing this. I know there are other ways to be, and I want to be them.

Just that I was driving and texting—caught in roadwork with two left lanes closed and a crawling thirty-minute backup at midnight—when I remembered Vaughn lived in DC. Why think? Just call. "Did I wake you?" I asked, abruptly realizing that New Life Vaughn might have responsibilities that included early to bed, early to rise.

"Still a night owl," he said.

"I shouldn't have called you," I said.

The pause tantalized: the time necessary for a judgy wife to nod begrudging assent, and he said, "Stay here. For a night or two. A night or two in the guest room, Lexie."

Victory.

An hour later I pulled into the circular drive of his McMansion. Motion detector lights leapt on, illuminating my car where I sat for a minute, combing my hair, fixing my mascara, trying to concoct some feasible, grown-up explanation

Vaughn could pass on to Abby that would make me a responsible person who *of course* would stay only one or two nights, who would never ditch her own birthday party, never string along an inappropriately young boyfriend who had been her student, never hope her powerful father's already dead and powerless, never a thousand different things. A story offering logical reasons to travel with no luggage and arrive deep in the night after a rushed phone call. There's no such story, because even the truth requires unwinding: the lies I'd told Vaughn about my past, the invented military dad who moved us place to place; I killed him with a heart attack to win pity once when Vaughn threatened to leave. I imagine Abby's sour face as I explain myself: Who's this wacko again? And you loved her? Then her relief: Thank god I came along with my big house and saved you.

Me thinking, Was that love?

Here in Vaughn's outstretched hand is a pink toothbrush, wrapped in clear plastic. A dentist's name stamped in gold. I imagine Abby's diminutive voice at her check-up requesting pink, accepting the free toothbrush not for herself but for guests, if any are stupid enough to forget their own or to get their luggage lost by the airline, neither something Abby would do.

I say, "So great now you're that guy with an extra toothbrush."

"Yeah, when did that happen?" he says.

"Maybe 2003?" I say. This is when I returned the antique ring; or rather, when he demanded it back, when I stuffed it down the kitchen drain, when I walked out, when I left, when he shouted out the window at dawn, "No one's better than me," when I got onto the back of a motorcycle, when I shouted back, "Fuck you," because he was right. I say, "Really. It's all great, the toothbrush, your house, seeing you." I sweep my hand upward and gesture in a semicircle.

He says, "I know you think I should disown this big fucking house, or call it all her idea, but I like it, and I like that it's big. I like everything about it, even those ridiculous columns out front and the portico that looks ripped right off an Italian villa. I like all that shit. If you don't believe me, I'll show you my office tomorrow. It's out back, a separate space."

In my mind, I fill in: and it's five times bigger than our closet apartment we shared on Second Avenue.

I say, "I loved your novel."

He stands awkwardly, flips a light switch that seems to have no effect. I'm distracted, wondering what's been turned on or off; why a house might have a phantom light switch. He says, "Why are you here, really?" There's coldness in his voice, maybe hatred. My heart races, cares. My therapist has said many times that anger isn't deadly to relationships: indifference is. I know—I know, I know, I know—I'm making a terrible mistake, and that I could walk down the stairs, out the door, and find a hotel.

Instead I say, "My father maybe is dying."

"Oh no," he says. It's too easy, isn't it, and I wait for his arms to open in sympathy, for him to fold me in. Then, "Hang on. Your *father*?"

"My real father," I say. "I never told you about him."

"Who the fuck was that other guy? Who ran the army base in Texas?"

"No one," I say. "Can you believe he was no one?" We're not talking about my father or my imaginary father in the military, the colonel, as I called him. We're talking about us. Too late at night and too late in time, and way, way too late to matter, not with his wife's ear pressed against the door. Must an apology be the words "I'm sorry"? Unnecessary, I've snapped at men; you're not the man who broke me, I want to explain, which is melodramatic, so all I do is be my broken self.

Such an awkward silence. *He was no one, they're always no one: only you are not no one.* Zen koan? Or Hallmark card?

What if I grab his hand? But I can't, not with this toothbrush in one hand and a tube of toothpaste from the guest room in the other. Doesn't occur to me to hold both items in one hand. When he turns and walks back toward that bedroom door, I'm glad I didn't signal my intentions, that (I hope) I signaled nothing. "Good night," he whispers, closing the door. A lock snaps harshly.

Make them come to you, is my father's motto, famous now on Capitol Hill.

"Good night," I whisper back. The black cat that I've been told fawns on strangers like a dog appears, twining itself between my legs. It has a people-name I can't remember, like Mike or Philip. "Good kitty," I say, and off it stalks, pushing open a cracked door with its face. This hallway is walls of doors. I'm so tired. And probably wrong about everything I read into the situation. I don't know what to do about my father, about my unraveled life. I wish the cat nosed itself into my room. I realize I should have asked for a T-shirt or pajamas, but which option isn't weird: sleeping in his wife's clothing, or in his? Bare naked it is.

The next morning, a wide band of sunlight sprawls across my face. It's 10:05, and I'm embarrassed for sleeping so late. Behind the door of the guest bathroom is a fluffy white robe hanging on a hook, so thankfully I don't have to wear the party dress downstairs. Thinking about this fact shapes my day: I'll find a mall and buy clothes. What a fine thing, having one problem I can solve. On a bathroom shelf sit several pairs of fancy, plastic-wrapped hotel slippers. Here, things are planned and prepared for. I choose an open-toed pair to show off the gold polish of my pedicure. Brush my teeth. Comb my hair. How desperate is lipstick? I examine the unattractive woodcut of a sailboat that hangs in the bathroom, certain it was purchased at a craft fair. Adjust the towels to hang perfectly straight. Slide on a light coat of lipstick, damn it. I've got to leave this room eventually, so I sashay downstairs as if everything here is very normal. Maybe the family's at church. Maybe I can leave a note and drive off, though the thought of shopping in my fancy dress is daunting.

I take the stairs slowly, followed by the black cat and a tabby I don't remember hearing about during last night's rundown. At the foot of the stairs, I pick the wrong turn, taking me not to the kitchen but to another bedroom with a made-up four-poster bed, picture window, gas fireplace, and a small sitting area composed of a tasteful recliner and a coffee table with a thick paperback, spine up. The lamp by the chair is lit, as if someone's returning soon. The décor is overly neutral, something I'm sure a realtor told them "shows well." The longer I stare, the more certain I am that I'm not supposed to know whose room this is, though surely it's the housekeeper's or an elderly parent's, someone who, like the tabby, will show up. I poke my head deeper, seeking clues, and am startled that one of my early photographs hangs on the wall where the door is. So he bought my art! But displays it in this impersonal room? Because someone equates my art with the crummy craft-fair print? The house is a maze, and so's the family. In the light of day, with sleep, and a glimmer of good sense, I see that coming here really, truly wasn't smart. Any hotel clerk could've handed over a toothbrush.

Keep complications simple, my father used to say. Whatever happens, he's a man who refuses to die, even if I watch his body fail with my own two eyes.

I retrace my steps and find the kitchen. The (I assume) wife sits at a kitchen island, cupping a mug between both hands as she gazes out the window. Of all the scenarios I've been expecting—me talking to Vaughn alone; me standing alone in the kitchen; me with a tense smile watching the two of them cozy over pancakes; me navigating the surly teen—this, wife alone, is unexpected. She doesn't hear me, meaning I could turn around and disappear, even drive away. My car's my new coping mechanism, I imagine explaining to my therapist. "Abby?" I say.

She turns. Her eyes are puffy and red-rimmed, and her dark hair is slopped back into a loose ponytail, but her smile remains controlled. "Good morning." She looks like hell and by the way she rests one hand across her face to shade my view, she knows it.

"Feeling better?"

"Thanks to the miracle of Imitrex," she says. "I just love strong drugs."

I'm not sure how to respond; her statement's almost a question, as if she's hoping I'll pull a lovely selection from my bathrobe pocket. I mirror her tight smile.

"The men are on a hunter-gatherer thing," she says, and I must look confused—because I'm imagining Vaughn with a shotgun—so she adds, "Getting doughnuts from the Sugar Shack, as a treat. The line's a mile long, but, you know . . ." She shrugs as if this behavior is beyond explanation. "The thrill is scoring maple bacon, their specialty, and always in limited supply. Do you like doughnuts? Vaughn will be so disappointed if you don't." She speaks in a rapid-fire murmur, with a small, almost-lost southern lilt.

"I love doughnuts," I say, which surely Vaughn remembers. Which maybe is why he's out buying them.

"Sleep all right?"

I nod.

"Coffee?" She jumps up to open a cupboard above the coffee pot and rummages through a clutter of mugs, plucking out two. She says, "In this family, on weekends, coffee mugs are thematic. It's silly, but nonnegotiable." A wry little laugh. She raises the first mug: a picture of a Georgia O'Keeffe cow skull: "Because you're an artist, or—" and the second mug is black with red printing that she reads aloud: "'Fear no art,' because, well—also because you're an artist. That's what I know about you. And that you arrived late at night."

It's fucking weird. But I say, "The black one, for the black of night."

She pours an inch, like she's rationing. "Half and half's in the fridge, and skim milk. I can dig up sugar, but no one here uses it." A threat? Or am I being paranoid? She sits at the island again, rewraps both hands around her mug like it's a life preserver. What's her theme, I wonder. Intruder in the house?

"Skim's perfect," I say. Normally I drink coffee black, but I'll scope the secrets inside the fridge. An art school friend once did a photo series of the interiors of people's private spaces, like drawers and refrigerators. Mine, she said, stood out for being so empty, which I pretended was a compliment.

Inside the fridge, it's a dull clutter of yogurt, Ziplocs of fruit and vegetables, Tupperwares with dates printed on strips of blue masking tape. The most interesting thing is a plate of fried chicken that looks homemade. There's a light drape of Saran wrap, but not the way you'd wrap something you cared about. I pour the tiniest smidge of organic skim into my coffee and let the door fall shut. Cold fried chicken—homemade, for-real, southern-fried chicken—gives me a pang. My mother's fried chicken was famous, her secret ingredient—which I happily reveal—was vodka, which she had plenty of, yet never enough. "I married her for that chicken," my father often said, maybe kidding.

I clamber onto the stool across from Abby. "What a beautiful home," I say, hoping to start a simple-minded conversation: pretty house, nice weather, come see the garden, talk about the garden.

But she says, "My mother's a decorator so I let her loose. Otherwise she'd criticize every choice I make, and that about sends me off a bridge."

"Um." My coffee tastes watery and sad, and there's an off-flavor to the milk. At home, I'd dump it and start over. Actually, that might be my theme, though I'm not sure how that translates to a coffee mug. Car driving away? Steaming pile of shit?

Abby says, "I'm so afraid of turning into her, I basically don't criticize anything."

I say, "Oh! Remind me what the cats' names are? They're so pretty." Pretty, pretty. Speaking of mothers' traits, mine did exactly this when she was uncomfortable, comment on how pretty everything was. When I was ten, my cousin Joel came home from college at Thanksgiving and announced that this new male "friend" accompanying him was his lover, and she said, "Y'all have the prettiest eyes."

Abby says, "Henry and Edith. As in, Henry James and Edith Wharton. You know, Vaughn's favorite writers."

Something's implied in her comment, but she speaks before I can sort out an appropriate answer: "How'd you meet again?" she asks.

Oh, that fake-casual "again," as if she doesn't buy whatever story Vaughn gave. I sip coffee, longing to start fresh with Georgia O'Keeffe. I say, "Vaughn didn't tell you?"

"He said in New York." She's staring hard out the window, over my shoulder.

"After 9/11," I try out.

"Okay." She's faux agreeable.

It's like a high-stakes poker game. Damn doughnuts better be worth it, Vaughn, I think, leaving me alone with her.

"He was the agent's assistant," I say. "And bartending."

"That first book of his . . ." Abby says.

"Yeah," I say. "He started it then. Wouldn't talk about it." No need to mention he read pages out loud every night while

I lay tucked against him in our single bed, my ear pressed to his chest, listening as the rhythm of his sentences echoed his beating heart.

She says, "I always wondered about his dedication."

"His dedication to writing?" I say, though I know exactly what she's talking about.

"The book's dedication," she says. "Who that book is dedicated to. To whom, I guess. To whom that book, the book that took eleven years to finish, the prizewinner, to whom *that* is dedicated."

"I don't remember." I raise my coffee, say, "Mind if I heat this? I'm one of those people who wants coffee to scald, to be dangerously hot."

She points to the microwave, and I punch in some numbers, let the machine whir. When I pop the door, the coffee's boiling and the milk looks curdled. What a mess I'm always making.

She says, "We own one of your photographs."

"I saw—by accident. I got lost looking for the kitchen, and the door was open, and there it was. I'm still obsessed with fire escapes. All the lines."

She nods as if she'll never believe anything I say. "In my bedroom," she says.

"Oh. I've read that's a thing, that couples want—"

"We're separated," she says. "The laws in Virginia are complicated, and even if they weren't, everything else is complicated. Everything is always so complicated." Anger flares each time she repeats the word "complicated."

"I'm sorry," I say.

"I thought he told you," she says. "I thought that's why you're here."

"Oh, god, no!" I exclaim. "I'm here because—well, because I got my own complicated, bad news last night, so, being me, my reaction was to immediately ditch my fortieth birthday party and do about a hundred terrible things to a bunch of different people, and also maybe hit a raccoon on the highway. I do things I know are wrong. I do them and do them."

I down the too-hot coffee, then add, "I don't think Vaughn wants me here, if that helps. We haven't seen each other for years. Just braggy postcards about our amazing creative lives, his more amazing than mine."

"Actually, his publisher canceled his last book," she says. "He might even have to give back the advance."

I arrange my face to look sympathetic. "What a mess."

She says, "Then it's someone else he's seeing, not you." She studies me.

I'm instantly jealous of "someone else." But I laugh, scoff, play cool, fool no one. It's pathetically clear—pathetically obvious—why I ended up here last night, tempted by the fuzzy past, wanting easy. Time to change the subject: "What about your son . . ." hoping she fills in the name, which I've forgotten. Melville?

"Complicated," she says. "But tell me I'm right about that book being dedicated to you."

This book is dedicated to two drifters: my huckleberry friend and me. I shake my head. "Sorry," I say. "I think he would've said if it was me." But there's telltale heat in my cheek as my face flushes. She nods.

"I mean, it doesn't matter, does it? Whoever you were to him? Whatever all that was. It's all, poof, gone." She flicks her fingers outward like two tiny explosions. "The canceled book is the one finally dedicated to me." Her turn with the awkward laugh and the flushed cheeks. "I thought we were okay," she says. "I thought we were forever."

There's the grind of a garage door opening, and she leaps up. "They're back. Don't tell him I told you. We're acting like everything's okay." Then she's gone, leaving behind her coffee mug, which reads, "Keep Calm and Carry a Gun." I'm unsettled, trying to decide whether to linger or not; which is more awkward, me in the bathrobe, me if I put on the cocktail dress from last night; and here's Vaughn. "Doughnuts!" he calls, slapping a pink-striped box on the island. I catch a whiff of sugary grease. "And—drum roll, please—maple bacon! Though some may have been consumed on the journey home. Casualties must be expected." It's a falsely jocular voice that's extremely grating, which I assume is on my behalf, until I catch the son, his son, slouched behind him, rolling his eyes. He's scant: thin and reedy, wearing baggy plaid shorts that a 1955 grandpa might mow the lawn in. The simple black T-shirt on top looks casually expensive. The kid tugs his phone from his front pocket and stares at it.

"No phones on Sunday," Vaughn says.

"You said no phone when we're getting doughnuts," the kid says. "Doughnuts—gotten." He points dramatically at the box with his middle, fuck-you finger. No comment from Vaughn. The kid shoves the phone in his pocket then scratches his cheekbone with that same finger, and still no reaction from Vaughn. The kid sighs as Vaughn pulls a stack of plates from a cupboard then grabs the coffeepot and tilts its contents into the sink with a splash.

"I'll brew something decent," Vaughn says.

"I like Mom's coffee," the kid says.

"Me too," Vaughn says, "but we have company today." And he nods my way, and it's a flash from growing up: my father barking, *Company*, meaning, everyone talk pretty. "You'll love these doughnuts, Lexie. They're the best." Vaughn extracts the used filter from a fancy coffee maker that's about the size of a Volkswagen.

I can't stand all this normal: kid, kitchen, breakfast, dad. I say it sexy, like I did that night in the East Village dive bar where Vaughn worked: "Doughnuts are my most favorite food."

This line's the first thing I said to him, me feeling reckless on shots of Absolut, rage-bored by the forgettable boyfriend next to me. Vaughn leaned over the bar and whispered in a silvery voice, "You look like you've got a secret," and I said, "Doughnuts are my most favorite food." Back then I smoked and turned my voice slow and deliberate, like talking around a mouthful of smoldering embers.

Now, I add the rest: "It's the grease. I love me some hot grease." The kid flicks his eyes my way, suddenly highly attuned to me, attention I shouldn't want, but which is pleasing. He lifts one eyebrow. It's boredom. Or showing off. We're all showing off, the three of us. The silence is luscious, awkward.

Vaughn runs water into my mug, rinsing it, as he stumbles out words: "This is the good stuff, from Swings. Best coffee roasters in town."

"'Best coffee roasters in town,'" the kid mocks. He sneaks a look to catch my reaction, so I puff his ego with a snicker, twitch my shoulder the slightest, shifting the way the robe folds over my body.

"You said it," Vaughn says, ignoring the kid's intention. Ignoring me.

But what if they don't come to you? My father belly-laughed at my question. "Hasn't happened yet," he said, and he's always right: here I am in my dad's town though he hasn't seen me—or cared about me—for how many years? I invited him to last night's birthday party, damn it, knowing, knowing not to; knowing, knowing he wouldn't show. Knowing there I'd be, looking for him. I take in a long breath, ease it out. Enough games.

"What mall's around here?" I ask. "I have to buy clothes and stuff. And find a hotel. I'm glad—"

"Thought you were company," the kid says. "You're leaving? Why don't you have clothes? What's that about?"

"Well, it's an unexpected—"

"Enough," Vaughn says. "We'll rustle up something you can wear." He grinds coffee, and there's only the buzz of coffee beans getting beaten up, the thick aroma of the best coffee in town. The grinding goes so long that I'm sure Vaughn's stretching the process, steadying the room. He measures four tablespoons of ground coffee into a clean filter. Pours in bottled water from the fridge. (Bottled water? Really, Vaughn? Remember the nights when dinner was nibbled-down pizza crusts out of a trash can in Tompkins Square Park?)

The kid says, "No, but seriously. Is 'company' now the euphemism for cheap hooker?"

"Enough!" Vaughn says. "Whitman, that's quite enough."

"It's Whit," he says. "I've told you a thousand times, I don't go by Whitman. Don't you even know who I am? Don't you know one simple, stupid thing . . . Dad?" So much scorn heaped onto that last word, and finally Vaughn's false bravado buckles: his face and body sag, then stiffen. He won't look at me, but the boy does, straight-on and hard, and that's not triumph he's showing, though maybe he thinks it is: it's pain.

Wrong for me to see this, a mistake to be here. Last night I thought I wanted Vaughn, or Vaughn's attention, or any attention, or anything. But nothing is the thing I really want; these things are only what I know.

I say, "Today's my birthday." If I'm not careful, I'll be sobbing. This sentence, repeated how many times, won't save me.

Vaughn says, "I remember."

"Yeah, I mentioned it last night," I say.

"No, I remember because I always remember," he says. "Forty."

His fingertip brushes the ridge of my knuckles, forward, back, exploring each rise and fall of my knobby, fluttery bones. His kid sees. His kid's right there. Vaughn's finger tickles, warms. Here's the simple, familiar ease of winning.

How is this the prize? This poor, sad man. This big house. This fake life. This boy's dad.

I snatch my hand away, tighten the already-tight knot in my robe, clutch both arms across my chest. Lock down my body before it betrays me. Vaughn's hand trails slowly along the granite counter, then flicks a switch on the coffee maker. Just like that, we're normal again.

The kid's face is stony. "Jesus Christ," he says, "we ever gonna eat?" He cracks his knuckles with noisy gusto, and Vaughn glances at him, as if startled by the crunching sound, the boy's presence, but says simply, "Pour juice for everyone, will you, kiddo?"

We eat the doughnuts, and the maple bacon are maybe not the best I've ever had, but very good, and the coffee is also not the best I've ever had, but very good. Everything's pretty. But what about the woman in the back bedroom faking a migraine? What about, "I always remember?" What about this fucked-up kid stuck smack in the middle? What about this all-alone kid, and all the all-alone kids, and the parents who fucked them up? I pretend not to feel Whit's eyes raking me over, despising me. I tell some jokes: easy to make people laugh. "Leave the dishes for Whitman," Vaughn says, "and I'll have Abby find something you can wear."

"Lucky they're the same size," Whit says. "Convenient."

"Better to be lucky than smart," I say. My father swaps these adjectives as necessary, believing he's both.

"What if you're neither?" Whit says.

"Then you better study harder," Vaughn says, and he stands, rocking his weight side to side, apparently unwilling to leave the two of us alone, because his words get pointed: "I'll bring the clothes upstairs." I lead the way out, and Vaughn follows as Whit calls, "Dad, it's like you've never been around a naked woman before." I glance back, and Vaughn's face is rigid. "Dishwasher," he shouts.

A robe's not naked, I want to say, but boys do that, don't they—turn women tiny any way they can. Not the kid's fault. Can't blame a child for grabbing attention when it can.

My father liked me best in a group. Birthday parties especially. For days, my mother fried chicken. Then a tent appeared in the backyard, and a bouncy castle. Two hundred guests—mostly his friends—bickering about politics, sloshing glasses of brown liquid that wasn't sweet tea, telling me in front of him how pretty I was. When he shouted, *What'd y'all bring my birthday girl?*, everything stopped while I ripped through presents: Tiffany charm bracelets, monogrammed pajamas, a glittery Swan Lake costume, guitars, kid-size French cooper cookware.

Overwhelming—uncomfortable—intoxicating: being watched by him. For too long, I wondered why those adults bringing these gifts liked *me*. "Doesn't matter," he said when I asked, "if the gift's got your name on it."

Fifteen minutes later, Vaughn knocks at my bedroom door, though it's already open. He's holding two Whole Foods paper bags stuffed with clothes. "The donate pile," he says. "Sorry. That probably feels . . ." He shrugs. "Abby's idea."

I smile. "It's really kind," I say, aware that it isn't.

"We're separated," he says.

"She told me," I say.

"I'm sorry about us," he says. "What happened."

I shake my head. "Don't you ever think everything is too late?"

He steps closer, nudging both bags into my arms. I smell piney soap. Paper crinkles. His hand cups my shoulder blade, slides down my spine. I feel all this without feeling it at all, as he kisses me, pressing himself in over the tops of the paper bags with urgency, me letting him. Not pity, not boredom. Obligation? Anger?

Who's he showing off for now, I wonder, in this empty room?

He steps back, and I say, for the millionth time, "Thank you," which I repeat until he backs away, into that hallway of doors. I imagine him walking through a different door, into another room. I got what I wanted, so now what? Your life builds around one core question, my father said, or was it one core answer?

A different door slams so hard the craft-fair print vibrates on the wall.

I roughly dump the first bag on the bed, root for anything good enough to get me in Target. Think about logistics, about my father's body in a hospital bed. According to the news, he's stable, but in a coma. Unresponsive. Finally, experts agree with my assessment of him.

I paw through a rainbow of fancy-labeled, jewel-tone dresses, many with price tags still attached. Cashmere sweaters—with moth holes. A knot of neckties. Unsuccessful experiments in leggings: velvet, pleather, denim, a tropical print. I'm desperate, so I set aside the garish tropical leggings.

The next bag holds the jackpot of a flannel shirt and several articles of faded black, blobby athleisurewear. Also a folded, gray, Nordstrom suit bag that I'm nosy enough to unzip. A sleek wedding dress, the waifish slip-style so popular after JFK Jr. married Carolyn Bessette: the exact dress my college-girl-self swooned over while studying pictures of their secret wedding. Maybe Abby loved the same photos.

I toss it onto my yes stack, as if this is the correct response to uncovering someone's abandoned wedding dress. *Vaughn murmuring, You're gorgeous. A father-daughter dance in the twinkly lawn tent, everyone gathered round.*

Abby stands framed by the doorway, perfectly centered. "Are you good?" she asks.

The question's askew. No, I'm not good. Every man marches forth with sin staining his soul, according to my father. But, "because I heard a door slam too loudly," is what she means, so I nod. "Guess it's come to this, me rooting through your discards. But I appreciate it."

She says, "Probably slim pickings since the housekeeper gets first crack."

If words could smirk, those do.

I say, "You know my father is the Speaker of the House. I'm not no one."

Less than twenty-four hours in DC and I'm that person: Do you know who I am? Works, but is her tiny gasp worth giving up valued information? Now she thinks she knows my whole story. That my father threw away his chance to be president because he wouldn't keep his dick in his pants. That my father threw away his family, that he threw away me.

"Vaughn didn't say anything about that."

"He doesn't know," I said. "My father and I are estranged. I've been lying about who he is for my entire adult life."

"Maybe you're lying now," she says.

Well, fuck. "Look," I say. "After I leave, you won't see me again, okay? I appreciate the clothes and the doughnuts and everything. The coffee. I really do."

"You don't look like him." She peers at me, and I smile his famous smile for her. "Maybe a little."

I stare back, trying to fix this woman's features in my head. But she's every unhappy, affluent woman. Maybe too much so, as if she works hard to be this way.

She says, "When she's up from North Carolina, his wife's in my Thursday yoga class."

"Be specific," I say. "There's so many."

"Current," she says.

"She's my least favorite," I say. "Though actually, they're all my least favorite."

"I imagine so." She shifts her eyes, settling them onto that Nordstrom bag. "Oh."

I say, "I loved that same dress, too, back in the day. From JFK Jr.'s wedding, right?" I wad clothing into the bags. "It's stunning. Don't get why the housekeeper passed."

"I guess I should take it back," she says. "I mean . . ."

While I wait to hear what she means, I sort through my keep pile and match the leggings with an oversize hoodie, the hoodie with some faded yoga pants, the yoga pants with the plaid flannel shirt.

She says, "I mean, the marriage is dead. Still, I don't want you having my wedding dress."

I pretend I'm surprised that that's what she meant. I pair the leggings and the flannel shirt, amused by the clashing patterns. I say, "Yet here it is, free for the taking."

"I get that you're messing with me." Her voice raises: "Honestly, I just want that dress to end up on a rack at the Salvation Army thrift store, or wherever things go when they're discarded. It's sort of wrecked. Vaughn caught Whitman wearing it."

Enough futzing with outfits because here's an interesting surprise in her life of complications. "Wearing, like . . . ? Cross-dressing? Or Whit's a transgender person?"

"Oh, no, my god, no. Nothing big and crazy and dramatic and permanent as that," she says. "He just likes attention."

The silence between us goes jagged.

I lift the dress, hold it out. The white silk drapes elegantly off my arm. JFK Jr. and his bride died in a foggy plane crash three years after their secret wedding. Never touch cursed things, according to my father. How can you know, we wondered, and he said, "Feels like that same gut burn when a hard decision hurts so bad you know it's right."

"I wouldn't really take your wedding dress," I say. "I hope I was raised better than that."

She shakes her head. "Vaughn came home late from wherever, and there's Whitman crammed into it, I mean, my god. This was maybe a couple of weeks ago. He was standing at the freezer, like he was perfectly normal, eating Chunky Monkey from the carton. Vaughn didn't even speak; he just left. What do you say? I can't have that dress around. I finally dug it out of the back of his bedroom closet."

"Is that so awful?" I ask.

"Well . . ." She pauses as if considering my question, but I realize she's only considering her answer, not wanting to sound the way she's inevitably about to sound. "It's not what a parent plans."

"What does getting rid of a dress do?" I ask.

"What does running away do?" She sweeps an arm across the room, encompassing me into its arc.

I drop the dress onto the floor, a silk puddle. "You know, your kid needs you," I say.

"Advice from a stranger," she says. "Always the best. Thank you."

I hold up the leggings. "No," I say. "Thank *you*." I smile, hard: my father's unerasable smile. Smile longer than necessary, he said, until you get what you want.

I do, at least now. She snaps her head in one curt nod and hurries off, as if someone's calling for her, though I hear nothing. Sure, but it hurts to smile. I remember my father at his bathroom mirror every morning, smiling, practicing, building those muscles. Back then, we just thought that was the nicest thing. We didn't know better.

What I do is wiggle into the yoga pants and slip on the flannel shirt. Stilettos. Collect my purse and phone. Balled-up robe tossed onto the unmade bed. Grab the wrecked wedding dress, my own cocktail dress, and dump them on top of one bag, along with the toothbrush and hotel slippers. But—what the hell—I crush both bags of junky clothing into my arms and teeter down the stairs, hoping no cats appear to trip me up. I'm quiet, tiptoeing on the balls of my feet, until I'm out the door and onto the circular drive, where the tap of my heels almost echoes. My phone's charged, its GPS programmed to a Target seventeen minutes away. Visiting hours at the hospital go to eight tonight. This is the map ahead.

Whit's sitting at the base of one of those portable basketball hoops that dads wheel into cul-de-sacs. He's hunched over his phone and won't care if I say goodbye. Of all the people I could just leave, this lost boy is that person.

Still. I walk partway over to him, calling, "Hey."

He doesn't look up but mutters, "Hey," which could be the end.

I embellish: "Your dad was in love with me a long time ago, and even though I loved him, I was shitty. Actually, I'm still shitty."

Now he locks his gaze onto me, squinting. I move to stand directly in front of him, my body blocking the sun from his face. He's pale, his skin almost translucent. "Yeah?" It's politeness, moderate interest, likely piqued solely by an adult saying "shitty" twice.

"Don't do that," I say. "Not to people you love. It becomes habit."

"I absolutely," he says, "hate my dad." His eyes flick back to his phone. "Aren't you going to say, 'no you don't, he's your father'?" he mocks.

I shake my head.

He swats at a fly buzzing his face. "Whatever," he says. "Thank you. Thanks. Okay. Is that it?"

"One more thing," I say.

I stand silently, listening to someone's lawn mower, distant traffic, two birds seesawing with song, the persistent fly. I'll wait. He'll ask. Learn to wait, my father told me, and that's what I learned first and best.

The kid says, "Okay, what? What's the one more thing?"

I take another second, until I'm certain he's looking up at me, and I hug both bags close to my chest to free one arm, which I use to pull the wedding dress off the top. And my cocktail dress. I bend and hunch—a painful balance in these shoes—and set both dresses in his lap, a light, shimmery heap, and his hand gravitates to those billowy folds. Sun bursts onto his face, and he shields the light away with his other hand. I say, "One day you'll understand you can leave all this behind, and nothing will matter but that, being gone. I left my father more than twenty years ago. Ask me if I've needed him since."

His mouth pops open, but he doesn't speak, maybe fearing any words that come next.

"No. Not once," I say. Easy to lie to this boy's scared, sad face. It's okay. He wants to hear this.

I straighten up and walk to my car, climb in, toss the bags on the floor.

Something else my father taught me: Looking back ruins it.

"Wait!" he's calling. "You can do that? How do you mean? You really did that? Left your family because why?" He picks up the handful of fabric and flings it at the empty space where I was standing. There's more.

But, whoosh, I'm gone, guiding my car along the curve of the driveway.

In the end, it turns out that what you need to save yourself isn't all that much, just someone's best advice.

ADMIT THIS TO NO ONE

Official DC is mindful of insignificant beginnings, of small decisions that escalate into epic downfalls. Five men break into an office one June night in 1972. A pretty girl wears a blue dress from the Gap, another pretty girl stuffs incriminating documents inside her boots, and a different pretty girl splashes her way into the Tidal Basin. A woman utters the phrase "basket of deplorables" during a campaign speech. A man is photographed sitting in an Abrams tank. Someone adds an "e" to "potato" at an elementary school spelling bee. It's announced that a "mission" is "accomplished." On July 25, 2019, a phone call is placed to Ukraine. A mayor waits in a room at the Vista International Hotel. Distressed at losing Iowa, a man howls into a microphone. "Read my lips," someone suggests. People pose on the *Monkey Business*.

Poof.

To claw back—if you can—is to arrive at a place that can never be the place you were; is to dwell within the shadowy gloom of *what if*; is to watch the world spin without you, after all.

What's the cleanup now, Mary-Grace thinks as a phone number flashes across the screen on her car dashboard. She's stuck in traffic on the 14th Street bridge, headed to—of all places—the mall at Pentagon City to meet with her personal shopper. In another city, it might be embarrassing to be dressed by someone, but here, with little room for error, she'll take the imprimatur of Meera's excellent taste. Let Meera dash around the store collecting jewel-tone dresses as if they're seashells, allowing Mary-Grace to wobble out judgment before capitulating: "They're pushing these sleeves this year? Really? Okay. You know best." Meera understands perfectly how Mary-Grace walks the endless wire of looking good without looking like she's working to look good. Half the women on Capitol Hill use a team of Meeras to create the illusion that a powerful woman can casually stride into a room.

No one in Mary-Grace's position ignores a ringing phone. The car's moving inch by half-inch, so how easy to accept the call and calmly announce, "You've reached me," her signature greeting since she started working with the Speaker, when she was young and still dressed herself. They should know who they're calling, she figures, so start them off-base. Four buzzes, then voice mail will grab the call.

She senses bad news. That familiar chill ripples the back of her neck, iciness tickles her toes. Bad news is her specialty, is why her job exists, why she exists: to mop it all up, to polish it into good news. Bad news is an opportunity. Who would ever tire of opportunity? To Mary-Grace, bad news is perversely good news, because it's a sure indication that she's needed and that she's important. That she's powerful.

The river below churns choppy and brown after last night's storm. So much lightning, she got out of bed and stood at her balcony, watching the jagged shards slice up the sky. Peaceful to watch rage storm itself out, and interesting, now, to contemplate how the river ends up roiling the next day, all that rage dumped here. Several people drown in the Potomac annually, usually overconfident kayakers and hikers at Great Falls who ignore the warning signs advising against scrambling out on the slippery rocks for selfies.

She's ready for that dang phone. "You've reached me," she says, now redirecting the trajectory of the car's inch-inching, nosing it toward the right lane and the eventual first exit in

Virginia. Whatever it is, she's needed. Whatever it is, she's in charge.

"Oh my god," she says immediately, then again and again and again and again. The lightning strike's sizzle, the whooshing suck of the currents, these words no one should hear. She crushes the brake pedal, barely avoiding smashing the Toyota in front of her and automatically raises one hand as an "I'm sorry," though it's likely they won't spot that via their rearview, likely they don't realize how close they've come to an annoying fender bender.

The mental list collects, which should calm her: who to call, who to text, who to inform, who to delegate what to. This traffic is horrific, likely sticking her on this bridge for a good twenty minutes before she'll exit in Virginia and then circle back to DC via the other side of the bridge, through different loops of snarl, crawling this goddamn car to GW Hospital.

Mary-Grace jams down the horn at the uptight Volvo SUV that refuses to let her squeeze by. Such a useless thought, but here it is: What if she had let the phone worry itself into silence?

Where is he? Sirens? Away drifts this gentle, blurry fuzziness, burning off like golf-course mist into buzzing, pinching, poking, stabbing, pulsing throbs, clicks, a curse, someone yelling, "He's stable," as if he's a fine horse, a stallion, a Derby winner, and that's a pleasant image, reminding him of something unplaceable. Maybe it's how the woodsmoke of a fireplace lingers in a sweater's weave through summer into another winter. He wants to speak—he always wants to speak—there's more to say—someone's always going to listen—but mess overwhelms his mind, fast and faster thoughts, until he's afraid, and he's a boy in his North Carolina yard, smelling the rain coming—no—his skin feels stiff and sour, he's hungover in tangled bedsheets, a strange shaft of sun raking his eyes—no—his fingertips balance lightly on his grandmother's cracked leather Bible, the gilt letters worn away—no—move the mic closer—no—none of it is right. Where are the faces? The goddamn faces, he asks, or maybe asks. Where's people on the other side, the bright white light, the beckoning voices? Where's God? Goddamn it, where's goddamn God—forgetting he no longer believes in God or religion, in anything, in anything not himself. No, he says, or maybe says. No one's listening, and he calls, again and again and again and again. Is death silent? If there's noise, can he be dead? He's not doing it right, whatever *right* is, whatever *it* is. He recognizes this mental chaos as fear.

For once, the Speaker is uncertain about what's next. The people he calls for are dead. No one comes to help his broken body, his flailing brain. What does he want to say? What if no one's listening, what if no one who matters is left to listen to him speak? What if everything he wants is wrong?

Her obedient mind—typically so docile, so readily steered and focused—rebels, circling in aimless wafts, turning time into taffy. Sure, she's the body guiding the Audi. But she's also supposed to be the icy shark-brain clicking on next, next, next, next.

Instead, she soothes herself with a particular memory back at the beginning, in 1992, when she's annoyed that:

The cardboard boxes come flat, needing to be constructed—tab A, slot B, flap C. This task she immediately assigns to the interns, huddled near the knot of tangled wiring that kept the phone bank buzzing between nine a.m. and nine p.m. (Eventually cell phones will kill these hives of volunteers armed with talking points, will transform the camaraderie of lively phone banks into individuals collapsed into armchairs at home, tapping numbers off an emailed list, dictating texts. Also, there's the rise of robocalling, which shouldn't work, yet does. But now, in Mary-Grace's memory, phone banks reign, a churning factory creating voice contact with the undecideds.)

Five or six or seven interns remain—not even Mary-Grace knows how many; the woman in charge of the intern program was the first to go, and anyway, the interns' work schedule is capricious, dictated by college classes and hangovers and boredom. Learning a name likely means never seeing that person again, so few staff bother. The interns sit on the floor, lined up like crows where the tables for the phones were. Their backs are propped against the white wall as they assemble box after box with grim determination, mentally revising the paper they'll write for college credit, berating themselves for interning with this candidate instead of another, conveniently forgetting they had no choice—their parent or uncle or godmother or etc. was a donor. This is how jobs come about, a connection opening the door. DONOR is an important word, more important than VOTER. The interns work for free, which is why they're still working.

A wall of fully constructed brown Bankers Boxes stack up.

Mary-Grace knows the interns are not to blame.

It's mostly women remaining, a core group of volunteers in their midthirties, wearing Guess jeans, Keds, and—in loyalty or defiance?—oversize campaign T-shirts they ferreted out from the way-back of the storage closet. What if *all* the shirts had been given away last August at the Iowa State Fair? What if more size Ms had been ordered, enticing women voters, instead of the vast quantities of XXLs for the white male demographic? What if many things?

But these women, with their straight teeth and straight noses, don't second-guess even the tiniest detail or action item, accepting that others make the decisions for a reason. They excel at removing posters from the walls with loving tugs at the tape holding each corner, the same light touch that strokes damp hair off the foreheads of feverish children. These women could rip down the posters, slash through his smile and his name written in the hopeful font preferred by the focus groups. But women intuitively understand that dismantling must be done gently. Their kindness might be reason to value the women, but unfortunately, like the interns, they work for nothing. They don't talk as they roll each poster tight, but maintain an agreeable murmur, punctuated with pecks of laughter.

Older women stand at the file cabinets, fingers tiptoeing along masses of labeled folders, remembering the pleasant precision of centering labels onto tabs. Occasionally, the dancing fingers extract records considered necessary for the next campaign—surely, dear Lord, there will be a next, pleeeease. Selected folders get slipped upright into a box, a phone book propped in back holding them tidy and upright. The rest are stacked flat in boxes labeled "Archives," along with the date and the year, as if anyone could forget either.

(It's understood that shredding has been completed. It's understood not to ask by whom. It's understood to have been Mary-Grace, here last night until three a.m.)

Mary-Grace knows these women are not to blame.

Paper clips glitter on the coffee-stained industrial carpeting, as if flung by the handful like poor man's confetti, and the communications director has assigned herself the peculiar task of picking them up one by one, which means she's crawling hands and knees in her black Donna Karan pantsuit, plucking up each paper clip and dropping it into a metal wastebasket adorned with hopeful-font bumper stickers. Plink. It's her fault, she thinks, though it isn't—Mary-Grace knows that—but it's convenient for her to imagine otherwise.

A couple of staffers wander desk to desk, scribbling numbers from Rolodexes onto yellow legal pads. A team of men appears with a dolly to silently load up the Xerox machine, rolling it away, one wheel squeaking fiercely. There's discussion about who's taking the microwave with its crust of scorched popcorn grease. The stained coffee mugs have been picked through, and the remainder are loaded into a box with the half-plan to donate them to a thrift store. "And the microwave," someone instructs, resulting in a lifeless argument about whether the Salvation Army accepts microwaves. Finally, the intern with carroty-red hair requests the mugs and the microwave for an apartment he and his girlfriend are moving into next week, and everyone is relieved.

There's no one to blame. There's no one to blame. The words rattle illogically in Mary-Grace's head, and she speaks them out loud at random: "No one's to blame." Sideways glances are exchanged, but no one dares utter the words being telegraphed. (He's to blame, entirely.)

Everyone understands that Mary-Grace is in charge of his desk, the antique oak rolltop he brought in, paying the movers himself with folded bills. So special, his elegant desk landing in this volunteer office, as if this office is more important than the others, these people more trusted. Everything feels special: the way he lines up blue pens on the left side of the desk pad like train tracks; his binder clips linked in a long chain; yellow legal pads, each with extrathick cardboard backing, stacked two inches high, some filled with his craggy handwriting, notes and lists no one dares read now; a pair of horsehead bookends propping upright a college dictionary and an empty datebook from a stationer in England. Now no one touches anything, not even the Puffs Plus with lotion, bought at the drug store across the street because the office supply company didn't carry the Puffs Plus he demanded. Not the bottle of Absolut in the bottom drawer. Especially not the silver-framed photos: wife, daughter, son, son, new baby. Perfect family, perfect in the brochures and TV commercials, at the rallies. No one wants to think about the family. Mary-Grace knows they're not to blame.

No one's seen him for four days. No one admits to feeling panic; "he's taking some time to reflect" is the story they slip to reporters. "We ask that the family's privacy be respected." But they speculate: he's perched on a stool at the nickel slots in Atlantic City; he's sleeping off a handful of Valium in a tent in the mountains of North Carolina; he's time-traveled back to his precious fourteenth-century Scottish highlands, wearing a kilt and storming a castle; he's stowed away on a Greek container ship en route to the Philippines. No one dares think worse. No one dares call him. If he wants to talk to them, he knows where they are: here, cleaning up this mess.

It's understood that Mary-Grace will not allow anyone to say or think or even half-think, *His* mess.

"I can't be mad at him," she whispers, staring too long at her calm face reflected in the ladies' room mirror. When she's checking tasks off the list in her head, she's fine: forward mail, cancel coffee delivery, hand over the philodendrons to a responsible woman. Yet the desk stays untouched. She won't dismantle it in front of the others, doesn't want them hovering about, scavenging the scraps. Also, as long as the desk remains, he's not entirely gone. She's not known for irrational thought, but she allows herself this tiny luxury.

At the end of the day, the interns are instructed to leave three empty boxes on top of his desk, "in case he decides to come in later," Mary-Grace says, though everyone knows the property manager and her team are sweeping through in the morning. There will be paperwork, and within the week the sign will be plastered across the window: FOR LEASE.

There's a long, enthusiastic round of "Let's keep in touch!" that Mary-Grace participates in, and she promises to join them at the bar around the block "in a bit," though they know she won't. They zip jackets, chatter as they depart in clumps: "I'm numb," someone says, "but mostly I'm exhausted." Someone else says, "Even when your head knows, I swear your heart never does." How dare you walk away, she wants to shriek at their backs as she smiles and waves.

Once everyone's gone, Mary-Grace turns out the lights and sits at the desk as she does when she's alone and crunching through tasks. The leather swivel chair is more comfortable than her folding chair, more important.

The shadowy room echoes, though no one's here. What's supposed to happen to her now? Go back home to marry someone or be a receptionist for some insurance guy? Someone else ends up president, and she'll care?

She tries to gouge her thumbnail into the polished wood, which is impermeable. It's not like any of this is personal, she thinks.

The phone rings, and she can't not answer, though definitely she called the phone company yesterday to disconnect the line. Because no one's there to care, she growls, "You've reached me," immediately thrilling to the arrogance of withholding her name. Booyah!

No one speaks, but she's certain she hears breathing behind the static. She loops her finger through the spirals of the cord, picks up one of his blue pens with her other hand and chews on the cap, something she's never done before in her life. There's no flavor; what's the appeal? She waits. And if she spends her whole life waiting? she thinks, unsure where the thought comes from, what it means.

Finally he says, "Mary-Grace? That you? You haven't left."

She untangles herself from the phone cord, feeling alive and alert.

"How bad is it?" he asks.

She wants him now to wait and wait, so she stays silent. She tosses the pen across the room, tosses another, another, until the whole line of blue pens has flown through the shadows.

He's patient, as if he knows she needs to finish this task. They're that aligned. In a meeting, she writes down his idea before he has it. He won't rip out newspaper articles, only cut them neatly with scissors, as she does, and clips the fringe off paper torn from spiral notebooks, also as she does. Neither can stand people who stir coffee fast. "You still there?" he asks.

What if she let the phone ring and ring? What if she were in her car, driving home? Or at the bar, with the others, the door slammed shut, no problem? "Uh-huh," she says. "Where are you, sir?"

"Have you ever been painfully, excruciatingly happy?" he asks. "Even for one moment?"

"No." Her answer jumps out quickly, with a deep honesty that frightens her. Those are terrible words to describe happiness, yet they're hers too, because they each know that's the only happiness worth having, the kind that makes you ache. She can't tell him this.

He says, "Well, I guess I don't mean . . . How 'bout let's say regular happy then?"

"Oh that, sure." These past years absolutely have been the happiest of her life. Working for him. People treating her like she's important because he tells them she is: "Here's the real brains," he introduces her, "here's my right arm." Imagining someone small and ordinary like her might end up with a White House office, a security clearance, an access badge of the right color. Everyone around her believing in big ideas and this big man carrying them forward. Being busy turns every minute precious, and days sparkle into weeks. Why's that not happy enough? What's lacking? She's abnormal. His questions disturb her. He rarely asks anything beyond the logistics of an event, a mailing, or a meeting. He's a stranger, even as he's the man whose sandwich order she could recite backward in her sleep.

His palm scratches against the phone, and there's a muffled, "I will in a sec." Back to her, he asks, "You should ask me if I'm happy."

"I'm not sure that's my business, sir," she says. After a moment, she adds, "I assume you are."

"Things blow over," he says. "Like any storm. Next day, there's the sun, rising."

Tree limbs crash through roofs, she thinks, as waters rise.

"I'll weather this," he says.

I, she thinks, I, I, I, I. I! "Of course, sir," she says. "Yes."

He coughs. "Well, I called to make sure you packed up my desk. Which you did because you're my marvel of efficiency."

"I'm about to get to it," she says, glancing at the empty boxes the interns left. Naturally, she'll do this final thing for him. He won't want much, maybe the . . . Abruptly she says, "No. Come pack it yourself." That thrilling surge of power. "Sir."

He laughs, as if she's funny, as if he doesn't jokingly demand at least once a day that she "lighten the heck up."

How does he not feel tension zinging the phone line? Her mouth turns tight and grim in the dark. He's her boss, her contract paid through the end of the month. The man believed to have a shining path to the presidency. She pokes a finger at one of the boxes on top of the desk, nudges it askew. She says, "You let everyone down." You let *me* down, she thinks, then says that, too.

He says, "Fine, so dump everything in storage, and the desk, too." His sigh is huffy, impatient. Worrying over furniture. She, Mary-Grace, is furniture.

A moment later he says, "Come on, Mary-Grace, sweetie. I need those bookends at least. And there are some files on—"

"No." She speaks very clearly so there's no confusion.

"Damnit," he says. "Do your job."

"I am," she says. "I'm telling you the truth. I'm saying what you need to hear, not what you want to hear. That's what you told me when—"

"Fuck you," he says. "I'm happy, and you're fucking fired."

He slams down the phone. She continues to clutch the receiver, waiting until she hears shrill beeps. Only the truth feels this way, she thinks, hanging up. She pulls out the bottom drawer and, her hands shaking, unscrews the Absolut cap and rocket downs a burning-hot swallow. Sifts out the four files she knows he means and drops them into one of the boxes. Hefts the two heavy, ugly horsehead bookends in on top. Adds the clay ashtray his daughter made in school that he likely meant to mention. Slips her purse into the box so everything's easy to carry to her car. Checks the trustworthiness of the seal on the vodka bottle, then adds that, cushioning it with her purse. She's angry, knowing he knows she's doing exactly as he asked.

The phone rings. Automatically, she reaches out, then freezes, her hand midair. It's a test. So insulting. What an insulting *pig*, and she flings the word loudly into the desolate room. Even so, even still, she wants so badly to pass, to please. She folds her arms across her chest.

The phone rings and rings. Sixteen times, she counts. Then twelve. Then six. Then twice, twice, twice. One last ring that, if possible, sounds angrier than the others. The silence is excruciating.

Did she pass the test?

No, because she imagines him wherever he is, worrying about his stupid bookends, so she picks up the box and heads to her car, locking the office for the last time. Waiting to turn left out of the parking lot, she flashes onto an exquisite moment of painful happiness, exactly what he was talking about, when the substitute filling in for Miss Clayton, the unmarried sixth grade teacher everyone knew got "knocked up," called her to the desk on the last day and whispered, "You're a smart girl, Mary-Grace. Smartest I've seen. And I'm begging you just to keep your own self out of the muck." The scorch of these words instantly confirmed everything Mary-Grace was afraid to feel about her shoddy family; the rows of stooped, quarter-wit students dozing at their desks; this forgettable substitute teacher, bulky in her shapeless cardigan, breathing oniony breath. "Yes, ma'am," Mary-Grace said politely, but her insides were Fourth of July fireworks.

Now, now, turning left out of the parking lot, it's another scorching moment where she understands what actually happened in the office, whose test it was: hers. HERS. He called her back from *wherever* (the hell) he is, called her again and then again, needing her, begging her to pick up, furious at the truth. Next time she'll say, "You've reached me," and be ready with demands. Next time—because whatever the *this* is that he's doing won't be forever. Mary-Grace can wait. If she needs him, he needs her more. This realization only seems like a small thing.

Wherever he is:

The Speaker is not in North Carolina or Atlantic City or fourteenth-century Scotland or tucked away on a container ship. He is not reflecting, though he approves that his staff floats this possibility. Mostly during these few weeks, he's in a king-size bed fucking his new fiancée (ignoring the tricky fact of his undivorced wife). If the two aren't fucking, they're talking about fucking, and if they aren't talking about fucking, they're dozing after fucking. It's a "do not disturb" pre-honeymoon, with no plan whatsoever except more fucking and random room service from the 24-hour menu, since their hunger pangs come at all hours, with no regard to the normal cycle of meals and life beyond the walls of the Greenbrier. "I want scrambled eggs," she might say after the eleven o'clock news; "How about fried chicken?" he asks at nine-thirty in the morning. The TV is on constantly, muted, and she likes fucking while their faces flash on the screen. She squeals: "Lookit me, I'm someone now!" Her voice has a jagged, husky edge, like the teeth of a saw. She tells him stories that she claims to make up, though they vaguely sound like the plots of movies he's read about, so he rarely pays attention to the words, just the patterns of sounds moving up and down, back and forth. What a delight. She's a delight.

He deserves this delight.

As long as he never leaves the Terrace Suite—the complimentary courtesy upgrade given to him when he checked in, alone, a decision the hotel surely regrets now—everything will be a delight forever and ever after, which is how she ends her stories because, she says, "Happy endings can't ever go out of style, aren't I right?"

Later, there'll be time for ponderous questions revolving around words like "self-sabotage" and "hubris" and "shame" and "self-loathing" and "supreme arrogance," and all the rest of the bullshit he'll bullshit through. "I love her," he'll say. "If that means I can't be president, I'm dying a happy man anyhow. Happy endings never go out of style in our great country, am I right?"

By then, he'll know every word's a lie. By then, he'll understand what his vicious grandmother crowed about, that he would be his own undoing, that the seeds of destruction are planted early and planted deep within. (He'll think himself unique in this regard.) He'll flail about, struggling to find fault and assign blame, secretly consulting psychiatrists and psychics, letting himself be hypnotized, paying a fistful of money for a natal chart from Nancy Reagan's astrologer that won't say squat. He feels himself born for great things, or so he's been told, and so he's told himself, and therefore, this, all of it, must be a "great thing." He can try again, beginning at the beginning. He spins platitudes. He smiles. He glosses over details. He denies. Too proud to ask forgiveness. Too selfish to understand what forgiveness means. Too chickenshit to say, "Sorry." No one who's anyone wants his phone calls.

Then, goddamn it, the baby dies. The baby *dies*. His son. Blake. (The special name she's been keeping locked and loaded, picked out back as a little girl playing dolls . . . "please, please," she said. The solution to "what to do about her" simplifies: ignore, until she disappears.) "No one knows why this happens," every doctor explains, but everyone in America knows: punishment. Fuck god, he mutters through the incessant nights, fuck me, fuck me, fuck me.

He's humbled.

He's humbled, and goddamn, Mary-Grace says it when he calls, says what he only thinks: *now he's got something to use*. She speaks the unspeakable words like each syllable's a rainbow, and he gags, yanking the phone from the wall. But she's right, and he calls her back to say so without saying so. So fuck you, god. He'll use it. He has no fucking shame: beloved baby *dead*, so now his calls go through. People pity him. Throw in the oh, ouch, twofer of being abandoned by this silly, two-bit wife. He's hauling in checks, exuding everyman pain, making his eyes go glossy like his soul's haunted. He mirrors compassion at the tales of woe unspooled by others. Recites in a whisper every morning when he wishes he were dead, "Bad news is opportunity."

It's her idea, he convinces himself, just a small thing.

Now, he can beg. He begs for forgiveness without believing a single word he speaks and just about falls on the floor when the American people lap it up, exactly as Mary-Grace predicts. He admires the forgiving American people. He admires the system that allows him this massively colossal fuck-up, allows this "scandal of the century" to shrink as more scandalous scandals press in, as the century turns.

Anyway, after the Dealmaker blows through, no scandal matters and the Speaker's cynicism solidifies. Having been forgiven, having been given an undeserved second chance (several times), he believes differently: it's not that he is destined for greatness, but that greatness cannot exist. *Forgive me* is something to say not because you're sorry, but because you've cracked the code.

"Being forgiven has made me feel God's love, has put me near godliness, has shown me how truly blessed I am." How has such a thing happened, he wonders—sometimes out loud—what hubris or fear or what *what*; what poisonous quality lives inside his heart that led him—leads him—toward such casual, wholesale destruction. He awaits punishment, but by whom? Logic is his comfort: If he refuses to believe in either a god who punishes or in a god who doesn't, then he's free to believe in nothing. If anyone asks, he can live with himself just fine. Who, in this town, asks?

Box up God. Box up Blake—a name he never liked much, not a name he would've chosen himself.

But these things happen in the future. This comes later. Now is the fucking. More fucking. He is fucking even as he understands, totally, that also he *is* fucked, yes, he knows how fucked he is. But: the fucking comes first.

The next morning, the property manager arrives with her clipboard and sees the desk and the silver-framed photos and the yellow legal pads and the pens on the floor in the sea of the empty room. She wants to scoff (she hates politics, never bothers to vote). Instead, she notices a more complicated response that's not quite sadness but maybe mournful yearning. Does she long for a man to give up all of his everything for her? Does she remember her own father abandoning her mother when she was thirteen, never to be heard from again?

Does she wonder how one man could rally millions, how millions of people might believe a single human could fix it all, could have something necessary to say? Does she glimpse something larger than herself? Does she think, "What if?"

She keeps the desk because it's solid oak and looks worth some money, and because her husband's got a pickup truck, which means she won't have to pay to haul it home.

Swirling lights and sirens technically are not unfamiliar, though this interior vantage point of them is, but they give way to the chemical smell of cold metal. A clattering hallway. Lights ablaze. Tubes, wires, an insistent clicking. Pale, forgettable eyes impassively regarding his mound of flesh.

His mind—joyfully assured; forcibly emptied of all doubt and most nuance long ago; elegant in its sculpted simplicity; razored into a narrow keenness—seizes upon what it knows, grapples toward comfort—the finger pressing the bruise, the tongue wedging into the emptiness of the missing tooth. His exacting mind latches onto a beloved image—which could've been that first January day he came to official DC or could've been yesterday—which is:

Pre-evening. Pre-evening is the preferred time for this particular walk, tracing the dozen or so long blocks of Pennsylvania Avenue NW amid a liquid glow of pinks and lavender-blues as the day's light settles and slips down into darkness. The between is where he feels comfortable, neither light nor dark, neither right nor wrong, neither Democrat nor Republican. It goes without saying that he will admit this to no one, least of all to himself. But he has been this way always, drawn to the middle, understanding that the world, that all of life, is middle more than edges.

The avenue is congested: heaving Metrobuses groan across multiple lanes; commuters whiz home like silver balls lighting pinball machines; cars and bikes dodge and careen in tandem; there's the crisscross of pedestrians texting their tardiness and tales of office woe. Only he is calm. Only he is serene, strolling the broad sidewalks as if they unfurl for him.

Like a king on promenade is how he pictures himself, a king strolling to his castle is the image in his mind. A homecoming after negotiating a treaty with the pesky French; or the Knights of the Round Table scattered, left behind, and he, the last warrior, returning from war. Odysseus. If only he were here on a horse, he thinks, he dares to think. Camelot hovers like mist in the back of his mind. *Camelot.*

Traffic lights scarcely interrupt his flow.

No one recognizes him, not the commuters, not the haggard five-museums-in-five-hours tourists, not the South Asian vendors hawking T-shirts off their boxy white trucks. A homeless man or two spins for a second look, but that's all, and is, perhaps, coincidence. He's anonymous, tap-tapping in his Crockett & Jones shoes, handmade for him in England, his head filled with . . . well, nothing beyond a pleasant sense of undisturbed satisfaction.

The light moves swiftly, coming earlier in the winter. He must leave his office by 4:30 to arrive at 1600 at the precise moment. There's urgency to this quest, to the way he calls to his staffers that he's headed "out" for "a bit" and they understand not to ask where or why, not to ask anything. Mary-Grace is to thank for their training, not that he is conscious of knowing this.

Most assume a love affair, a tryst: woman, man, boy, girl, girls, women, men, boys. "Nothing would surprise me," some of the staffers sniff, but this, actually, would surprise them, his love affair with the falling light, with this place, with this lost and dead dream, the thing that once was. Many staffers are too fresh, too certain of themselves to fathom this journey. Others were, he thinks, when he thinks at all of this team of people who work for him, who run his life, who run him, these others—and maybe most—are too programmed, lacking any wilderness in their souls. He wouldn't be quoted saying this, ever, but in his deepest heart, he knows that his secret, what keeps him going, is that tiny bit of wilderness still alive in his soul.

It's fashionable to bemoan the closure of Pennsylvania Avenue, a consequence of the everlasting threat of terrorists—but he likes feeling dropped suddenly out of city streets, straight into Lafayette Park: its earnest kooks to his right; joggers lacing their way through the block with grim determination; and to his left, the tourists gape-mouthed and slow-moving like fish cluttering a cold aquarium; Secret Service and stiff-backed cops; the black bars of the iron fence; and now a new and irritating safety fence creating a fresh perimeter. Encompassing all this, a certain unique glow. The day's last gleams receding into unknown depths, streetlights flickering to bright life, the tourists tilting their phones and iPads into shimmering rectangles trying to capture it all, their faces slack with awe—"There it is," they murmur—gawking as if the president might pop outside to toss a football or fire up a grill, as if the president might be ordinary—and the godlike silvery-white glow of the building itself, a beckoning, like yearning in a dream, the thing or the essence of the thing he has chased his entire life, what he sacrificed for, before he was conscious of what sacrifice or pursuit truly meant.

The thing he will never have.

He is not a king returning to a castle nor a king battling for a castle. Camelot forever belongs to someone else. He's only a man standing on the outside, looking in. This is who he has been from the very beginning. Not that he understands this.

Not that he could admit it to himself if he did. It's just a walk, an ordinary evening walk. Nothing epic.

And there . . . just that quick . . . oh, how the light shifts; he sees the light shift. What if he hadn't—? What if he had—? If only.

Don't worry.

The American People forget their presidents too. "Who is the" quickly autofills to "president" in a Google search. Here are twelve names. Which is not a former president, was not—once—the most powerful man in the world?

Chester A. Arthur ~ Herbert Hoover ~ James Buchanan ~ John Tyler ~ Martin Van Buren ~ Millard Fillmore ~ Rutherford B. Hayes ~ Samuel Johnston ~ Thomas Hawkins Hanson ~ Warren G. Harding ~ William Henry Harrison ~ William McKinley

The American People forget because the American People prefer their slates clean. Time tidies messes, and history writes and rewrites, saving asses again and again. What politician doesn't run on some form of "A New Beginning"?

If they forget the presidents, they'll forget you. Instead, ask yourself this: Then who *will* remember? Speak that name, say it, call it: insignificant as it is. Understand that in the end, there's always power in the small and the ordinary.

KILL THE FATTED CALF

Memory leaves us helpless.

When I turn eleven, sucking in too much breath for the big blow-out-my-birthday-candles moment and wishing in my head, *horse-horse-horse*, my father interrupts: "If you want something vast, Lexie, you start out on something small."

The first gift I open is a pair of iron horsehead bookends, too heavy to hold in one hand. He tells me he selected them from a furniture store, a set for me, and a matching pair for his office. My lined-up Baby-Sitters Club paperbacks suddenly look important on their shelves. When he works late, scribbling on a yellow legal pad, unconsciously spinning his leather desk chair that way he does, jumping up to pace, I imagine the horses' dark eyes following him. I imagine the horses offering the advice he's looking for, unlike my horses, which stay silent despite the secrets I share. I name mine Pet and Pal, and his Blackie and Ghost. I imagine he tells them the things he tells me: "I'm going to change the world," he likes to say. "Wait and see. I'll be president someday." The truth of these words burns in my heart, grows into facts. "Congressman first," he says. "Start with something small."

"My dad will be president," I tell kids at school as I divvy up bumper stickers printed with his name.

"He's going to be president," my mother tells me. "So, no, you can't expect he has time to watch you in *The Nutcracker*."

Sundays are best because he won't dare miss church with us. Sundays are the two of us walking hand-in-hand up the aisle to the pew his family has sat in for generations, me in my shiny-white shoes and white eyelet dress. Admiration ripples from the ladies wearing pastel suits. My brothers behind us, my sister not yet born, my mother at the back. Once I whisper that I'm going to grow up and marry him, and he says, "You better." Afterward, we watch as he stands on the sidewalk to talk, ringed by clusters of people. "You'll be president one day," they say.

When he leaves us, when he leaves me, I grab Pet and Pal off the bookshelf and heave them with a tremendous, rattling *thunk* into the kitchen trash can. Their weight whooshes the plastic bag off the rim. My mother dumps coffee grounds on top, eggshells, the peeled-off casings from sausages, orange rinds, and then the entire breakfast none of us eats that morning.

This afternoon at the hospital, my father's wife, #4, tells me, "You know, in DC, we're more than one thing."

"No one anywhere is only one thing," I say. "DC's not so unique."

"Here we have to remind ourselves," she says. "Because here we're expected to choose, right *or* left, red *or* blue, this *or* that, one *or* the other."

"I get it," I say, to stop her from going on.

She's claimed the only chair, and though she's dauntingly thin, she sprawls corner to corner, no upholstery visible. She crosses and recrosses her legs, trying to lure my father back into consciousness by flashing her bronzed and burnished skin.

A moment later she adds, as if here's the important part, "What I mean is, he's in there somewhere, even if he won't respond."

"I understand what a coma is."

"But that's not what we're talking about," she says. "Right, Lexie?"

Once, I was my father's favorite. Experts say that girls who enjoy close relationships with their fathers grow up well-adjusted and often take leadership positions. There are other wonderful outcomes, long lists of famous women who were "Daddy's girl."

I was his favorite: which is different than having a *close relationship*. What I understand now is that I became his favorite because I didn't push to be close. He counted on me to stay content with what was given, leaving room for others.

Late on summer nights—later than a child should be awake—my father let me play solitaire with a deck of cards, the two of us side-by-side on the screened-in porch. Cicadas buzzing, a cone of lamplight, me cross-legged on the floor, him on the slouchy sofa. He with his martini, me with the Tab and skim milk my mother let me drink because she said she knew I wanted to stay skinny; an "ice cream float" she called it, and I had no idea it wasn't. He'd watch me set the deck, flip cards until I lost or won (no cheating with him right there). Game after game, because he said he needed these dark hours to think through his day and tomorrow, rerunning and anticipating conversations with people; "How's he helping me now, how's he going to help me eventually," was always the calculation, and, "Is he with me, or just another bastard?"

I slapped down cards with authority because he liked the *whap*, and after each game, I passed the deck to him to shuffle (he perfectly arched the bridge of cards in a way I couldn't, not even with practice, not even now). Sacred time, these nights. My mother fussed that he didn't point out the plays I was missing, wouldn't suggest, "red eight on the black nine." "She's a kid," my mother said to him, "and you're an adult. You're supposed to help her."

"This little girl's way too independent for that," he said, and I imagined I was.

This afternoon. It's a hospital with valet parking. "Take my car," I tell the man wearing the fluorescent yellow vest, "and keep it." He laughs because surely he's heard it all. I'm exhausted: the unexpected drive up from North Carolina, the surprise of being in DC. Adding up time to understand I haven't spoken to my father for a dozen years. My important father. My father who's Speaker of the House. My human father. My father in a coma.

"Ma'am," the valet murmurs the way people address hurt animals backed into corners, because I'm clutching my car keys. I offer my clenched fist, wanting him to pry back my fingers one by one, peeling me open. He looks into space, and my mind forces my hand to loosen, forces me to drop the keys on the dash. "Thank you," he says, as if I'm doing him the service.

Whatever's going to happen is finally happening.

I chat with various people at various desks, with suited men wearing earpieces; I walk and am walked through airless corridors, following the red path, the blue path, stopping in a bathroom just because there it is and I figure I should; I present my ID, speak with immense persuasion to prove I'm who I am: his daughter. Real family. ("Oh, we thought . . ."; I know exactly what they thought. "Yes, there are other daughters," I grit out, "and other wives and the other woman, yes, it's all complicated. My father's very complicated." Meaning, my life is very, very complicated.

At long last, I'm in an aggressively generic private waiting room: bland walls lined with bland furniture, a carpet that's forgettable even as I gaze at it, a beige Kleenex box centered on a coffee table. It's a room built for crummy news and sadness, the sort of room with no focus beyond what's at hand: sickness, resignation, tough luck, anxiety. Not even a blathering TV; I don't want one except as something specific to hate. My options are glaring at the prints of simplistic ocean views, two hanging crookedly on each wall, or the hand-sanitizer station by the door. I could dredge up my phone, but apparently, I left it in the car. I half-hope the valet steals it.

It's likely the girl is here too, that they brought her to this same close-by hospital.

That waterfall of emptiness, having a sister I don't know, don't want to know, can't know. I don't understand how I feel about her, beyond an ache if I think of her, or the others, each from a different woman—the new toddler twins, or the baby boy who died—or my own scattered siblings.

My lips stiffen into an indeterminate grimace, I glance wildly for a clock or watch. Is a family made of memories or of blood? Is "family" a fairy tale we tell or are told so we can sleep at night?

She has a name. Which is . . . won't kill me . . . say it . . . Madison.

"I wouldn't have lifted one finger to try to save him," I announce, though the room's empty. This teenager, this girl, this half-sister of mine who's also not mine was with my father during the attack and leapt into the path of the knife, ending up stabbed. (According to the internet.)

I'm sorry, but I can't suddenly care. I mean, beyond vague hopes of general good wishes that she's okay and doesn't die.

I understand that I'm furious at this girl, at my phantom sister—let me count the ways—for thinking herself brave, for believing she's suddenly important, for not yet knowing all the things I know about our father. I repeat myself: "I wouldn't have lifted one finger." How great to shout inside a hospital!

I imagine someone wise murmuring, "Is it possible you might surprise yourself?"

I shake my head, hard. Let Madison grab all the glory. Let her think she saved him, let her believe none of the rest of us tried.

In the car, driving through last night to reach today, I imagine asking him to forgive me. I imagine him begging me to forgive him. I imagine us simultaneously saying, "Let's leave the past behind." Imagine my heart melting and his heart growing three sizes. My voice awakening him—a medical miracle! Him dead before I arrive. I imagine a swirl of feeling everything and also the blankness of feeling nothing.

Imagine myself spinning reporters a poignant story of reconciliation. Or grunting, "No comment," and scribbling avalanches of thoughts onto the empty pages of a journal. Telling no one or walking into a bar afterward and telling everyone everything. Finding a man to fuck and telling him to hurt me, telling him harder, no, really: *harder*.

I imagine a jam-packed hospital room, laughter, and shared stories. Pulling up a hard chair, just us two. Spooning him soup. Machines beeping and nurses spilling in, elbowing me aside. A window in this room, a cardinal in a tree. Darkness shrouding the room, shadows, a chill, a distant train whistle. Sunlight, wafting breezes, chattering kids on swings in a park across the street. My father saying, "I knew you'd come. I knew you'd be here." Or saying, "I never thought you'd come." Or, "No one asked you to come." Or just, "Who are you?"

I'm driving to see him because I imagined I'd have a father to hate forever.

"It's believed that people in comas hear us speak," the doctor tells us, meaning me and my father's wife. We are three women standing outside an ICU bay, nothing in common beyond the body of the man in the coma. "Talk to him," the doctor says. "Familiar voices definitely help." She punctuates her command with snapping nods, someone accustomed to orders being followed. Her eyes stare at a space above my head, perhaps a trick taught in med school to safely avoid eye contact.

"Is *my* voice familiar?" I ask, too nervous to keep wrong words from leaking out.

Same series of nods. The wife nods. Everyone knows the answer to this easy question.

I hold back other words: Do I want to help?

Later the waiting room door opens, and a woman steps in, then lets the door click gently shut. She's too old to be anyone my father would marry; maybe a careful fifty passing for forty-three. She reeks of officialdom: efficiency combined with undercurrents of urgency and stifled anxiety. I'm both soothed and alarmed to see her, certain she's from my father's office. She's got to be that person who knows everything and does everything, meaning even this, especially this—dealing with the surprise appearance of the surprise daughter (the original surprise child—one of several; people say, "Too many to count"; people say, "Ever hear of birth control?"). (Yes, my fetal appearance is why he married my mother, and why she married him; I'm the surprise child who wasn't scandalous because he wasn't Very Important back then.)

I ponder how this woman was selected to deal with me. Versus a white-coated doctor, someone impersonal and professional droning medical terms. Versus the actual wife. Likely this woman selected herself with, "I'll take care of it," an assurance she undoubtedly delights in.

She sanitizes her hands at the dispenser, rubs her palms briskly, then goes finger by finger. My hands suddenly feel dirty, but it's not like I can jump up and copycat sanitize.

She makes her way to the chair directly across the coffee table from me and pulls it close, as if future conversation will be whispered. We do the size-up, eyeing each other. She sits perfectly still, except for the sanitized fingers of one hand, which fiddle at a triple strand of pearls around her neck. Excellent posture, ankles crossed, the way southern mothers teach girls to sit. She's someone who pulls out answers, versus me, unable even to ask proper questions.

I'm sitting here, yet I'm falling, spinning back through time, my father in North Carolina, announcing at an otherwise normal Sunday dinner, "Your mother's kicking me out," no sugar helping send those sour words down, nor my mother's immediate retort: "Your father cheated on me and won't make the girl get an abortion because of his so-called political career." To this day, she denies saying it. It's true, but *she* didn't tell me, she tells me.

"So you're Lexie," the woman says, dragging me back to now. "I'm Mary-Grace Ledford." We lean in to shake hands. Her grip is strong, practiced. Mine must feel vague and random, so I smile brightly to compensate. She's not wearing any rings, which is disorienting, as if she's breaking a law, though I'm also ringless.

I say, "I'm here to see my father."

Mary-Grace says, "That's the thing. This is sort of a shock, you here."

"I'm his daughter," I say. "From the first family."

"I know who you are," she says.

I try joking, as if something here is funny: "The prodigal daughter."

She shakes her head slowly. "His wife doesn't want you here." Her turn to smile brightly, pretending her statement's palatable. Her teeth could use some whitening. I'm happy seeing this flaw in her perfect face, so I can forget my own myriad flaws—my awful leggings that barely match my awful flannel shirt, my general dishevelment from this awful, unplanned trip, the trail of bad decisions made last night, this morning, throughout my life.

That quick spiral through various regrets doesn't let me escape the words: the wife doesn't want me here.

I agree. I don't want to be here either. Yet here I am.

The biblical story that obsesses me as a child is that of the prodigal son: the younger brother who squanders his share of the family fortune on wine and women. Once the money's gone he slithers back home, willing to live with the pigs. The dutiful brother is pissed because Dad's thrilled at the younger brother's return and commands the servants to put out a fabulous welcome-home feast, nailing the decision in a line I whisper: "Kill the fatted calf."

So unfair. (Says the dutiful daughter.)

My father explains: "Remember when you lost your Cabbage Patch doll, then found her two days later in the sandbox? You weren't mad she was gone. You were only happy she was back. Right?"

Wrong. I despised the responsibility of that doll; my mother bought it, knowing I'd never ask for one. I buried it in the sandbox myself. But I give my father an agreeable nod, so he'll grant approval: "There we go."

Now I'm the prodigal.

Now my father's become—surprise!—some sort of militant atheist, which is why he was attacked by a conspiracy nut at the Kennedy Center, knifed and knocked over, his head smashing against the marble floor, which became more the problem than the stabbing. No one knows why he gave up on God except for rumors of dementia, and what he says, which is, "I'm gosh-awful tired of pretending something other than science is all-powerful." Fringe religious groups targeted him instantly.

"Two things that don't mix," I imagine Mary-Grace advising him, "are politicians and atheists," which of course he knows. Yet he ignored this good sense, seeking another path of self-destruction.

Consider if it's the father leaving, the father squandering the family's money and pride, squandering the family itself. Why return if other doors fly open and someone else dishes up heaping plates of fatted calf?

Or consider the story from the point of view of the calf.

Mary-Grace says, "I know you. Your childhood picture's on his desk."

"Posed," I say. "For brochures. How long have you worked for him?"

"*With* him," she corrects.

Fine. Let her feel valuable.

"From the beginning," she says. "That first run for president, when everyone compared him to Kennedy."

"But you actually stuck around," I say. "Through the slop. When he fucked himself and his family and the 'true believers' over with the scandals and the everything. Are you crazy in love with him? Or do you just love punishment?"

She says, "There's the photograph of the two of you, where you're sitting on that stunning black horse. And he taped up the picture you painted when you were four, with the splotches and zigzags. There's a clay ashtray you made with yellow-green glaze that's always in the upper left drawer of his desk. I remember—"

"Stop," I say. How many times have I heard a laundry list of checked boxes, him demonstrating love in approved ways? "What about any of this is sincere?"

She nods, as if something has clicked into place, and says, "How lucky to be his favorite."

Can't help it: my easy-sleazy heart beats tra-la-la-la, pounds loud and happy. Not that I want to believe any of this. Life's straightforward with my father locked in the narcissist box.

Mary-Grace sits with unmoving eyes, as if there's an oil portrait superimposed on her face. I've identified the accent peeking out as North Carolina: the south, the past, someone who didn't start out as this gristly DC woman with whatever pompous DC title she has.

"Then why haven't we spoken in more than ten years?" I ask.

"Why are you here?" she asks right back.

Like every politician, my father often proclaimed, "Family is everything," even as he destroyed each of his various families, one by one, as mindlessly as me scraping aside the grainy anthills bubbling up through the cracks of the sidewalk in front of our house. "Get your hands out of the dirt," my mother would say. "Nice girls don't play with bugs."

I say, "Family is everything, I guess."

She says, "To be close to an important man, allowances are made. That's understood here in DC. We don't need to say it."

Someone advised him. *Cut your losses* now. *They're fine without you.* I imagine Mary-Grace, dewy and sweet, making a decision back then to say, "Starter family," in her North Carolina drawl. Now she says, "He told me that losing you was the only regret of his life."

No. No, no, no. No. This ache is the bones I've built my life upon. This scar proves I exist.

What he used to tell me: "When you grow up you'll have a beautiful baby girl who's going to be the only person in the whole world I could ever love as much as you."

What I tell myself: One more year. Next year. This guy'd be a good father. That guy. Next year. Next week. Suddenly I'm forty.

I slump back into the sofa, pushing hard to make the cushion give and give, ready to focus on moving the immovable force of Mary-Grace. Maybe I'm unsure about why I want to see my father, but I don't want to not see him. I came all this way, I think, I drove all night. No, wait, I drove four hours. Talk, or she will.

"I could donate blood," I say. "I've got quarts and quarts." I know blood doesn't come in quarts, but the right word's a blank because time's rocketing me backward: "How do I even know she's mine?" my father shouts, and my mother shouts back, "Just look at her. That's your damn blood like poison in her veins."

Mary-Grace slips into her accent: "The Speaker has plenty of blood. But thank you. I'll pass along your offer to the doctors."

"And his wife," I say.

"This is your message to her?" she says. "You came here to donate blood?"

I hold my breath. Doing that turns you invisible. "Did it work?" I asked my mother, who said, "Yes, to your father we're invisible." My breath rushes out way too loud. "I need a message to see my own father?"

Mary-Grace runs one hand through her short, expensively colored hair. The stack of bracelets on her forearm clinks, the only sound in the room. She clutches them into silence with her other hand, leaving her arms awkward and twisted above her head, paused as if she's an anguished marble statue, a figure in a Greek myth. She says, "Sorry. It's typical DC think: What's the message?" She unfolds the peculiar arrangement of her arms, pleating them neatly against her chest. "It's the wife you're up against, not me," she says. "I'm on your side."

"You know him best," I say.

If a one-shoulder shrug could be proud, hers is.

"If I may," she says, "all you want from this situation with your father is a little bit of peace. That's what you want. What you deserve." She studies me, then nudges the tissue box my way, knowing I want to cry before I do.

I sob, slammed by a hurricane. I don't know why. I hate my father. Those words don't scare me. I often say to any well-meaning, do-gooder friend, "I hate my father." How is that also *I love him*? How is it?

My hand rakes tissues out of the pop-top: institutional, functional, lacking comfort. Perfect for how people cry in this terrible room. Wipe eyes, blow nose, blow, blow. A half dozen used tissues pile up. She walks to the corner of the room and carries back a small metallic trash can that she extends. It's partially filled with tissues and I add mine.

She stands in front of me, suddenly taller than I thought. "You need to hear this," she says, and my muscles tense solid. She repeats: "Losing you is the only regret of his life. He'll never stop loving you."

I laugh, hoping to piss her off. As if I hadn't heard this tired line a trillion times, as if I hadn't whispered it to myself, believing it until so much time ticked away that I couldn't. "Oh, please," I say. "This particular problem isn't solved by paying off a girl or marrying one or divorcing another one or dumping a family into oblivion. This isn't buying a sad girl a horse."

She bites her lip, looks away, looks back. "Don't tell anyone, but . . ." she says. "They told me you're the name he called in the ambulance. Not his wife. Not"—she pauses with her mouth open, not finished, then finishes, each word its own outraged sentence—"Not. Even. Me." The trash can slips, knocking against the coffee table and tipping a cascade of used tissues onto the floor. The sound's dramatic in the small room. Immediately, Mary-Grace grabs two fresh Kleenexes from the box and, bending, uses them to pick up tissues with her hands, tossing them back into the trash. Mesmerizing that she doesn't flinch. Anyone would leave this mess for some unseen person to clean up. Could be she's too used to being that person. She plops next to me on the couch, forsaking good posture.

"I don't believe you," I say.

"I find it's hard to hear something that possibly changes everything," she says.

My stupid, hopeful heart. I want to squeeze out all that soppy happiness, wring my emotions back to desert-dry.

"That's why his wife doesn't want you here," she says. "Jealous."

"Of me."

"She doesn't want me here, either." She cocks her head and studies me with X-ray attention. I'm guessing this is the conversation she's been planning since before she walked into the room. Like she's playing chess and I'm the kid in pajamas with a deck of cards.

"Look," I say. "I don't know or care what your deal is with his wife, but he's my father and I've got a right to see him, and if you're not taking me to where he is, I'll talk to someone who will. I want to see him." I let that bit of clarity settle my brain. I've said it. I *know*. I can hate him, and I can want to see him in case he dies.

"She's adamant," Mary-Grace says, "which means we should work together."

Which means let her run everything, I'm guessing, this liar with her confusing statements about my father's regrets. I'm not anyone's simple child anymore, and I can lie too: "Here's my message. I'm pregnant. It's a girl, and I'm naming her after him. Tell her—" I fizzle into silence. I imagine sitting on his bed and making this announcement; I imagine him squeezing my hand, him sitting up and hugging me and saying I love you. I let my mind imagine all the whirling, impossible things. See, I imagine saying, you're happy. I've made you happy.

She stands. "This is the story? You're sticking with it? Baby girl?"

I want to ask if it's a good idea, if it will fly. "It's not a story," I say.

"Congratulations." At the door she turns and says, "A baby. She won't like that much."

My father is famously generous. Buying ponies for little North Carolina girls with brain cancer. Paying the bill for everyone in line at the checkout at the Dollar Tree on Highway 15. A section of his Wikipedia entry is headlined "Legendary Generosity." I check often for updates.

Imagine the entry that might follow "Legendary Generosity," maybe titled "Aftermath." What happened to that pony—named Spotty by six-year-old Kaylee—after Kaylee died? I'm sure my father paid for several months of boarding; let's be optimistic and say a year—but ponies live what, twenty-five, thirty years? How long did Kaylee live? How did her parents feel, knowing Spotty was trotting around a field while their daughter was in a hospital bed, in a grave? What did they think when that boarding bill showed up in their mailbox?

Or at the Dollar Tree, why only one checkout lane? Why not all? What if you were the person who'd plucked out every last quarter from your fistful of coins, and you were at the electric door sensor as my father made his grand announcement: "Everyone in line at lane one, it's all on me"? What if you were the person who showed up too late, after he spoke? What if you weren't chosen?

Politicians don't need to be loved. They only need to *believe* themselves loved, to feel loved. Or maybe that's what someone once said about me.

"Why can't I go live with him?" I ask my mother, who answers, "Because he doesn't want you either."

"When's he going to be president?" I ask my mother, who answers, "After shitting on me like this? Never."

"I hate you," I tell her, and she says, "I hate me too."

I start a scrapbook of pictures of him from newspapers and magazines, carefully cutting away any faces that aren't his. That lasts a week.

I call his office five or six times daily, first thing and sometimes late at night. "I'm sorry," the pleasant woman says, "but your father's out right now." That lasts about a month.

Gifts arrive the day before my birthday, the day before Christmas. Cards come on birthdays, Halloween, Valentine's Day, Easter, and Sweetest Day—a holiday we've never heard of. Every spring and fall, a check arrives loose in an envelope, with "school clothes" written in swirling cursive on the memo line. Always a flag stamp; I imagine someone sitting at a desk with a drawer filled with rolls of them. The generic birthday cards typically feature a drawing of a cake and "Enjoy your special day!" printed inside. His name signed the way it looks on the constituent updates that arrive quarterly in the mail. I keep every card in a shoebox. Saving cards lasts nearly seven years. Now I glance and toss.

My mother says to me, "There'll come a day he's sorry for everything he put us through, mark my words," and I answer, "How will we know, if he's ignoring our existence?"

As soon as they can: My brother joins the marines. My other brother moves to Alaska. My little sister marries a Brazilian man twenty years older. My mother remarries, then divorces, then remarries, then divorces, then remarries, then divorces.

As soon as I can, I dutifully attend college; move to the East Village to become an important New York artist; get spooked when friends tell me the only reason I want to be an important New York artist is to prove something to my father; slink back to grad school; shamefully use the cachet of my father's name to snag a teaching job at a respectable university; change my name really for real, finally; mistrust any art I produce.

What he shows up for: graduations, weddings, baptisms, funerals.

Why he comes: to eventually insert himself into the scene in a public and dramatic way, i.e., the heartfelt toast bringing tears to everyone in the room who's unrelated to him.

Why we invite him: Because this time will be different. Because this time really will be different. Because this is the time that will be different. "Because he'll show up anyway," is what we say. Because—damn it—we want him there.

How I feel: too numb to be angry.

How I want to feel: too sad to be angry.

How I really feel: furious.

The door opens and I recognize #4, the "this time it's love" wife. The mother of the adorable twin toddlers (Bug and Ducky, until they grow into their pretentious names). The high-powered C-suite executive who left Duke Energy the day my father proposed. The calculatedly trustful, faux-naïf who deems prenups "unromantic," who looks "the other way" and sees "the bigger picture" when journalists ask about my father's past. The ultimate true believer and schemer, certain this tarnished man will still maybe actually possibly be president next election cycle. Face, smudgy with tears. Hair, like she combed it with her fingers a minute ago. Purposeful dishevelment.

"Dear Lexie," she says. "Forgive this wait. The doctors are so . . . Such a surprise. And a baby! There's a bright spot of news during this horror. I'm shocked and so embarrassed now's the first time we meet." She runs together all her words, and I can't gauge her sincerity. Both arms extend, hover. As if they're magnetized, I'm pulled into standing, drawn deeply into her embrace, inhaling a fresh squirt of Chanel wanting to mask sweat. My eyes close briefly. I don't want to like her, and I don't, I don't. But this embrace is enchanting.

She steps back, brushes both hands against her hips, smoothing herself, easing me out of her orbit. I remind myself that she's younger than I am, and smarter. Remind myself that if I were welcome here, I'd have heard from her first.

"Things are dicey," she says. "I haven't been home since I got the call. What a wreck I am. Look at me—no, don't! But do come along, and I'll let you see him for a quick minute. Sorry I'm such a mess."

Mary-Grace stands behind her, blurring into the background. Her face is pale, the two streaks of blush crossing her cheeks abruptly seeming garish. She sweeps one arm in a *be my guest* gesture that's both impersonal and highly personal, as if I'm betraying her deeply, when how can that be? I've just met her. I don't know her. How dare she think she knows me. I look away, refusing to thank her.

I thought New York would be easy, or easier than it was. I thought I was talented. Thought I'd use my father's famous name to dance onto the walls of any gallery I wanted. Thought something about being related to him would be useful. Thought that if I didn't get love, I'd at least get something: gallery, *New York Times* write-up, sparkly parties. "That guy," the gallery owners said. "What fuck-uppery, blowing up a whole presidential campaign over some girl." I nodded, agreed that my father was fucked up, laughed at the talk show hosts' jokes they whooped and repeated. Then they said, "Nah, sorry." I thought their mockery would be easier than explaining I'm nothing but a birthday marring his calendar, an address, some secretary's handwriting scrawled on flag-stamped envelopes.

Bagels are at the nurse's station, a fancy tray that apparently just arrived with a giant blue bow, cream cheese, smoked salmon, capers, the whole getup—reminding me I haven't eaten for hours. The nurses dig in, rooting out favorites.

"See how little it takes to make people happy," #4 says, resting her hand on my arm. It's something my father would say in an unguarded moment to someone trusted. Likely she's parroting him.

My stomach grumbles. We watch the nurses swarm, maybe because neither of us wants to be in the bleak room containing my father.

"Mary-Grace's idea. She did it all," she says, watching the tableau. She sounds resentful, as if bagels should be her idea. "I said to her, what about the Secret Service, but they don't like that kind of thing."

"Bagels?" I ask, a genuine question, genuine surprise.

"Kind gestures," she says. "Not in public. They're so professional. They don't even want Christmas cards according to Mary-Grace. She knows everything, runs everything, so of course we listen to what she says. No one gets far without someone like Mary-Grace around." It's possible her fingers tighten around my arm the tiniest bit.

"Oh," I say, wilting under her glare. "Yeah."

She finally slides her hand off my arm, places both hands on her hips, an oddly aggressive stance, the stance you take when you're gearing up to impose your will, to *make* those Secret Service agents eat bagels, *make* those agents slit an envelope, read a preprinted sentiment for happy holidays, and display that damn card on their fireplace mantel. She lets out a gusty laugh. "Everyone's annoyed by her," she says. "But no one says so. Let's go before she's even more furious that you're seeing him."

"She's furious?" I ask.

"Perpetually fuming," she says. "I try to be amused, try to rise above. Mostly I do. I love that you showed up, rattling her. Ha—her face when they told me you were here. Utter shock. Squawking, 'Let me think, let me think,' before zooming off to the bathroom. Ten minutes later, it's all buttoned-up organization: 'Of course we'll tell her no,' she said. Hearing Her Royal Smugness say that *guaranteed* me changing my mind from not wanting to see you. It's unnatural how protective she is if you ask me."

What a tangle. I'm in only because she can't stand Mary-Grace.

"He's your *father*. I'm not getting in the way of that." A raised eyebrow suggests that for all her overtalking she knows not to tack on the next part, which I guess is along the lines of, *Not now, anyway.* Or, *Not over this.* And, *Don't push me.*

She corrals a wandering doctor, and they confer; medical words flow beyond me, out of reach. "He's in there," the doctor says. "Talk to him." Then the doctor leaves, and #4 says, "Okay, let's go," and I hear myself ask—though I already know the answer: "Then he didn't say my name?"

The way she stares at me, like physically slamming me up against a wall. "What? When? He's in a coma. I don't think you understand how serious this is."

"In the ambulance," I say, embarrassment torching my face. I could be twelve, a child alone inside this big moment.

"Mary-Grace said that, didn't she?" she says. "To lure you up to DC. What the actual fuck. I should have known she dragged you here to mess with me. I said to her, don't call any of you people until we knew something."

I shake my head. "I heard it on the news, so I started driving."

"Fuck," she says. "What do you want, anyway?"

My mouth opens, closes. I say, "Guess I was just hoping."

"If anything," #4 says, leaning in so close that her minty breath overwhelms me, "mine's the name he would say."

9/11.

My father didn't call me—though I was in New York.

I didn't call him—though he was in Washington.

That's what I say when I tell the whole story.

"Did you want to call him?" someone always dares to ask.

No, motherfucker. I wanted *him*—my dad—to call *me*.

This man.

His eyelids look thin, pinned shut. Those hands can't be his; surely they were sliced off a mannequin. I don't know my father, but he's not this slack body in this sad bed. Where's his famous smile? Where's his . . . everything? Where is he? How long is more than ten years? I feel his pissed-off wife watching carefully. I lean in and kiss my father's dusty cheek, playing my part in a scene. "Here I am," I murmur. "Right here." No one cues my next line, so I stand silently.

The room is barren, lacking bagels, balloons, flowers, cards, photos, cozy blankets, ancient stuffed animals. It's all machinery and institutional décor. A TV hospital room: that unreal. No one wants to settle into here, whatever "here" means.

She takes the only chair, sinking quickly into it as if going limp. She grabs her phone, half-scrolls for a second, then drops it into her lap. "Thoughts and prayers," she says. "My god. When the man's turned atheist. The irony. That's why he was attacked, you know. Some religious nut. The last thing this man wants is anyone's prayers." She barks out a rough laugh that's almost affectionate.

"I was praying for him," I say. This is not quite true, as the word ringing my head all along the crazy, breakneck drive up from North Carolina was "please." Please what?

"You're late on that," she says. "Late maybe on all of it." She leans back, balancing her head on the wall, and closes her eyes, maybe unwilling to see hurt on my face, or, actually, not wanting to acknowledge I'm not hurt. Like I need to care about anything she says. "Look, I didn't mean how that came out," she says. "Your baby. Tell him that. There's some good news. Right?"

I could confess that I lied. That Mary-Grace finagled. That I shouldn't be here.

"Tell him," she commands.

I say, "A girl."

"Who wouldn't take a real live baby over a stupid prayer?" she says, eyes still closed.

I pray for a horse. Four birthdays in a row, I birthday-wish for a horse. I shooting-star- and eyelash-on-the-cheek- and dandelion-seed-wish for a horse. I beg for a horse. Do extra chores to seem responsible. Hoard allowance. Even plant carrots in a garden to feed the horse. I pray for a horse. I pray and pray.

The week after he leaves us, he buys me a horse. I sit on it one time, exactly once, for that photo Mary-Grace remembers. The velvet of his nose against my cheek. That warm, springy smell. My mother says, "You don't really want something from *him*, do you? Now? After what he did?" I thought the only, only thing in the world I wanted was a horse. But: "Sell it," I say, the worst words I know, worse than curse words. "You sure?" she asks, "because you're not getting a horse from me," and I say, "I'd never want a horse from you either."

Selling my horse isn't the blood sacrifice that brings back my father. Or that hurts him. Nothing could do either, I conclude, but then I live my life as if something could and would, because all I want to do is blame him harder.

Now's the moment I've pushed myself into.

I try to imagine his rickety voice calling for me in an ambulance, begging, someone noting the simple syllables of my name amid the complexity of medical wizardry, someone thinking, Better pass along that information to whoever's in charge.

I imagine believing Mary-Grace, believing her *just because I want to*.

Also, I imagine Mary-Grace glancing at the photo on my father's desk, coolly assuring him, "Losing you is the only regret of her life."

Can I welcome my father back?

I never imagined this about the story of the prodigal: me being the father.

There's a window, and outside the window is a view of a maple and on the maple is a flashy red cardinal, exactly as I imagined. "See the bird?" I ask the man in the bed, my father. His wife rustles in the chair, shifts it so the legs scrape the floor, makes a show of studying her watch. Already #4 is bored, wanting quick wrap-ups and joyful reconciliations, wanting love and understanding. Or, I don't know, could be her message is that she's tired and afraid.

"I'm having a baby girl. Like you wanted." Should be impossible to say the words, but nope. Lying beats candy for empty calories. "I'm thrilled. You'll come visit in Durham and meet her."

The bird lifts into the air, disappears.

It's hard to talk to someone who doesn't answer. Also, it's easy. Nothing I say can be wrong. Also, everything I say must be right. "Today's Sunday," I say. "Remember us going to church?"

The inhuman whir of machinery. The queasy stink of sick. His feet splayed sideways. Tubes, lights, flashes, pulsing.

"Remember us playing cards?" I say.

Being here is like time never passes. Like all the time the world holds narrows to this single moment. Every minute I've spent waiting for him to respond to me is right here. Each grain of my own silence. One half-breath might blow it all away.

Can anything that matters be said?

Please, I want to say, then say it: "Please. Please be happy. Let's both please be happy, maybe starting now."

It would be nice if something happened, but the only thing that happens is #4 butting in: "That's sweet. Keep talking. Say some more. Tell him about the baby. Tell him how you feel. Now's your chance, Lexie. Forgiveness!" She beams at me as if she deserves credit for orchestrating the whole damn, dumb thing. Oh, the picture in my mind of her fabulously perfect life with her fabulously perfect parents.

Time to piss her off too. "There's no baby," I say. "I lied to Mary-Grace. I want a baby. But there's only me." I brace for her fury, look forward to her kicking me out.

"Jesus fucking Christ," she says. "Now I've—" She stops, draws in a deep breath that seeps out slowly: classic stress management. And again. The moment feels long.

I punish myself, but why?

She resumes: "I'd lie up the wazoo for one more minute with my own sweet daddy, may he rest in peace. Here you are. Here we all are, and honestly, everything's going to be fine. Ask me how I know."

I touch my father's hand, the rigid, lumpy line of his knuckles. For some parents, for some children, love and pain become the same thing, or almost the same thing, or maybe the only thing. We hurt, we hurt, we hurt, we hurt, we hurt. We don't waste time, we hurl it aside, glancing up only when there's no baby, no one to respond in the ambulance, no great god above to steer the lost child home. I say to my father's wife: "How do you know?"

That bark of a laugh. "You're not really supposed to ask. I'm just talking."

How could it be wrong to *want* to be loved, to admit *needing* to be loved? Why did I never just tell him that, in words? Wouldn't a father—*my father*—know? Here I surprise myself, understanding suddenly how a sister, my *sister*, my sister Madison, might want, need, expect, hope for the same from this man we share, our father.

And maybe even from me.

Is any answer simple—and if it isn't, what makes it seem so, now, too late?

That night, before leaving, I check the private waiting room: empty. The garbage can of tissues: empty. The air there feels like it's been replaced by air from somewhere else. She works with him. So why would she wait in a waiting room to say goodbye to me?

I get it: Mary-Grace selects and sends the Christmas gifts; signs his name on the birthday cards; keeps my addresses—first on a typed card in a Rolodex, then in a computer file—as I move from Chapel Hill through East Village sublets to Phoenix to Carrboro to Durham. Dutiful Mary-Grace chose him and got me instead.

While my car careens through interstate blackness, heading to my empty condo in North Carolina, I imagine Mary-Grace alone in her own empty condo, pouring a tall shot of bourbon, grabbing a fresh box of Triscuits for late dinner. She toasts herself, gulps at the booze. I'm imagining so hard that her whisper cuts through the dark, "Fixed it. Finally."

EVERY MAN IN HISTORY

Several years from now

Saturday night. I love putting my body on the line, he says, but not flirty: serious. He glances around this dumb party like he's hoping someone tossed a bomb he can leap on.

Show-off, I think, arrogant, I think. Startling green eyes, I think, gloriously long swoops of glossy, black-black hair.

He says, Actually, my toes are my best feature.

That's flirty.

That's comfortable ground. I do my bored smile and check out his feet, clad in high-end, orange Piñatex sneakers.

What are you? I ask (not the DC classic, *so, what do you do?*). What are you is really *who* are you, polished to palatable. Like me, at this party I didn't want to go to. My in is knowing a former housemate of the people living in this group house in Columbia Heights . . . though she texted "sry" ten minutes ago, so she's a no-show. What are you? I ask again, because either he didn't hear or doesn't understand. A cop? I ask. Soldier? Not Secret Service? Where's your earpiece?

I heard the question the first time, he says, then adds, When you trust people, they'll come through.

Okay, I say, let me try that. I pose thoughtfulness on my face, fake-prop my jaw against my folded-up fingers. But honestly, he's making me feel right now like maybe I want to trust him. Like, I never feel this way, but here he is making me. I steel my eyes.

He says, I'm a soldier for justice.

Figures. Yet another idealist assuming he'll change the world. DC swarms with them. This helps. He assumes he's so special and he's not. I can walk away from that.

I let my hand fall away from my face and turn, but he grabs my arm, hard. Wait, he says, who are *you*? Who really, really are you?

His grip on my bare skin prickles up goosebumps. Bet he feels them too because there's a sideways smile like he caught me. A boho girl drifts by, watching us more closely than she should, protectively, like his hand squeezing into me is turning into the new Rape of the Century or something, and I'm about to tell her to mind her own business, but I catch on that it's him she's protective of, not me, not me at all.

He lets a little half-nod slip, which she decides is an invitation to horn in, and he says, This is Caf, and I say, Like caffeine? And she rolls her eyes because I guess I'm so horrifically unoriginal to ask that, and says, Not exactly. She tiptoes herself tall enough to whisper straight into his ear, but he's still got hold of my arm, though distractedly so, not with intent, and I use the time to examine the width of his palm, the rounded knuckles. No rings but a series of small, navy-blue ovals tattooed in the middle phalanges of his fingers, *phalanges* being a useless word I learned once. The ovals don't line up evenly, as if it's purposeful they don't. Two leather bracelets, one with knots, one woven.

She's whispering and edging closer, her hand clutching his arm, entwining into him like an invasive vine, like the English ivy people love in front of their Logan Circle rowhouses until they try digging out its endless ropes. Maybe I don't want him, this soldier for justice, but it's not like I want her having him, or her thinking she wins. As his grip loosens, about to slip away, I take my Solo cup that's half-full of ice and tap water and rest it on the top of his hand, the metacarpal bones to be specific, and he howls and jerks away, shaking off water droplets of condensation, trying to dodge the burning, icy jolt I gave him. He says, Jesus H. Christ, what's that about?

Dope-faced Caf slumps, fizzling out, twitching her weight from hip to hip, and if I ever felt such a look of longing for any guy shadow my own face like that, I'd have to shoot myself.

I'm Madison, I say, and Caf snarks, After the slaveholder president? And I go, After the avenue, though she guessed right. He laughs, and I join in. Nothing's funny. Still, a laugh's better than a whisper because it's loudly public, and he says, Serves me right for bragging about putting my body on the line.

Caf huffs out a nonresponse, and she doesn't stalk off right away but soon enough.

I text "sry" to the married K Street lobbyist-man who loves my ass. He'll convince himself I'm working on a paper, a presentation for my upper-level lit class, something that'll get a good grade because he needs to imagine me smart, that if I'm not someone now, I will be someday. (Even as he also likes me for being absolutely no one so he's untroubled about the things he wants to do to my body, the things I let him do to it, to me.)

I'm not "sry," not at all. Not for any of it.

The next morning. Dak lives in a tiny English basement in Petworth scattered with dinged-up furniture pulled off a curb on garbage night. Doesn't bother me that someone's gotten to a bed first. Whatever.

I love that you have only tea, I say to Dak, though what I wouldn't give for black coffee. I'm wearing nothing but his old Yosemite T-shirt he told me is from high school as I stare into his cupboard, and it's like a tea dictionary: rooibos, matcha, chai, fair trade, organic, ginseng, antioxidants, bergamot. Plus a whole shelf—in this tiny kitchen—devoted to tea accoutrements. Some girl, I think, with money. Also, the hard seltzer cans in the recycling bin are the girliest pink flavors.

Dak slides up, wrapping his arms around me. His body's warm, smelling faintly of cinnamon. I love tea, he says, the words a caress that make me long to love tea—or anything—with equal fervor.

He shuffles out a box from the back, an herbal blend that smells mostly of cinnamon. My current favorite, he says, and I imagine him absorbing the scent of all he comes in contact with, including me. He waves me to sit on the only stool, and I do.

You drank water at the party last night, he says. Are you in recovery? It's okay.

I shake my head and say, I like being in control. And because I suspect he wants to be asked, I ask, Are you in recovery?

He plugs in a half-full electric kettle and seems melancholy as he says, Nah. I admire people who do that, though, quit the thing they think they need to live, who tear out their defining structures.

When you put it that way, I say.

I know lots of people, he says.

He doesn't finish, so I take a stab: Lots of people who should be.

Recovery is a thing you've got to be ready for, he says, so *should*'s always the wrong word.

I say, Like last night when you said, *Should* we go to my place?

He laughs. The sound makes me think of tumbling puppies. He's one of those people who laughs a lot, for different reasons, but mostly because he likes the effect he has. Why isn't that annoying? I should be annoyed. He says, I like clear rules to live by.

I say, I like no rules.

He says, I mean like a moral code, like an internal moral code.

I say, I mean like no rules, no moral code.

He says, This tea's killer, you just wait.

He doesn't believe me because I sound contradictory: no rules, yet in control. Nothing about me adds up. I like that. People are that way, not adding up.

We talk some about the tea, like it's the only amazing thing on earth. Are we really talking about tea? Maybe I can't read his signals, which hardly happens. I try not to tangle with things I don't already know the answer to or outcome of. Lobbyist-man told me that's the number one rule of his life.

I interrupt: How'd you know it was water at the party?

He says, I saw you run the water at least a minute before putting the cup under, and I was pissed at you wasting a precious resource, but then it was cute, you sticking your pinky in the stream like the Queen would.

Do you wish I was in recovery? I asked. Do you need to save me? Are you one of those?

I state my question casually, but he's got to know it's important.

The kettle clicks off, and he takes two mugs off the rack over the sink. There's Ivory on the counter, and a fresh sponge. Someone is clean. My mind's registering two mugs drying, not one, one mug that's Man United and the other that's pale pink, with a rounded, expensive shape. He holds the pink mug by the handle when he gives it to me, and I latch onto that hot ceramic like I'm being tested.

He's standing next to me. We're immersed in awkward, self-aware silence. He picks at a fingernail; I sop up a drop of tea off the counter with one finger, which I wipe on his T-shirt. It's fluttery-soft, perfectly worn—clothing I'd steal if I didn't think he'd truly miss it, if I didn't like him. The tea tastes like pie. I'm uneasy, liking things about him, noticing details. I don't even remember if lobbyist-man is right-handed or left, if his big-deal watch is gold or silver.

I should go, I say, standing up.

That hateful word, he says, tugging me back down, finishing, *Should*. Anyway, your question: what I really think is that recovery's bullshit for most people. My sister died after years of the rehab revolving door. That's why I ask.

I'm sorry, I say. The silence turns reflective and purposeful, becoming the moment to talk about dead people, the complications we live with. Instead I say, When I was growing up, the water in DC contained lead so we ran it to clear the pipes.

Deer Park, he says, and he points to the corner, an apparatus for giant water jugs. He watches me not adding up bottled water + him. Then he says, Jesus, all that plastic, but . . . then finally admits, Someone else set it up.

She *insisted*, I say, air-quoting.

Well, he says, she pays for it.

Your girlfriend, I say, feeling mean.

My wife, he says, so that makes the money stuff okay, not transactional, right?

He peers in, waiting for my reaction, which I compress. Give him nothing, I think. But I give him everything: I thought you were someone, I say.

We have an arrangement, he says, for real. She works for an NGO and travels a lot. Right now she's in Mumbai for three weeks.

No, I say. I stand up, for real, hating how melodramatic it is to stalk off like a bitchy hookup. All that's missing is me knocking over my tea, liquid gliding across the counter.

He says, This is why I didn't tell you.

I shake my head, hoping he begs, hoping he doesn't, hoping he does.

He says, Just please try, please, please.

He tugs the hem of the Yosemite T-shirt, and I twist away, wrenching off the shirt, letting it drop to the floor. I'm bare and exposed. He looks me over, and I let him, so he'll feel cheap and lonely, though I already know he won't. Maybe that's how I want to feel. Or how I do feel. (Lobbyist-men and lawyer-men don't count; they're not this.)

Whatever.

As I say, Okay, he says, You should see your face!

There's that rollicking puppy-dog laugh I already love. He says, Obviously, I'm joking. Who'd marry me? It's my mom who insists on bottled water. My *mom*. She's like you, terrified of lead. Wait, what did you say? Okay?

I shake my head hard and fast, smack my fist onto the counter so my spoon bounces. Who'd buy his story?

He says, Do you believe me? Do you trust me? Or do you have trust issues?

You fucking asshole, I say, and I call him all the names and combos, inventing new ones. I don't believe him. His mom? But that laugh. And he reminds me: You said you like no rules. Inevitably, we tumble ourselves back into his bed, where we stay and stay and stay until Monday threatens to make everything real because there's an early phone call from her that he takes. Turns out that Mumbai's time zone is offset by thirty minutes, which, well, I admit I didn't know. Five-thirty at night in Mumbai is seven a.m. in DC. See, I tell Dak, this is me learning something new.

Also new: these unsettled feelings, wanting to see him tonight, wishing the girl would stay in India, wanting to smash her pink mug to pieces, caring.

Two weeks later. Nine-thirty dinner reservations at lobbyist-man's favorite place in the world, The Palm. He's so important his caricature is painted on the wall, along with like a thousand other important people. He's got way more hair in the picture, but my mouth's shut on that topic. Tonight, we're seated across the room from the spot where his face is on the wall. First time here, we sat by his picture, but that table's jammed with people in suits busting their asses to impress some out-of-town couple.

Lobbyist-man asks, What, I'm nothing but a bank to you kids? (meaning twenty-year-old me as a "kid," meaning all kids, his kids, who are at Sidwell Friends, and anyone's kids, whoever looks at him and sees white male, sees privilege). I work hard for my damn money, he says, not waiting for my answer, not wanting it.

Because I ordered lobster? I say. Because you specifically said, Order lobster.

Of course, order goddamn lobster, he says. Why wouldn't you?

So I did, though I wanted rib eye. But I know he likes to be seen showing off. I'm usually in a good mood at these late-night dinners: he's winding down, and I'm waking up. In my mind, this is the last time. I'm going to tell him about Dak, I swear, at dessert.

Would I like your kids? I ask. Would they like me?

Of course, he says. They're very popular.

Usually I hate anything that's popular, I say.

He shrugs. Why talk about this? he says. You'll never meet them. They won't meet you. It's moot.

There's a pompous word. So I say, What's that mean?

It means don't go looking them up, he says, suddenly interested in our conversation. It means let's just keep them out of this. He windmills one hand wildly, nearly knocking into the goldfish bowl of a martini we're sharing—supposedly—because the prick waiter wouldn't serve me, even when I said I was his daughter. I say that sometimes to avoid pawing in public. Or, Thanks, Dad, I'll announce loudly, good idea, Dad.

Moot, I say. What's *moot* mean? (Obviously, I know, but let's see what he says. Also, obviously, I googled the shit out of his wife and kids ages ago.)

Irrelevant, he says. Not the point.

Is there a point? I ask. You don't want to pay for my lobster? I'll never meet your kids?

I swear I'm telling him this time about Dak, how with Dak (maybe) there finally is a point, how (maybe) feeling something good is good. I enjoy thinking lobbyist-man will be happy for me, though it's more likely he'll call me a goddamn slut, which is what he called his daughter after he told me his wife found birth control pills in her bathroom (my same brand BTW). Whether he's happy or he lashes me with *slut*, I'm fine or whatever.

You kids, he says again. He does this sometimes, gets real drunk real fast, like he's been coiled all day, anticipating that first drop. He says, The point is that you're the one thing in my life that has no point. That's the point. You'll understand when you're older.

Again with the wild arm. I grab the martini to protect it. He usually orders me extra olives but forgot tonight.

That's the point for you, I say. What about for me?

His eyes glaze because like he always says, his whole day at work is questions, same with his whole night at home, and one hundred percent of all questions are bullshit.

I just want a night out, he says, without bullshit questions.

I sit back, fluff my hair with one hand. Now's where he tells me I'm gorgeous, that I should walk to the ladies' room so he can gawk at my ass.

You're gorgeous, he says.

What a broken clock. I say, Oh my god. I put on like I don't like hearing it, but I do like hearing it. It's maybe one of my favorite things. Still, I don't want him to know that, so I say, There's more to me than you know.

I'm sure, he says. Tell me one thing. He leans so close I see cheek pores in the flickering candlelight, leans in like he's really, really interested, like I'm about to tell him some actual deep secret. Which is mean. He knows all I am is lost, which isn't secret. I'm too sad suddenly to make up anything, mostly because why bother? He'll just believe it.

I say, I'm going to the big protest on Saturday. (I don't say that Dak insisted.)

Oh yeah, he says, so many roads closed.

It's social justice, I say.

He says something I don't expect, which is, I admire people who put themselves out there.

Here's where I could tell him about Dak. Instead, I say, Are your kids going?

His eyes laser me. Enough with my kids, he says. Anyway, who got you into this? It's not like you. When did you start caring about monuments being named after slave owners? That battle's over, and every man in history's a fuck, so what's the big deal?

Here's where else I could tell him about Dak. Instead I say, Those confederate statues came down.

Statues are easy, he says. I just don't get why you care all of a sudden, *Madison*.

It's kind of ugly, how he says my name, like I'm the old-time slaveholder the other Madison was.

I repeat, Like I said, there's more to me than you know.

He grabs my hand. Tear gas is real, he says. Cops are real. It's not the way it looks on video. Christ.

I imagine him saying these words to his fancy kids with their fancy lives, warning them with sweetness in his voice, not with the anger I get. Then, still leaning in, he adds, I want to fuck you right now. Let's go.

Across the room, suits are jostling out of their table, laughing like everything's so funny. I call out, pointing to lobbyist-man, Hey, his picture's painted on the wall, right next to where you're standing!

Boy, he leans away from me so fast. It's like I'm exhaling poison.

The clattering restaurant drops into a quick hush as heads spin to stare, but almost immediately the room's normal again because a lost girl shouting is easily contained. Several of the suits peer at the wall, and the out-of-town woman exclaims, There, and smacks her palm flat onto his painted face. You're famous, she calls over to us, how about that?

I give her a big, dumb, double thumbs-up as she snaps a selfie with the picture. Now that's funny, that she chooses the picture with the picture, not with the real man. That sums up this night and every night. I have to tell him about Dak. I have to let go. I have to give this up.

You're famous, I murmur.

Look, lobbyist-man says.

I wait a moment, which is another moment where I could tell him about Dak, then say, Where? At what?

Christ, he says. I'm paying for your lobster, aren't I? Who else is doing that for you?

I get an image of Dak's pretty face in my mind, Dak and me sitting in this corner banquette in The Palm, Dak saying, Order the lobster, but as an invitation, not a command, Dak holding a straight flush of credit cards. To lobbyist-man, I say, No one.

So it's settled, he says. You get lobster and I get—more arm waving—all this. We're all happy. Seems fair to me.

Fair to Dak, too, I think, when he's the one getting the leftovers later, peeling open the aluminum-foil swan I hand over at three a.m., him asking, What the fuck is this? And the way his eyes widen and glow when I say, Lobster. Eat as much as you want, I tell him. I can get us more.

In my head, always. If I were going to tell Dak one thing about myself, it might be this: For whatever extra-credit reason, I was on the lighting crew for *West Side Story* in high school, and a single lyric railroaded through my brain the entire time, "Something's coming, something good." My mother laughed at me when I told her. She said, Tony's dead at the end, and Nardo too. Plus, you'll never convince me Anita wasn't gang-banged to pieces in that drugstore.

Or this one thing: I grow up being assured that my famous father's other, realer children and ex-wives hate me and my mother. She doesn't give a shit, and lawyers get fat skimming the lawsuits scraping money for us, as she tries to weasel an official DC entrée for me. Why meet my dad for lunch if he hates me? I might ask, only to get back, He does hate you, which is exactly why.

Or this: Once, at some awful, rushed burger-and-fries mall lunch at Shake Shack, I ask my father straight out: Do my half-brothers and -sisters hate me?

He barely glances over and says, I'm sure they do, but why don't you ask them?

(I'm twelve years old then BTW.)

Me being sassy catches his interest, so I reply, Okay, I'll ask you. Do you?

Do I what? he says, the master of buying time.

Do you hate me? I ask in the throaty, flirty voice I (still) use to make people uncomfortable. I copied it off my mom, who—I swear—would come on to a squashed cup in a gutter if she thought it would buy her a drink.

Sweetheart, he says, lifting his hands in surrender, I barely know you.

So, I could say some things. Doesn't make me special.

There's also this: lots of times I imagine myself extraordinarily famous, my face breaking the internet. I imagine my half-siblings studying my cheekbones, the angle of my blue eyes, the tiny widow's peak denting down into my forehead. Maybe they'd say things like, Look how she looks like us. Maybe they'd notice that my smile is pretty much exactly our famous father's famous smile. They'd have to say, She's one of us. I'd let them think that. Maybe I'd even like it or whatever.

Thursday before the protest. She's a girlfriend, not a wife, and she's flying into Dulles on Monday. Bet she's pissed at missing the protest, I say to Dak, who nods and explains her boring job as I fake-listen. I want to make clever signs, but Dak says signs aren't how he gets the point across, that he's not some selfie-loving, virtue-signaling Facebook mom bragging that her picture's in a "50 Best Signs of the Protest" listicle. I don't bother asking what happens when the girlfriend is back. That night we stream an old Vampire Weekend concert and hold hands as if we're a very old couple, and Dak's face is intent and beautiful, and I wish I could draw so I could draw it.

Okay, so later, I do try telling Dak one thing, about one half-sibling, Lexie, the oldest girl, and how I cyberstalk her. How I don't trust the Google alert I put on her name, so I do a search every couple of weeks to see if she's up to something—maybe a museum buying her art (finally), or maybe she's getting married (finally) or something, or she's (finally) on social media, but nope. It's only old things she did, who she used to be. Her PhD dissertation on JSTOR. Closed-up exhibitions of her photographs in a Durham gallery. Syllabi from the teaching job she used to have. And always, those pictures of her from our father's failed presidential campaign, where she's a sweet-faced little girl with a photogenic, curly ponytail, holding his hand at a horse show. Like she's the ghostly ancestor who came before me.

Why doesn't she do more? What kind of loser is she? Yet seeing how little she's accomplished soothes me. I worry the next thing will be an obituary, and oh snap, there's the end of me imagining I'll talk to her.

Why her, Dak wants to know.

She's lost like me, I say.

Stop creating a victim narrative for yourself, he says. You're better than that.

Stop telling me what to do, I think automatically, and no, I'm not.

Why her, really? I'd never tell him or anyone. I feel we met already, in another life, or a dream life; her voice drifts along my brain edges, wanting me to know something I never quite all-the-way know. If I smell a carnation, I see her ponytail, which I don't understand why. I feel she likes black coffee and M&Ms, but I couldn't know this. She's a phantom, wandering free, unfettered.

There was a different sad mall lunch at Maggiano's with my father where he called me Lexie by mistake, then told me today was her birthday and how he could never forgive her because she stopped talking to him, because, as he said, maybe he fucked up a little bit in his personal life, that way he does, that way his grandmother warned him about, how the seeds of destruction always root from within. I held my breath so he'd keep talking, and for once he did: My girl Lexie stomped my goddamn heart, he said that day, his body deflating and slumping like living it all over again. I never should've, he said, I should've, if only. I didn't know what I could possibly ever say, little useless, forgotten me, how I could dare compete with that. I never had a chance, I said, and he half-nodded, said, No one does with me anymore. You know what they say about true friends in Washington, he said, and I didn't know, but whatever. That's when I decided I wanted to know the girl who could break this big, famous father of ours without breaking herself instead.

Saturday, spilling into Sunday. It's not wire binding my wrists but feels like it. Usually pain's whatever, but this is different since I didn't pick it. We're all sitting on the curb, under a streetlight, lined up like ugly dolls no one chooses. The cement's hard and feels germy—dress for common sense, Dak told me, dress anonymously, but I only half-obeyed. Leggings are comfortable, but the leopard print feels stupid as I stare at my ripped-up knees extended out in front of me, the blood crusting over smears of scraped skin. Everyone else is in black or gray, jeans and hoodies, closed-toe shoes, and not sandals like me. We've been sitting here how long, like fifteen minutes, and no one's explaining what happens next or when. A cop walks past and spits into the street. My throat's raked raw, my eyeballs feel scoured too bright, my crummy back's ready to snap like a stick.

Dak and I ended up being shuffled a dozen people apart on the curb, and it doesn't seem possible to walk over and demand to squeeze in next to him. Plus, he's mad at me, or I'm mad at everything. Him there and me here works fine.

Day's the peaceful part, Dak told me, and it was: walking, shouting, speeches, people with phones (not us) taking photos of clever signs, crackling sound systems, a thousand rainbows of pungent smells, waterfalls of anger about the wretched history of the wretched country and the wretched sins of the wretched past. Our fortune's based on a crime, a white girl hissed at all of us in the porta potty line, on sin. Dak traded a joint for some buttons: Jefferson = Rapist; Cancel George; Black Genocide 1619 – 2day; First Lady Sally Hemings. I agreed with everything I heard, but it's not like anyone's dragging nineteen feet of bronze Thomas Jefferson down out of that rotunda. More walking, walking, walking. I followed Dak, listened to him tell me I was doing great at my first protest. Whatever. It was such a DC day.

Then it wasn't.

Right when darkness edged in, we turned onto K Street, part of a splinter group of a hundred or so, and the chants spiraled loud, hard, twitchy. Even I felt something: currents meeting, melding; a simmer rising. Originally, I wanted to carry a sign, but maybe I wanted this more, whatever this was going to be. Dak yelled for me to cut out NOW, because the energy was unstable; the cops were a block over and closing in; supremacy a-holes clustered up ahead, waiting for us; and everything was going to *explode*, he said, he just felt it, the charged-up crowd, the gravity falling out from under, the hydrostatic pressure jamming up. Now's when to get the fuck out, he said, and stay safe.

A joke, I thought, to leave when it's getting good, to think about being safe, so I laughed, wanting him to laugh with me, to remind me we're here together. Nope.

At least hang back, he said. Stay back and be ready to run. Side streets are good, but never alleys. Pull off your shirt if you have to; you wore layers like I said, right?

Nope again.

I glanced at the back—white kids, old hippies, moms. That's who I am to Dak.

The group tightened, surged, pressed shoulder to shoulder, rippled like an ocean gathering itself up. The air thickened. Noise swelled. I felt what Dak was feeling. I inhaled the sharpness of my own sweat. Do I love these people? I remember thinking. It was a clear, chemical moment in my brain, a light suddenly on.

You can't be here, Dak yelled, goddamn it, leave right now, and he gave me a hard, mean shove, and I shoved back harder and meaner, so he stumbled out of step, and space bubbled open around us, the crowd moving forward into a jog. I longed for a rushing swoosh of time to show me with certainty if it works out between me and Dak, even as my untrusting brain murmured, no-no-no, the way this protest wouldn't fix anything either. Whatever. Goddamn it.

No justice, no peace, I shouted over and over in perfect cadence.

I'm begging you to leave, he said. Don't you get that I could love you if you'd let me?

Goddamn it again. I'm to blame.

There must be reasons to do things, even when we don't know what they are?

Maybe I wanted to prove that ACAB or maybe I wanted to prove that I'm not worth loving or probably it's the self-sabotage rooted in my genes. All I know is I double thumbs-upped Dak, but a second later, someone brought by a tote bag loaded with bricks, and Dak reached for one, and so did I. And when Dak heaved his at a grinning man wearing White Power 1-6-21 body armor, the brick sailed way wide, and when I threw, goddamn right I smashed all the blood out of that smug motherfucker's pale, hate-filled face.

The rest was me vanishing into a churning roar, into damp, humid darkness. Bodies tumbling and pressing in, and a kaleidoscope of white and Black faces cartwheeling past, sirens and megaphones, running and zagging. Plumes of tear gas blistered and burned. The indulgence of feeling rage swell and spill, of making pain manifest, of action overtaking thought, overtaking everything.

We could burn it all down. And that's what we shout. I hear nothing else. I want nothing less.

The next morning. Abruptly, we're all released. The sun's bright, the sky an angular blue.

People have phone numbers Sharpied on their arms: family member, friend, a social justice group. I mentally laugh, betting Dak saw me as the number he'd call, the rideshare to the rescue, bringing granola bars and a credit card. There's a role for everyone, Dak explained back when I was slipping into leopard leggings. Not everyone, he said, has to do everything, though clearly he believed he did.

The girl next to me extends her forearm to me and I nod with gratitude, memorizing the numbers. She's with a clutch of AKA sorority sisters, women with little time and zero compassion for lost girls like me, and I get it. They've got all this work ahead of them. Dak is I don't know where, but I can't count on him waiting outside. He said, If we're separated, worry about yourself and get home, and I'll be fine.

I'm sure he will be fine, just like all the men in history who were fucks—the country's history, and yeah, my history.

As for me, those sorority sisters or anyone would accuse me of using this important cause to serve my own selfishness, and I'll confess: Yes, maybe I am. But also, maybe, yes *finally*, I would add. Finally, I understand what giving up one's body might mean and *should* mean; understand there's something worth giving up a body for. That's where to begin.

This city holds things greater than me. Here's my freed-up heart, still beating and ready.

ACKNOWLEDGMENTS

Family first, so thank you to my husband, Steve Ello, who supports all my endeavors with good grace, and who "found me" here in the DC area; and to my parents, who insisted on making that long-ago family trip to "our nation's capital" when I saw the Capitol dome for the first time as we exited the train station; and to my sister and her partner, who are definitely worth driving halfway around the Beltway to visit (even in rush hour traffic).

Upstanding literary journals and anthologies gave many of these stories a home along the way, and I'm so grateful to them and their fine editors and staffs: Ploughshares; Southampton Review online; Southern Review; Arts & Letters; Little Rose Magazine; Story Magazine; Phoebe; Boog City; River Styx; This Is What America Looks Like: Fiction and Poetry from DC, Maryland, and Virginia (anthology); Pushcart Prize XLIV: Best of the Small Presses 2020 Edition; and visionary Kelly Abbott, creator of the Great Jones Street literary app, gets a special nod.

Can't forget my agent at Curtis Brown, Kerry D'Agostino, and my editor at Unnamed Press, Olivia Taylor Smith, for their wisdom and excellent counsel and good cheer and patience and for helping me find the book within the pages.

Kisses to Nancy Carson, who lent me the sanctuary of her meditative house to write in when I most needed the space; and to Lisa Couturier, Maribeth Fischer, and Mark Wisniewski, who nominated my work for the Pushcart Prize; and to W. T. Pfefferle, who was enthusiastic at exactly the right time; and to these loving readers: Gerry Romano, Veronica Grogan, Harriett McCune, Dan Wakefield, and Cynthia Weldon.

Take me far, far away, and these residencies did, offering blissful space where I wrote and revised many of the stories included in this book: Appomattox Regional Governor's School (ARGS), Hawthornden Castle International Retreat for Writers, Fairhope Center for the Writing Arts, and the Sandhills Road Trip Writer's Residency (cohosted by University of Nebraska at Kearney and Chadron State College and the Mari Sandoz Heritage Society).

Real life means a teaching job, but mine is more "joy" than "job," and I'm delighted to have spent so many happy years with my student and faculty family at the Converse College Low-Residency MFA program in Spartanburg, SC; I adore y'all, and I'm so grateful to Rick Mulkey and Susan Tekulve for starting this program more than ten years ago.

Untold friends along the way have critiqued a story or two, spilled the gossip I needed to hear, assured me I would finish the book, allowed me space to whine and vent, and made me laugh until I cried . . . especially these long-time stalwarts: Marlin Barton, Dan Elish, Marty Figley, Rachel Hall, Carolyn Parkhurst, Amy Stolls, and Paula Whyman.

My monthly prompt group is a constant source of inspiration and support: Michelle Berberet, Nancy Carson, Mary Daly, Joanne Lozar Glenn, Lisa Leibow, Mark Morrow, Lauri Ploch, and Nina Sichel.

Perhaps I should end with the answer to every burning question that haunts me—what will teach me, what will inspire me, what will guide me through a pandemic—and that answer is, simply, books; and so my eternal gratitude goes to books and to the writers everywhere who write them.

A Book Club Discussion Guide can be found at
www.lesliepietrzyk.com